V

from A to Z

Suddenly I envisioned the torture of hammering out a custody agreement and knew I could never divorce him. I may be celibate and miserable for the rest of my years, but I will not leave Roger. If only I could have it all, a husband and a lover. The French manage it, don't they? Or is it only French men? What do I know?

Eddie wants me. That's all I need. He caught me staring and winked. As I watched him, I realized this guy isn't even my type. In retrospect I realize that what attracted me to Eddie was his attraction to me. I saw his desire and suddenly it didn't matter what my type was.

'Til next time,

V

"You'll absolutely love V—in fact, you'll wish you were her friend. But since that can't be arranged, you'll happily settle for reading her diary and discovering her most private thoughts and all the outrageous things that happen in her life."

—Kate White, editor-in-chief, *Cosmopolitan*

THE DIARY OF

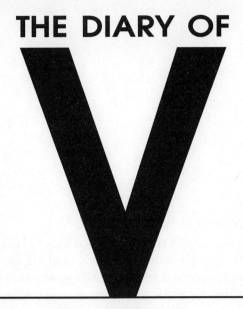

V

The Affair

DEBRA KENT

WARNER
VISION
BOOKS

A Time Warner Company

Warner Vision is a registered trademark of Warner Books, Inc.

Jacket design by Diane Luger
Book design by Stanley S. Drate / Folio Graphics Co., Inc.

Warner Books, Inc.
1271 Avenue of the Americas
New York, NY 10020

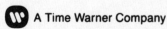 A Time Warner Company

ISBN 0-7394-1807-6

Printed in the United States of America

For Jeff, Adam, and Lisi
And for my parents,
Martha and Donald

Acknowledgments

This book would not be possible without Jeff Isaac, my husband and biggest fan for two decades, the person who pushed and prodded and ultimately convinced me that Valerie Ryan deserved her own book. I also want to give special thanks to my delightful children, Adam and Lisi, who love me even when I appear to be joined at the hip with my iMac.

Kate White is my patron saint, as intuitive as she is adroit, always supportive—a gem.

My agent, Sandy Dijkstra, who must have been my favorite aunt in another life, is tireless and wonderful and exquisitely patient.

Amy Applegate has filled the dual role of dear friend and wise counsel, and I'm grateful that she found her way to our dear little town.

My editor, Maggie Crawford, is a writer's dream: smart, enthusiastic, insightful, and always in good cheer. I adore her.

I thank David Salzman for his guidance, and Peggy Northrup at *Redbook* and Judy Coyne at Women.com for their commitment to V, online and everywhere else.

Andy Mallor is the best-dressed attorney I know, and I'm grateful for his help with the legal plotlines. He is brilliant. Any missteps are strictly my own.

Donna Wilber, Lorraine Rapp, Lisa Kamen, and Alisa Sutor are my personal pom squad, true allies and confidantes, the finest friends a woman could ask for.

Chelsea, Poe, and Joseph P. Kendicott are perfect exactly the way they are, even if they'll never read anything I write.

Love and gratitude go to Teresa Coleman, my favorite aunt in this life; Brian Kent and Richard Spitzer, talented and honorable men; Hy and Sylvia Isaac, who have supported me in every possible way; Carole Holton, a true alchemist and treasure; and Ann Smith and Vivian Counts, my beacons, my fellow travelers.

I thank Martha Spitzer, who inspires me with her spirit and passion and strength.

And I thank Donald Kent, a fine poet and writer who left us too soon and will always be missed. This one's for you, Daddy.

THE DIARY OF

October 3

Worked late last night, trying to catch up on paperwork. It's just me, the Hungarian cleaning ladies, and the guy who waters the plants. I couldn't help but notice his arms, thick and hairy (nice hair, not gorilla-man hair), and his torso is a perfect V. He is sex in a pair of blue jeans.

I realized that he was spending a lot of time around my desk, which didn't make sense since I only have one sad little ficus. Then he smiled and said, "Working late again, huh?" He was on one knee, tamping the mulch around the base of the tree. His fingers were thick and strong. "You ever find time for a little fun?"

A legitimate question, actually. Since my promotion from staff therapist to "senior partner in wellness" here at the Westfield Center for Mental Wellness, I've had little time for anything but thrashing through heaps of paper and going to management meetings where I get to vote on such critical management questions as Does Filomena Perez in reception deserve a nineteen-dollar-a-week raise? (Yes.) Should our holiday staff party be catered or a potluck? (Catered. Who the hell has time to cook?) Should we start a softball team next spring? (God no.) As senior partner I was responsible for generating new "wellness bridges" to physicians, divorce attorneys, school counselors, and others who were in a position to send new clients our way.

"Nah, you don't get out much. I can tell."

Wait a minute. Was this guy trying to pick me up?

My whole body prickled to life. It had been two and a half months since Roger and I had sex, so it wouldn't take enormous effort to get me interested. His name was embroidered in neat cursive over his pocket. Eddie. "You have a cute mouth," he said.

Flirting! Oh joy! I straightened up and smiled at him. I licked my lips. "Excuse me?" I said disingenuously.

He pointed to my computer. "Your mouse. Cute."

He was talking about the fuzzy mouse cover I'd bought at Staples. "Oh. Yes. My mouse." I was mortified. The man leaned across me to pet the mouse and I could feel the heat radiating off his forearm. "Well, I'd better get the rest of the floor," he said. Then he winked.

Roger was in his study when I got home. He didn't turn around when I walked into the room. It's been a week since I lightened my hair and he still hasn't noticed. I moved closer, bent to straighten some papers on his desk, flipped my hair in his direction. "Valerie, I'm working on a critical scene. Later, okay?"

I would have slammed the door but my anger was suddenly tempered by simply this: Eddie.

'Til next time,

V

October 10

It took me exactly twelve minutes to get home from work and that's with "traffic," a word that we invoke with feigned exasperation because we know that five cars stuck behind a tractor on Middle Street is nothing compared with rush hour in the Lincoln Tunnel. In this midwestern college town, everything is situated twelve minutes away from everything else, regardless of where you are or where you are going. It takes twelve minutes to get from my house to the health club. Twelve minutes from Pete's preschool to the pediatrician's. Twelve minutes from my office to the Dairy Queen, or the dry cleaner, or the supermarket, or the mall.

This calculus only works if you live in one of the two main residential areas: "in town" or in one of the subdivisions. If you live in town you can walk to campus, which is why professors covet this pricey neighborhood, and you can buy an older home made of something real and sturdy like stone or brick, but you only get one full bathroom, and the windows on these homes don't close right and all the rooms are drafty and you live in mortal terror that your World War II–era furnace will blow up on the coldest day of the year.

If you're willing to live in the suburbs, you can buy, for significantly less than the price of a house in town, a big new house with a new furnace, five bathrooms, a nice yard, a walk-out basement, a cedar deck off the family room, another cedar deck off the master bedroom, and windows that close properly. So the good news is, if you live in a subdivision, you can pee in five different toilets. The bad news is that your house is made of the lumber equivalent of Spam, an unnatural amalgam of chips and fillers. The houses look stately, but they're like those propped-up facades at a movie studio theme park. God forbid we should have a tornado in my neighborhood, these stately Spam houses will be flattened like roadkill.

When I got home, I snarfed down dinner and got Pete in bed for the night. I yanked on that itchy black teddie Roger bought me four years ago, yet one more attempt to resuscitate my sex life. I stood near his desk, cleared my throat. He looked up. "Hi, hon," he said, absently. He was looking right through me, his mind clearly on his work. Then his eyes focused and he sighed. "Oh. I get it."

Maybe another woman would have persevered, but I felt too self-conscious to continue. "Forget it," I told him. "It was a dumb idea."

I headed to the kitchen, clicked on the TV, and opened the pantry in search of anything chocolate. I found an orange plastic pumpkin behind a dusty waffle iron. Pete's Halloween candy left over from last year. Three Hershey's Kisses and a roll of those tart candies kids reluctantly accept when they'd much prefer anything chocolate. I unwound the tiny foil wrappers one by one and let the candy soften in my mouth. The irony was not lost on me: If I couldn't have my husband's kisses, Hershey's would have to do.

Three cheers for Roger, I thought bitterly. Mister Playwright. Mister Broadway. It's been nine years since his play *Basic Black* hit it big. Critics called him a genius. They had great expectations of him. We all did. But Roger hasn't managed another hit. He sits at his Mac and stares at the screen. He types. He scratches his stubble. He deletes. He types. Scratches. Deletes. He did manage to squeeze out a one-act play in the summer of '94, but it was so bad that some people walked out within the first fifteen minutes, and there was booing and giggling during the curtain call. Roger went to bed that night and stayed there for two weeks.

I'd feel sorry for the guy if I weren't so angry. Instead of turning to me as an ally, he has turned away. I feel like such an impostor. Big-shot psychotherapist. How can I possibly help my clients when I can't even manage my own marriage?

The good news is that Eddie came by to water my tree this morning. Since when does he work in the morning? And why did he tend only my tree and no one else's? Am I wrong to think this has something to do with me?

He was wearing a baseball cap, chinos, and black high-tops. He looked like a street kid but I could tell that he was about my age, maybe a little older. Black hair, olive skin, and—yes!—slightly bucked teeth, that orthodontic imperfection I happen to find attractive. I'm no gardener, but I could see that he wasn't doing anything productive with my ficus. Then he said, "So, uh, you think you'll be working late tonight?"

"Actually, I have an appointment this evening," I answered, wishing that I could cancel the dinner we'd planned with that vulgar producer and his wife.

"Uh-huh." His back was toward me so I couldn't see whether there was disappointment or indifference on his face.

'Til next time,

𝒱

October 17

My first appointment wasn't until 10 so I stopped at McD's across from the Center for a cup of coffee. I was scanning the local paper (Council Approves New Stoplight. Charity Run Rescheduled Due To Flooding. Farmer Reports Pig Theft) when he walked in. I didn't recognize him at first because he looked out of context without his watering hose. He said something goofy like, "Is this a private party or can anyone join in?" I swept my newspaper off the table (a bit too eagerly, I'm afraid) and he sat down.

It seemed like we talked about everything: white-water rafting, tobacco companies, *Chicago Hope,* micro-brewed beer. He was so easy to talk to. He talked about his kids (three, all girls), but not his wife. I told him about Peter, but never mentioned Roger. I saw his wedding band. I caught him glancing at mine.

I looked at Eddie and wondered if this is what his wife saw when she fell in love: celadon eyes, sun-toasted skin the color of cafe latte. As he talked he ran a finger around the rim of his coffee cup, and I found myself hypnotized by that finger, going around and around and around.

I raced back to the office and almost crashed into Millie, the coffee lady. (She carries this picture of her dog on the cart, wedged in between the bagels. She's convinced that the dog is her mother, reincarnated. "Just look into those eyes," she tells me. "What kinda dog has eyes like that? I swear, it's Mama." The really weird thing is, I'm beginning to believe her.)

Millie grabbed my sleeve as I ran past her. "Hey, where's the fire?" She looked into my eyes and smiled slyly. "Hey? What's all this? If I didn't know better, I'd say you're in love."

"You're nuts, Millie," I told her. "I'm a married lady."

'Til next time,

V

October 24

Last night I dreamed about a man, a stranger. He was older, tall, strong. No sex, just hugging. I vaguely un-

derstood that I couldn't be with him because I was already married, but I couldn't remember my husband's
name. I fleetingly worried about my stretch marks. The
overwhelming feeling in this dream was pure astonish-
ment and gratitude that anyone could love me so profoundly. When I woke up my arms were curved in an
embrace. I cried when I realized it was a dream.

I had lunch with Elaine yesterday. She's been single
for years and it's beginning to dawn on her, horribly,
that she may be single for the rest of her life. She looked
at me with tears in her eyes and said, "You don't know
what it's like to be alone."

I wanted to tell her, "You bet your ass I do." It's possible to be married and still feel alone, and in some
ways that's the worst kind of solitude. Little Pete gets a
surfeit of cuddling and attention; we snuggle him on
the living room floor, Roger on one side, me on the
other. I watch Roger stroke Pete's hair and think, at
least someone in this house is getting Roger's affection.
I suppose he could say the same about me. I have little
interest in touching my husband now.

Yesterday was our eighth anniversary. I could barely
find the motivation to pick out a card, let alone buy
him a present. He hired a sitter; I almost feigned illness
to avoid going to dinner. What a farce. What are we
celebrating, after all? He bought me a sweater in a color
he knows I cannot wear (peach), and I bought him a
book. We ate at Pico's in silence as I mentally clicked
through all our material possessions and imagined how
we'd divvy them up. Suddenly I envisioned the torture
of hammering out a custody arrangement and knew I
could never divorce him. I may be celibate and miserable for the rest of my years, but I will not leave Roger.
If only I could have it all, a husband and a lover. The

French do it, don't they? Or is it only French men? What do I know?

Saw Eddie flirting with Gail, my secretary, and felt an awful rush of jealousy. She seemed to glow under his gaze. He caught me staring and winked. Why do I care? This guy isn't even my type. All my boyfriends, and now my husband, have been pale and rangy. In retrospect I realize that what attracted me to Eddie was his attraction to me. I saw his desire and suddenly it didn't matter what my type was.

'Til next time,

V

October 29

Lauren Chapman, another senior partner, cornered me after the management meeting last night. "You gotta hear this," she says, giggling. Lauren has three kids and easily fits into her high school gym shorts (this I know because she wore them to the family picnic). And after fifteen years of marriage to her investment broker husband, she still comes to work with marks on her neck that look suspiciously like hickeys.

She pulled me aside and told me a story I'm sure was meant to entertain but only made me more depressed. Last night she went to meet her husband at his office for a quick bite before heading back home. Living up to his name once again, Randy insisted they make love in the conference room. On the table. "Can you believe him?" Lauren cackled. "He's got the hormones of a fourteen-year-old!" I wanted to slap her. I know I shouldn't let this get to me. I'm a therapist, for God's sake.

I can hear Roger lifting weights in the next room. If I didn't know better, I'd think he was having sex. All that grunting and gasping. He's having this love fest with his pectorals and I'm alone in the bedroom watching *Lucy* reruns.

I haven't given up altogether. Inspired by a magazine article (and, I suppose, Lauren's tale of unbridled conference room lust), I crept up behind him tonight while he was loading the dishwasher and reached for his fly. "What are you doing?" he asked, genuinely perplexed. "Relax and enjoy," I whispered, determined to get him into bed. He turned to face me, pulling up his zipper. "Honey, did you forget that tonight's *NYPD Blue*?"

I know I should have "communicated my needs in a non-threatening way using 'I' messages." (How many times have I given that advice to my own clients?) But in a perverse way, I'm glad he reacted the way he did. Now I can savor my fantasies of Eddie without guilt or remorse. It's an amazing feeling, knowing that somewhere in this world there's a man who really desires me. Right now, I need that.

'Til next time,

V

October 30

Tomorrow is Halloween, and as usual, Pete still hasn't picked out a costume. First he wanted to be Captain Hook, so I ran out and bought a pirate costume at the party supply store and even found a stuffed alligator I'd planned to rig to his pantaloons. Then last week he decided that pirates weren't cool and he'd rather be a policeman. So I ordered a cop costume from the Lillian Vernon catalogue, paying extra for overnight delivery, but when he put it on, inexplicably he started to cry, so I shoved the whole damn costume back in the plastic bag and told Pete he could go trick-or-treating stark naked for all I cared, which only made him cry harder. Now he wants to be a pepperoni pizza. I've just spent the last two hours on my knees in the garage trying to cut a giant circle from a refrigerator box I pulled out of the Dumpster at Sparky's Appliances. I've painted it, I've glued on construction paper pepperonis, and I've devised an elaborate harness so he can wear it and walk without tipping over. And if he decides he'd rather not be a pepperoni pizza after all, I will have no choice but to strap the damn thing on and go trick-or-treating myself because I will, most assuredly, need the chocolate!

'Til next time,

𝒱

November 7

This morning I found a red velvet heart hanging from a branch of the ficus. It had to be from Eddie. I felt a hand on my shoulder and turned. "I see you have an admirer." It was Diana Pierce, the Center's comptroller and, as it happens, an old college buddy of Roger's. I always suspected Diana had the hots for Roger. She's divorced, testy, flamboyant, always on the offensive. "It's that studly plant guy, isn't it?"

"Huh?" I tried to sound confused.

"I've seen him hanging around your office. I mean,

how much time can it possibly take to water a plant?"
Diana threw her head back and cackled, her mouth
opened so wide I could count her fillings.

"Diana, I really don't know what you're talking
about." (At this point I'm wondering if I look as guilty
as I feel.)

She reached out and chucked me under the chin.
"Baby, I love it when you lie." She started for the door
and then turned around. "By the way, how's Roger?"
She left before I could answer.

I spent my lunch hour with Eddie. We grabbed hot
dogs and found a green spot four blocks from the office. I kept expecting Diana to pop up from behind a
bush. He hinted at a stagnating marriage (he mentioned
that his wife is usually asleep by the time he gets
home), and I hinted at my own (I told him about Roger's obsession with his play). When we got back to the
building I asked him to take a different elevator. "You
know, so people don't start suspecting things."

"What kind of things?" he asked, his eyes glittering
wickedly as he grinned. God, I love his teeth.

"You know." My face hurt from smiling so much. An
elevator chimed and Eddie hopped in. I could see him
staring at me as the doors closed.

Roger was unusually animated when I arrived home.
He had the cordless phone in his hand. "Guess who's
coming to dinner?" He waved the phone in the air.

I put my briefcase down and rubbed my shoulders.
"Tell me it's a masseuse."

He smiled. "It's Diana. She just invited herself over.
Two weeks from today. Says she wants to catch up with
me. I mean us."

Now what am I going to do? Diana is totally unpredictable. What if she says something about Eddie?

'Til next time,

𝒱

November 14

Oh no. I can't believe this. Two minutes ago I heard the phone ring. Roger got to it first. He held his hand over the mouthpiece as he offered it to me. "Some guy wants to ask you about plants for your office. Sounds like a phone solicitor. Should I tell him you're not interested?"

I held my breath. "I'll take it."

Roger shrugged and went into his office. As long as I could hear him hammering away on the keyboard, I knew it was safe to talk. I tried to sound casual. "Hello?"

"Hi. It's me. Eddie."

"Eddie? From the office?" Who was I kidding? I knew exactly who it was.

"Yeah, Eddie from the office. How are you?"

Scared, I wanted to say. It felt as if Eddie had violated some fundamental tenet of fantasy and flirtation. How could he call me at home, the place where my husband and son live in happy ignorance? Eddie had upped the ante. "Fine," I answered. "What's up?"

He cleared his throat. "I'm buying new plants for your floor and wondered whether you had any favorites. You know. For your office. I mean, before I place the order, I just thought I'd ask."

I took a deep breath. "You've got to be kidding." I felt dizzy.

"Huh?"

"What is this, junior high school? I know what's going on here."

There was absolute silence on the other end and for a moment I thought he'd hung up. But then Eddie's voice came through, hushed and soft. "If you know what's going on, then you must know that I can't get you out of my head. Especially the way your mouth curls up at the corners, even when you're not smiling." I could feel my lips tingle the way they do when the novocaine starts to wear off. I bit my lower lip hard.

"I have just one question for you and I want you to answer me honestly. If your answer is no, I'll never bother you again."

I couldn't bear that thought. "What's the question?" I whispered. My head hurt.

"Are you attracted to me?"

I knew that my answer could change my life. Everyone's lives. I could hear Roger tapping at the keyboard in the other room.

"Yes. I am attracted to you."

"Mommy?" Jesus. It was Pete. How long had he been standing there? I pressed my mouth to the phone and whispered, "Gotta go." My heart thumped frantically. "Bad dream, sweetheart?" I led Pete back to his room and tucked his dinosaur blanket up to his chin. He smiled at me and fell back to sleep. I watched him guiltily. It's almost as if I'm betraying him too.

'Til next time,

V

November 21

It's 1 A.M. Pete and Roger are asleep and I've just spent the last half hour with my head over the toilet. When Roger asked, groggily, if I was okay, I told him I thought it was the sweet-and-sour shrimp I'd had for dinner.

I lied.

I know it's the guilt. Even when there was nothing left in my belly, I heaved the bile. When that was gone, I just shook and gagged. My cheeks are flushed and I've got the chills. It's the guilt.

Roger had reached for me in the night, then pulled me against him so we nested like spoons, his arm around my waist. I felt the stirring in his briefs, felt it against me. He was sound asleep. If he could touch me now, why not when we were both awake?

I felt his warm breath against my neck and suddenly I was overcome by pity. I thought of his receding hairline and his futile efforts to grow a goatee. I thought about the failed plays, the success that has eluded him season after season. I imagined him hunched over the keyboard, convinced that this time he was golden. I thought of his one positive review, published in the *Times* ten years ago, now pathethic and yellowed in its frame. I thought of the wife whose heart hungered for another man.

What would he say if I told him about Eddie? Would he be arrogant and ridicule Eddie's lack of education, his lowly profession? Would he crumple in pain? Would he cry? Would he fill with rage and, for the first time in our marriage, raise a hand to strike me? Or, worse, would he silently pack his things and take Pete away?

I felt his heart beat against my back. He murmured in my hair. Did I hear him say he loved me? I held my breath and listened keenly like a birdwatcher for the call of the loon. I was wide awake now. I actually hoped he would mention some other woman's name Diana, Cameron Diaz, anyone but me. I wanted a reason to want Eddie. I wanted to level the playing field. Roger said it again, unmistakably. He said, "I love you." It was at this point that I felt my dinner roil and surge and I staggered back to the bathroom.

As I write this I can feel the anxiety ebb, finally. I need to get back to sleep. I've got back-to-back clients all day tomorrow and a session with a married woman with four kids who thinks she may be lesbian. I owe it to her and all the rest of my clients to be awake and alert. Maybe I'll take something to help me get back to sleep. I think I've got some melatonin in the medicine cabinet.

Wait. My computer just chimed. Who could be e-mailing me at this hour?

'Til next time,

𝒱

November 28

Even before I checked my in-box I knew that the new e-mail was from Eddie. But how did he get my e-mail address? Wait a minute. I know. I'd seen him flirting with Trish, the new receptionist (implants, I'm sure). She'd handed him something. Red cover, yellow lettering. Damn that devil! He must have sweet-talked her into giving him the directory! That list is as closely guarded as the Pentagon—lest any of our particularly unstable clients try to track us down at home.

I clicked on the envelope icon and his name appeared, highlighted on the screen. Edward Bennedetto. I stared at his name for a long time before I got the nerve to read his mail. Just two words.

"You awake?"

He was on-line. I could have ignored it, could have deleted it. But the seventh-grader in me could not resist. I had to write back. "Mmmmmm. I'm here." Not "yes" or "yup." But "Mmmmmm." Flirting in cyberspace. What am I doing?!?

He fired back a response. "What are you wearing?" Oh God. Don't go there, Eddie. I guess I provoked him with that "mmmmmm" business. By now it's 2 A.M., and I'm so tired I'm seeing bugs on the wall and the drone from my printer is beginning to sound like music. Sheryl Crow, actually. I could have logged off. I *should* have logged off. But this was too delicious. "T-shirt. Panties. Black, by the way." Actually I was wearing a Gap sweatshirt and leggings, my bedtime attire of choice these days. Eddie responded: "Mmmmmm."

This was too much fun. And so illicit. Then I thought of Roger snoring upstairs in bed, his chiropractically correct foam pillow wedged under his neck. I could feel my stomach clench, the beginnings of another session of guilt puking. I couldn't handle much more of that tonight. "Gotta go. Get some sleep!" I logged off before I could see whether he'd written back.

It's late. We signed Pete up for peewee basketball at the Y and it starts tomorrow evening. If I don't get some sleep myself, I'm going to be zombie mom in the bleachers.

'Til next time,

V

December 5

I feel like crap. It was one of those days when I hated everything. I hated the wasp-like cyclists in their Lycra, riding three across, hogging the road, so physically fit I wanted to slam my Jeep right into their tight little butts. I hated the women who jogged in the freezing drizzle with that glazed "runner's high" look in their eyes (damn fanatics). I hated the mothers who came to the preschool holiday party in their size four Talbot's plaids and shiny loafers, all permed and perky and so damned happy. Can anyone possibly be that happy?

And I hated the fact that Eddie didn't show up for work today. Forty-five minutes spent getting dressed this morning. All that effort, wasted.

I've noticed that I've started to see myself as I imagine he sees me. The image that holds no fascination for my husband now ignites the lust of another man. I touch my lip and think, this is the lip he loves, the lip that curls up at the corners even when I'm not smiling. He said it was catlike. I straddle a bench and see the curve of my leg and think, this is the leg he wants to stroke. I slip off my T-shirt and imagine him watching me from the corner of the room. Is this sick, or what?

Betsy, my dear old college roommate, wants me to do this. I mean, have an affair with Eddie. I e-mailed her last night and told her everything. (Not that there's so much to tell: I have a crush on the office plant guy, he has a crush on me, and we flirt like junior high schoolers. End of story.)

She e-mailed back this morning. "You only live once, kid. You're young. You're beautiful. You deserve to feel loved and desired. Get him into bed!" I was stunned.

This was coming from Betsy, the only girl in my sorority house who didn't own a fake ID and actually studied for exams while the rest of us were at keg parties with the Delta Chi boys. Betsy, the good Catholic, the only friend who could legitimately wear white at her wedding.

On the other hand, Betsy could be viciously sarcastic. Maybe she was just playing with me. I e-mailed her back: "Are you kidding?" She must have been on-line just then because the phone rang a moment later. "Not on your life." Her voice was hushed. Her kids must have been in the room. "You go, girl!" (Now that this hip urban expression has finally made it to Betsy's prim hamlet in suburban Iowa, "You go, girl" has, shall we say, lost some of its appeal.)

She couldn't talk: Child No. 4 was wailing in the background. But after I hung up the phone, my old friend's exhortation stayed with me. With good Betsy's blessing, the possibility of taking Eddie to bed felt tantalizingly real.

'Til next time,

𝒱

December 13

Wound up having lunch with Eddie today. He jumped into the elevator just as the doors were closing. "Mind if I join you for lunch?" No one else was in the elevator. I could feel myself flush. "Sure." Truth is, I hate eating alone. It could have been anyone and I would have said yes. (I'm aware that I sound as if I'm rationalizing now.) I had the sudden impulse to hit the emergency stop button and pin him against the wall. Judging by the look on his face, I think he was thinking the same thing.

We found a quiet booth in the back of Peking Palace. It felt so illicit sitting back there. Eddie pulled a little box out of his coat pocket. "Got something for you," he said, smiling. I looked at his beaming face and I felt . . . I don't know how to put this . . .

I just felt this overwhelming pity for him. Yes, I've imagined slipping my hand inside his briefs. Yes, I've even concocted complicated stories in which his wife and my husband just happen to be on the same plane, which tragically explodes in flight. Yes, he makes every nerve ending in my body come alive just by walking into the room.

But I never thought he'd actually give me presents. Gift giving comes with a relationship. We don't have a relationship. Or do we? Do I want him to love me? Or just lust for me? Do I want him to be my second husband, or my first lover?

So I take the box in my hand. I shake it. I try to smile. How could he know me well enough to buy me something I'd like? And what's he doing buying me presents on his plant-guy salary? I open it and pray it's not jewelry. I look. Oh no. It's a tiny brass bust of Sigmund Freud.

Poor Eddie. Does he think all therapists are Freudians? I've never been especially fond of Freudian theory (especially that penis envy nonsense). I could see Eddie looking at me with a hopeful, expectant look on his face. He so badly wanted to please me. I realized then: he's really falling for me. I don't want that. I don't want his adoration. I want his body. I don't want to see Eddie as a puppy. I want him as a wolf.

After lunch, I ran into Diana in the rest room. We're both fixing our makeup in the mirror. With her trademark arched eyebrow she says, "So how's your garden stud?" I tried not to let her see the terror on my face. What, exactly, does she know? Then she says, "Has he shown you his hose yet?" I tried to sound light. "Good one, Diana. But you know I only have eyes for Roger." She smirked but I left before she could say anything else.

What's really nerve-racking is that this woman is coming for dinner in six days! If she's like this when she's sober, what is she likely to say after she's had a little wine?

'Til next time,

𝒱

December 19

The night I'd been dreading for weeks is finally over. I feel strafed. Almost everything that could have gone wrong, did. Pete woke up from his nap with a fever. My in-laws were supposed to take him for the night but he was so miserable I couldn't bear to send him away. He spent most of the evening in my arms, sweaty and irritable, while I labored to reach around him with my fork. My period hit in the middle of dinner and leaked through my pants and onto the upholstered chair (I don't think anyone noticed but I almost died when I saw the stain). I got my foot tangled up in the Christmas tree lights and pulled the tree down (Roger caught it before it hit the floor but two glass ornaments smashed).

But none of this compared to the agony of having

Diana in my dining room for three and a half hours. Diana is what I call a "nonporous surface." Every conversation is strictly one-way. She can talk about herself ad nauseam but has zero interest in other people, except to the extent that they have something to offer—if you can get her a courtside ticket to the basketball game, she's your best friend.

Worse than her self-absorption is her sadism. As I'm serving the salad she says, "These greens remind me . . . have you told Roger about your new friend?" I froze.

"Which new friend is that, Diana?" Roger looked up quizzically, midbite.

"You know, your *friend*." I tried hard to seem confused. After a long, painful pause she said: "Maggie Belky, the new social worker. Nice girl." Roger, uncharacteristically, must have been paying attention, because he said, "What does that have to do with greens?" Diana looked at me, smiling. "I don't know. Just some weird train of thought, I guess."

It was like this all night. She'd gesture toward the potted azalea on the kitchen counter and say, "Your plant doesn't look so hot. Anyone you can call for expert advice?" Or, "Can you recommend a good landscaper?"

After she'd finished off the bottle of wine, she wrapped her arms around Roger's waist and told me, "You take care of my Roger, you hear? If I'd had any brains I would have grabbed him when we were juniors at Penn. I was such an idiot." Roger blushed and gently extracted himself from her grip. He moved to my side and muttered something lighthearted. I felt a wave of guilt as I contemplated his loyalty. Diana finally left at 11. I practically had to shove her out the door.

As I loaded up the dishwasher I remembered that

next week is the office Christmas party. Everyone's invited, including service staff (computer tech people, the coffee lady, and, yes, Eddie). Significant others are also invited, but Roger hates these things so I usually go alone. Just then a song came on the radio, a song about a furtive kiss, the flicker of a tongue, an affair. I put another plate in the dishwasher.

'Til next time,

V

December 21

The Christmas party was everything I'd hoped and feared it would be. Eddie and I made small talk most of the night. Diana trapped us by the buffet. Beer in one hand, unlit cigarette in the other. "You know that song," she started, hooking a painted fingernail into my sweater. "Oh, you know that great Bonnie Raitt song. I just love her, don't you?" My mind clicked through every Bonnie Raitt song I knew.

Which one could she possibly be thinking of?

Then I realized. Oh no. Not *that* one. "People are talking . . ." Diana began to sing. "That's right, Valerie and Eddie, they're talking about you," she crooned, lounge lizard style.

I could feel a stinging wave of heat pass through me. Eddie, on the other hand, seemed completely unruffled. He smiled and raised his beer. "Diana, I think you missed your calling." She curtsied and sidled up to me. "He's a peach, kid." She paused and looked me in the eye. "But then again, you already have a peach at home, now, don't you?"

Some peach. Roger has said barely four words to me in over a week. We sleep back to back, without even a perfunctory good-night kiss. He is animated and happy when Pete is in the room, but when he's alone with me he seems to die by degrees. Our marriage is in a free fall. So am I.

It was during this gloomy contemplation that I felt a warm hand on my arm. "Meet me in the stairwell," he said. I'd never seen him so serious. My heart felt like the engine on my old Mustang, racing so hard and fast I thought it might explode. When I got there he was sitting on the stairs. Even in my crazed state I could step back for a moment and admire him. God, he is sexy. And so big. Everything about him (as far as I can see) is just so deliciously big. His neck. His arms. His legs. All muscle. When I'm near him I just want to curl into him. Roger is so pale and slight sometimes I think I'd have to protect him if we ever got attacked by muggers. With Eddie, I feel so sheltered. It feels so unfamiliar and so good.

"You look beautiful tonight." I could feel him taking me in. "I have something for you." He had nothing in his hands. I was confused. He stood up and moved close to me. He smelled of beer and Eternity. I thought I was going to pass out. He dipped down and put his mouth on my cheek.

A kiss.

"Don't look so scared," he said, touching a finger to my cheek. The spot that he'd kissed felt warm and moist. "We're friends, right?"

"Of course," I answered, unsure of where he was going with this.

"Well, friends kiss, don't they?" he asked, smiling

wryly. "It's not like I kissed you on the lips or anything." My lips tingled at the thought.

He held out a hand. "Friends?"

I reached out and shook his hand. "Yeah. Friends." My voice wavered. My hand felt scorched. He started to pull me toward him—I felt an almost imperceptible tug—then he stopped. He must have sensed my terror. I wanted it so desperately. I was not ready.

I have replayed that kiss a hundred—no, a thousand—times since then. The office has been closed for the holidays. I'm almost afraid to go back.

'Til next time,

V

December 24

I am sitting here in the same clothes I've worn all day, the same clothes I slept in, sweatpants so rank I can smell them. I haven't showered in forty-eight hours because I haven't been able to carve out the six minutes I need to hop in the shower, blast my hair with the dryer, and slap on some makeup. Instead, I've spent the last forty-eight hours preparing for this most joyous of holidays. I've assembled Pete's new Fisher-Price workshop (Roger, as usual, pleaded mechanical incompetence), I've hauled out the Christmas dishes and set the table. I picked up the Santa costume Roger insists on renting every year (though vanity prohibits him from faking the fat belly, which invariably leads Pete to ask, "Mommy, what's wrong with Santa?").

'Til next time,

V

January 8

The sky is white, the air is wet and cold. I have such a hunger to be held. I imagine Eddie's thick arms wrapped around me, imagine burying my face in his broad chest. I try to picture myself in Roger's embrace and just can't do it. The desire isn't there. I lost it when he stopped wanting me. Are there women out there who can lust after a husband who clearly has no interest in them? I can't.

I remember when he would fix his gaze on me as I undressed. He'd say, "You look good," and I knew he wanted me and his wanting stirred my own lust. Now I undress and his eyes are fixed on the hockey game and I'm just another piece of furniture. Granted, I don't have the body I did before Pete was born, but that shouldn't matter, should it? I've known all kinds of women—my own clients—fleshy, jiggly, round women who have sex with their husbands. It can't be about my body, can it?

So I don't imagine Roger holding me now. I imagine Eddie. I see the wisps of black hair trailing from his belly to beneath his pants and wish I could run a finger along that trail. I smell the soap on his skin. I can almost feel the softness of his lips on mine. It feels so good to know that somewhere in this city is a man who wants me. Why am I torturing myself like this?!?

Last night I was determined to talk to Roger about our marriage. I had the name of a therapist I respected (we both worked at the hospital after I got my degree), and I wanted to make an appointment. So what do I do instead? Like a crazy woman I ask—in the middle of *NYPD Blue*—"Are you having an affair?" He mutes the

TV (he would never actually turn it off) and says, "What in the world are you talking about?"

"Well, I mean, you never want to make love anymore. Is there someone else?"

He rolled his eyes. "Is it that time of the month, perchance?"

I knew what was happening. Obviously, I was projecting. But I couldn't stop myself. "No, it's not that friggin' time of the month, Roger. Just tell me, are you screwing around?"

He laughed and clicked the sound back on. "If you want to have a conversation about why we're not having sex, that's fine. But if you're going to make up some crazy story about me and another woman, forget it."

I rolled over and switched off my lamp.

'Til next time,

V

January 16

Now this is interesting.

Just after I got Petey into bed I heard the phone ring. Roger picked up. I listened for a moment, trying to discern if the call was for me. Apparently not. He was talking in a familiar tone. Who could it be? His mother? His sister? I walked by the bedroom and saw him stretched out on the bed. He looked comfortable, as if he was settling in for a long conversation.

I went downstairs to check out the Caller ID. A. R. Elkins. Then I did something I haven't done since high school. I picked up the extension in the kitchen and listened in. It was a woman. A very young woman. I heard her say, "I hate this weather." I heard her say, "My dog threw up all over the living room rug."

Then Roger said, "Wait. Someone just picked up the phone."

Busted.

"Petey, is that you?"

I disconnected the phone from the wall. I listened as Roger's footsteps moved across the hall to his office. I went upstairs. I tried to sound casual. "Who called?"

"Was that you who picked up the phone?"

I suppose I could have lied. I could have told him I'd scheduled a fax and it was just the computer breaking in. But something impelled me to be truthful.

"Yeah, it was me. I was just curious to know who you were talking to."

Roger swiveled around in his chair and stared at me. "I can't believe you. You actually eavesdropped on my phone call?" He shook his head in disgust. "You're crazy, you know that?" His voice got louder. "You don't trust me, do you? Well, do you?" He was yelling now. I was afraid he'd wake Petey. "I trust you fine, Roger. I just wanted to know who was on the phone."

Turned out it was someone named Alyssa, one of the students in the playwriting class he teaches at the Learning Attic. I told him I thought she sounded rather chummy. "*All* my students like me. I can't help that, can I? I don't see why you have a problem with that." He is practically screaming now. His face was red and a thick vein bulged along his forehead. "It so happens that Alyssa needs a little fatherly attention. Her parents are splitting up. I can't believe you have a problem with that!"

"Gee, Roger," I told him. "The gentleman doth protest too much, methinks. And do me a favor: Stop screaming!" I slammed the door as I left his office. I headed back to the kitchen, looking for something sweet, chocolate specifically. Just for the hell of it I went back to the Caller ID.

Jesus. A. R. Elkins had called every day since last Wednesday, sometimes three and four times a day! Here I was, tormenting myself over a chaste kiss at an office party, while my husband is messing around with his student? What the hell is going on?

'Til next time,

V

January 30

It is 3 A.M. I haven't had the guts to ask Roger about the girl. She hasn't called again unless she's figured out how to disable Caller ID. I picture her: leggy, busty, blond, full lips, and so damn young. I am torturing myself.

We did the family thing today: made pancakes for breakfast (Petey helped), spent an exhausting day at the children's museum, went to Applebee's for dinner. What a farce: the two of us, trying to be civil for the kid's sake, interacting with a minimum of words, gritted teeth, and zero eye contact. In the restaurant I watched an older man stroke his wife's hair. It was clearly a familiar gesture; she leaned into him and tucked a hand in his back pocket. Like a teenager, I thought. Such tenderness. Such affection. How I have wanted that.

My parents had it. I'd find them making out in the kitchen or in the car at the end of an evening out when they thought I was asleep in the backseat. Or I'd catch Daddy playfully grabbing for my mother's ass. She'd shoo him away—only halfheartedly—then he'd pull her close and nuzzle her neck. My sisters and I would shriek: Yuck! But the truth is, I liked it. It made me feel safer, somehow more secure, knowing that my parents were truly *together*. And they still are.

I always assumed my marriage would be like that. I'd had four intimate relationships from my freshman year in college—when I lost my virginity—to the month I'd met Roger. Great sex in every case, natural and routine, like brushing your teeth (but a lot more fun). But it wasn't just the sex. It was the sense of being profoundly desired.

And it was like that with Roger for the first year or two. Things began to deteriorate the year he left his job at the ad agency to devote himself to writing plays. Emboldened by the success of his first show, he chucked everything, bought a new Mac, and holed up in his office. But the second try was a flop and I remember how it cast a gloom on our lives, as if he'd been diagnosed with some terminal disease.

For a moment there, in the children's museum, I almost reached out to Roger, almost squeezed his shoulder. Would it have changed things? Could it have been the beginning of a reconciliation? Why didn't I do it? Pride? Fear? An unwillingness to relinquish the fantasy of Eddie?

'Til next time,

V

February 6

I can barely breathe, let alone write. I have made such a mess of things. Eddie came by my office at one o'clock, slipped a note under my door while I was in session. The note read: "Play hooky with me. Movies and a beer? Meet me at 2 on the corner."

The prospect of cutting out for the day felt deliciously wicked. I'd never cut a class, never missed a homework assignment, never failed to send a thank-you note. Skip out on two clients? I glanced out the window, noticed a pigeon on the ledge, the sun glinting off its iridescent feathers. Suddenly, impulsively, I grabbed my coat and headed out the door.

"Call my four o'clock and reschedule," I told Gail. I knew it was too late to reach my three o'clock. She came straight from school. She was probably already in the cab heading for my office. "And when Alice gets here, tell her I had an emergency and set up another time this week."

Right then I could feel the guilt swelling in my throat like a black balloon. I should have paid attention.

Alice is fourteen and clinically depressed. Last summer she found her father in bed with the au pair. He begged her not to tell, even bribed her with a new puppy, but Alice spilled it. The parents divorced, plunging the mother into near poverty. Alice blames herself. Last month she started cutting herself, first with paper clips, now with a pocketknife. But she never missed a session. She told me I made her feel safe.

I thought about the mysterious Alyssa Elkins. It had been a couple of weeks since I'd eavesdropped on that phone conversation. I didn't have the nerve to ask Roger if he's having an affair with his student. I fleetingly imagined her straddling my husband on the desk in his office at the Learning Attic. It had been six months since Roger and I had had sex, even longer since we had a real conversation. I *needed* to be with

Eddie. This would be *my* therapy, or so I had myself convinced.

We spent the afternoon like a couple of kids, giddy and free. We caught a matinee, then headed to Pony's for a beer, and then on to Space Cave to play video games. There was a kind of underworld element in that dark and noisy room. Who were all those grown men huddled against these arcades, and why weren't they at work? Eddie stepped behind me, presumably to help me aim the rifle. I felt his breath against my neck, his groin against me. "You smell so good," he whispered. I'd never felt more aroused. "Let's leave," I heard myself say. By now it was 5 P.M.

Then my pager beeped. I found a pay phone and called the office. "It's about Alice," my secretary said grimly. "She stepped in front of a bus. I mean, right here, outside the building. There were witnesses. They say it was no accident. She's at Memorial. She's critical."

At this point I didn't know if I'd vomit or pass out. Was I really responsible for this girl's suicide attempt? What if I'd been sick? What if I had crashed my car on the way to work? Why should it matter how I spent that hour?

It matters.

'Til next time,

𝒱

February 12

Like an alcoholic bargaining with God—get me through this hangover and I'll never take a drink again—I'd promised to end my "thing" with Eddie if He would let Alice live. Today she's out of intensive care and I'm already dreaming of my next rendezvous with Eddie.

I saw him this morning. I'd come in early to catch up on paperwork, but when I came across Alice's file, I fell apart. He found me sitting at my desk, and I'm sure he noticed I'd been crying. He locked the door behind him, pulled a chair close to mine, and held my hands in his. After a long silence he said: "Talk to me."

"My life is a complete disaster. I feel totally out of control."

He wiped a tear from my cheek with a callused thumb. "This isn't your fault. The girl was suicidal. It could have happened anytime, anywhere." He traced little circles across the top of my hand. The early-morning sunlight streamed through the blinds. I'd never noticed the flecks of violet in his eyes.

We spent the next hour like that, talking about our lives, our expectations, our disappointments. His eyes never left mine. We didn't kiss or even embrace, but after he'd left I felt as if we'd spent that hour making love.

If it was his raw male sexuality that first attracted me to Eddie, it is his ability to truly *listen* that now keeps me captivated. It's impossible not to contrast Eddie's interest in me with my husband's profound lassitude. To wit: When I came home last Friday, convinced that Alice's suicide attempt was a message from God, I was ready to start anew with my husband. I put Petey to bed and walk into the family room. Roger is watching ESPN. "Can we talk?" I ask him. He cranes his neck so he can see the TV. Apparently, I am blocking the view. "Can it wait?" he wants to know. For a split second I see the two of us sprawled on the bed with cartons of

Chinese food and the Sunday papers. We used to read the paper aloud, then discuss the issues of the day with the earnest intensity of a couple of graduate students. We didn't even own a TV then. It seems like such a long, long time ago.

"Well, no, it really can't wait." I try to sound assertive. It's what I teach my clients, yet it's the thing I find most difficult to do. I hate begging for attention. I mightily resist the urge to say: Fine. Watch your damn TV. Instead, I say, "I really want to talk. Now."

Roger snaps off the set and crosses his arms over his chest. "You're on."

"Something terrible happened. One of my clients tried to kill herself. I had canceled out on her. I think that's why she did it." I am not ready to offer all the details.

At this point Roger is tapping his fingertips on the table and jiggling his foot, signaling that he's losing interest or patience or both. I had interrupted the hockey game. The meter is ticking and I am just about out of time.

"So what do you want *me* to do about it?" he says.

"You? I don't want you to do anything. I'm upset. I just wanted to talk." By now I want to throttle him.

"Look. You work with a bunch of crazies, and crazy people do crazy things. She's a sick kid and you're taking this way too personally." I can see him looking past me at the dark TV screen. "Okay?"

"Yeah, Roger. Okay." I grab the remote. "Here. Let me do this for you." I switch on the set and fling the remote to the floor. It cracks apart and the batteries roll out. "Hey!" Roger cries. "Whadja do that for?"

I find myself counting the years until Petey is old

enough to handle our divorce. I've got to get out of this marriage.

'Til next time,

V

February 20

Thanks to a flat tire, I now know exactly what Roger is doing with his young student. My Jeep wheeled over a broken beer bottle in the parking lot as I pulled into my spot this morning. The tire was completely deflated by the end of the day. I hadn't fixed a flat since college and wasn't sure I remembered how to do it. So I pulled out my cell phone and called Roger.

He didn't answer—and it didn't make sense. He'd always been home by 6 P.M. I worried that Petey had been hurt—God's revenge for Alice's accident—and saw a fleeting but vivid picture of Roger in the hospital emergency room, crumpled over the gurney as the nurses covered the small body. When my clients do this, I call it catastrophizing. Yet the truth is, I do it all the time. Ever since I was a little girl, sitting on the window seat in our living room, watching for the headlights of my father's car, I've always conjured horrific possibilities.

I had to hurry. I managed to fix the flat myself, then sped home, taking streets instead of the highway to avoid rush-hour traffic. As I rolled through a yellow light at Washington and Seventh, I saw them: Roger and a young woman lingering outside the Learning Attic. She was a girl, really. I slowed as I passed them, knowing intuitively that they would never see me. They were in the kind of glass bubble new lovers create for themselves, impervious to outside distractions. She wasn't the blond cover girl I'd imagined, but had a Stevie-Nicks-witchy-woman look: spiraling hair, almond eyes, red-painted lips, long skirt, cowboy boots. Very different from the cool, Waspy, Talbots look Roger always said he favored. As I passed them, I saw her lean toward him and adjust his scarf. An intimacy. I'm still in shock.

I picked Petey up from day care, knowing Roger would be momentarily panicked when he arrived and didn't see his son among the other kids. I wanted him to panic.

It's now 7:36 and he still isn't home. Is my marriage over? I allow myself to contemplate the possibility. I never thought he'd have the courage to make the first move, but it looks like he fooled me, didn't he? I'm scared. I am not ready to live alone. I am not ready to end my marriage. And crass as it may sound, without Roger's money I'll be broke—almost as broke as Alice's mother, who went from caviar to food stamps almost overnight.

Roger is a trust-fund baby. The money his parents made in the stock market—buying Disney and McDonald's and IBM when these companies were young and green—has made it possible for Roger and all his siblings to live comfortably and pursue the careers of their dreams. Hence, Roger the Playwright. My client load changes every month so my income fluctuates, and ever since the managed care revolution, most of my clients leave treatment after the allotted six or eight sessions.

I couldn't have a house, couldn't afford a car, probably couldn't afford health insurance. I'm not ready to live like a grad student again, cinder-block-and-plank shelving, hot dogs for dinner. To know profoundly that I am alone, that I am not loved, that my marriage may be ending . . . it's all so chilling. And suddenly, in light of these possibilities, there is nothing sexy about Eddie. The prospect of poverty has the effect of a cold shower.

I'm aware that by focusing on my finances, I conveniently avoid the real issues. Forget about losing money—what about losing my life's companion, the father of my son? What about Petey? Do we really want to live with the burden of knowing we wrecked this child's life? If nothing else, isn't Petey's well-being worth fighting for? I resolve to confront Roger when he gets home. I'll be cool, controlled. I will not cry. I'll tell him it's time to work things out.

When I heard Roger's key in the door, I was prepared to employ the interested-but-detached voice I use with my clients. ("I got a flat today," I'd tell him. "I tried to call you but you weren't home. Leftover lasagna okay for dinner?")

But the moment I saw my husband's face, flushed and happy—and actually heard him *whistling*—I knew I'd never make it. "Where were you at six o'clock?" I said, already accusing. I felt my outrage roil, then surge. "I saw you. With her." I sounded like Elizabeth Taylor in *Who's Afraid of Virginia Woolf?*

"I see we're moving up in the world. First eavesdropping, now spying." He sorted through the mail, chuckling derisively. He had on one of his trademark expressions—a razor blade smile, grotesque in its insincerity. It made me want to pummel him.

"Damn you, Roger. What the hell is going on?" I could hear Petey humming in the other room as he rummaged through his crayons. I didn't want him to walk in on this. One of the kids in his Saturday play group told him his parents were getting a divorce because they fight too much, and now every time Roger and I argue, Petey asks pitifully, "Are you going to get a divorce now?"

"What do you think is going on?" Roger narrowed his eyes, waiting for my theory.

"Don't play games with me. I saw the girl." Already I was crying, my voice choked as phlegm clogged my throat. "I saw how she touched you."

"She wasn't touching me. I don't know what you're talking about."

"Was that Alyssa?"

He stopped flipping through the mail and stared at me. "How did you know her name?"

"Caller ID."

"God. You and your Caller ID." He wiggled his fingers in the air and made Twilight Zone noises: "Ooooh . . . I guess Big Brother is watching me. I never wanted to get that thing in the first place." He left the room to play with Petey, left me in the kitchen, alone and trembling in my rage. I began banging pans and slamming cabinet doors. With a sweep of my arm I pushed mail and papers off the counter and onto the tile floor.

It's a blinding kind of turmoil, this anger. I imagine it's how a two-year-old must feel in the throes of a temper tantrum. I was out of control and terrified, knowing I must look like an ass, but simply incapable of regaining my calm. In retrospect, I know what fueled the rage: it was the belief that this man who had deprived me—no, starved me—of physical affection in all these months had somehow found the capacity to give the gift of his attention and touch to another woman.

This idea (and that's really all it is—I have no proof of an affair) had captivated my imagination in the cruelest way and catapulted me from a relatively sane wife to a raving shrew. And as I raved with red eyes and a swollen red nose, I thought, "How could he love a woman this needy, this pathetic? How could any man?" I shoved the lasagna into the microwave and heard Roger's footsteps behind me.

"You've got no right to spy on me, you know," he began. I refused to turn around.

"Look. She's a flirt. And she's cute. But there's nothing going on. I swear."

I turned now and searched his face for the truth. I didn't believe him. Suddenly I thought of Eddie, his body against mine in the video arcade, and I felt guilty and ashamed. A childish phrase sprang to mind, and it's never been more appropriate: It takes one to know one.

'Til next time,

V

March 3

Last night I felt a powerful need to talk, but there was no one to talk to. Betsy is always asleep by nine. I was too embarrassed to tell either of my sisters about Eddie. Teresa is too critical, Julia too self-absorbed.

So I did something I thought I'd never do: I went online. First I found a chat room for mothers; all they wanted to talk about was getting Kool-Aid stains out of the carpet. Then I joined a group of singles, where I got an instant message from some guy who wanted to know what color panties I was wearing. Finally I found a chat room for newly divorced women. Thinking they might have some cautionary tales and sound advice, I lurked for a while, then introduced myself and shared my sorry story.

I can't believe the response. One person urged me to dump Roger ASAP and move in with Eddie. Another suggested I give up on both men and become a lesbian. ("You've never been loved 'til you've been loved by a woman," she insisted.) Another woman said I'd be crazy to give up Roger's trust fund and offered to trade places with me any day. And one ex–New Yorker told the group that she'd given up everything—husband, house, job as a high-powered publicist—to become a waitress in Texas where she's now dating a cowboy and having the best sex of her life. On one hand I thought: You slut! On the other hand, I found her story tantalizing. It was as if she'd thrown a stick of dynamite into her life, fled from the rubble, and started anew. Of course, she didn't mention whether she'd also left behind children.

I teach people how to communicate, yet my husband and I still haven't sat down to discuss the mess we've made of our lives, and I go on-line to reveal myself to total strangers! I'm paid to help resolve marital conflict and my own marriage is a shambles. How many clients would I have today if they knew? Then again, nearly all my colleagues face similar contradictions. Michael leads the anxiety disorders workshop and I know he takes Xanax for panic attacks. Nan can't maintain a friendship longer than six months because she's pathologically self-centered. Avery's a family therapist who hasn't spoken to her mother in twelve years. And James is one of the leading experts on marriage and infidelity and he's been carrying on with his research assistant for years. Perhaps that's what makes him an expert.

'Til next time,

𝒱

March 6

After Roger insisted that he wasn't sleeping with Alyssa, I decided to leave the issue alone, thereby deferring the painful but necessary process of deconstructing our marriage in order to rebuild it. I don't have the energy for that. I'm also scared. There's too much venom under the surface—his and mine. I've opened these wounds before in hopes of a reconciliation, then suffered the assault of Roger's acrid hostility. ("What do you mean I'm not affectionate?" he'd scream. "How about you? When's the last time you offered to rub *my* back? And what do you expect when you wear sweatpants to bed every night?") I'm not ready to put myself through that again.

My eleven o'clock canceled today. I thought I'd take the opportunity to meditate, but I wasn't alone for long. I heard a soft rap at the door.

"Do you accept walk-ins?" It was Eddie. He ducked his head boyishly. I opened the door wider to let him in, then closed it. Locked it. "I normally see clients by appointment only," I said, playing along, "but I'll make an exception in this case." He stretched out on the leather sofa and rested his large hands across his belt buckle. His biceps bulged, even in repose. He stared up at the ceiling as he spoke.

"See, Doc, I've got a problem."

My heart thwacked wildly in my chest. I knew precisely what would come next. "There's this woman. I can't get her out of my mind."

"So, what's the problem?"

"The problem is, she's married. So am I."

"Hmmm. Tell me more."

"She's amazing, Doc. She's smart . . . sexy." Eddie turned to stare at me. I had to look away. The word ricocheted in my head.

Sexy? Me? I decided to take a risk. "Tell me about your wife."

Eddie was quiet for a long time. He looked up at the ceiling again. "Patty. You want me to tell you about Patty?"

I swallowed hard. I wanted to say, No, not really. Let's get back to that sexy woman you can't get out of your mind. What was I afraid of? That he'd say he still loved her? Or that his words would turn this phantom wife into a flesh-and-blood woman. A mother. Like me. His stories would make her sympathetic, and then inviolable.

I was wrong. By the time Eddie had led me through his marriage and its demise, I cared nothing for Patty. And for once I understood completely how a gardener and a clinical psychologist could be locked in this lover's knot. Damage attracts damage; pain finds pain. We had reached almost heliotropically toward each other, knowing intuitively that we would be accepted and perhaps even loved.

He told me so much. I want to write more about the details of his marriage but I'm already late for a haircut appointment.

'Til next time,

V

March 13

As Eddie lay there on the couch, I imagined myself stretched along the length of him. I imagined him gripping me with his strong, tanned arms, then maneuvering me so I was under him, which is how I like it. I wanted to be overwhelmed by him. He glanced at me as he spoke, and I prayed that among his talents, telepathy wasn't one.

"I married Patty in high school. She was pregnant. I wanted to do the right thing. But we'd only been together four months. I didn't love her." I felt relieved, then ashamed. If I really cared about this man, wouldn't I want him to resolve his marital problems? Did I really want him pining for me?

"We were both raised Catholic," Eddie continued, "so divorce was out of the question. I don't think I'm Catholic anymore." He turned to look at me. I tried not to react. "Keep going."

"You know what they say—a woman is either a devoted mother or a devoted wife, but never both at the same time." I'd never heard this particular maxim but it gave me a guilty little shiver. I didn't have to think hard to know which category I fell into. "Well, Patty's always been a devoted mother to our three girls. Wouldn't even have sex when she was pregnant, convinced that it would hurt the babies." I quickly calculated, three pregnancies times nine months . . . that's over two years without sex. "Then Patty's mother moved in with us last year and . . . well . . . I'm last in line. No, it's worse than that. I'm not in line at all."

There was no yearning in Eddie's voice, no hint that he wanted his wife's affections. He talked as if he was describing something that happened a long time ago, in another life. "Patty's a nice girl. Helluva mother. But I can't tell you the last time we actually had a conversation. When I left my last job to start my business, she barely noticed. Not like I wanted a party or anything, but it was a big move, you know? I've got twenty-two employees and she couldn't care less."

I was confused. I hadn't realized Eddie was in business for himself. I'd pegged him for a community college dropout. He quickly read my face. "You're wondering why I'm always here if I'm the boss. Right?" I nodded. He *was* telepathic! "The day we met, I was filling in for one of my guys. His wife was having a baby." He looked away sheepishly. "After that, I kept coming around just to be around you. I like talking to you." Then he laughed. "You think I'd be playing hooky if I wasn't the boss?"

I felt such turbulence. It had been years since I'd been the object of any man's desire. I needed Eddie's attention the way the willow root seeks water. I had been parched and my very survival depended on his desire. There were many things that drew me to Eddie: his machismo (so different from the fey and cultured boys I'd dated in school), his tenderness, his smoldering stare. But above all, I was attracted to the simple fact that he was attracted to me. And the truth is, I find that troubling. Am I so profoundly needy that all it takes to get me going is a man who wants me? What am I willing to trade to have that steady infusion of desire? My child? My husband? Can I possibly have both: the stability of married life *and* the passion of an affair? What price would I pay for my greed?

When he had finally finished talking about his decaying marriage, he pulled himself up and patted the couch, gesturing for me to sit near him. It was risky. My next client was due in five minutes; she was a strongly intuitive woman whose husband had, in fact, been unfaithful. I was sure she'd scan my face and know instantly that Eddie and I were having an affair. And yes,

I do believe that's what this is, even if his body hasn't entered mine. I feel as if I've surrendered my soul to this man. With a rush of adrenaline, I think of him first thing in the morning, and as I fall into the dim twilight between sleep and wakefulness, he is my last thought. When I shop for clothes, I choose things I think will please him (the short black skirt I found at Ann Taylor). When I dab on perfume, I imagine him inhaling the scent with his face against my neck. When I lift weights at the club, it's the fantasy of Eddie watching from a corner of the room that enables me to finish the set.

There, on the couch, Eddie reached for my hands and held them lightly between his own. "We'd be good together. You realize that, don't you?" I nodded slowly. I felt locked in his gaze. He reached over to brush the hair from my eyes. "Don't we deserve some happiness?" I didn't know what to say. Frankly, I never thought I deserved to be happy. The only clear message I got growing up was: Work hard and do whatever it takes to succeed. No one ever said: Do whatever it takes to be happy.

"My old man died when he was forty-one. I don't think I ever saw him really happy," Eddie said. He held my hands tighter now. "He hated his job and hated his marriage, but every morning he went to work and every night he went to sleep in the same bed with my mother. He had a heart attack on the Fourth of July. He'd been scrubbing the barbecue while my mother stood in the kitchen, nagging at him like always. 'Scrub harder, Joseph! You expect me to eat off that thing?' I remember it like it was yesterday. He looked at her like he was going to say something, then dropped to his knees. I thought he was joking around. Then he flopped over and I knew he was dead. I was nine years old."

Eddie ran the back of his hand across his eyes. Impulsively I reached up and touched a finger to his lips. He turned quickly and kissed me full on the mouth, and in a moment had me beneath him on the sofa. His tongue was cool and tasted sweet and he moved his hand expertly under my blouse. My body arched to meet his, he pulled me closer, roughly. Whatever moral compass I might have possessed was quickly corrupted by the power of Eddie's magnetic field.

Just as quickly, I heard a knock on the door, then a key turning in the lock. Then, a woman's husky voice: "What the *hell?*"

Diana.

Thank God for the small foyer between my door and the rest of the office—by the time Diana came into view, Eddie had pulled himself off me and I'd managed to sit up. I quickly ran a finger over my blouse to check the buttons but there wasn't time to smooth my hair.

"Oh-ho! What have we here?" Diana moved into the room with the authority of a headmistress. A corrosive smile spread across her face. A key dangled from her hand. Eddie knelt by the window, pretending to be fussing with the ficus tree.

"You can tell lover boy he needn't bother," she said, gesturing toward Eddie. "I know what you're up to and it sure ain't gardening." As her eyes scanned me, I felt as if I was undergoing an MRI. I've never felt more exposed. I could have responded with rage—this woman had no business breaking into my office—but I was too consumed by shame and panic to take the offensive. I managed a feeble, "What the hell do you think you're doing in here?"

"Now, this is rich." Diana moved closer, her eyes fixed on me. "Your hair's a mess, your lipstick is smeared across your face, and you're asking *me* what the hell *I'm* doing? You make me sick."

"Screw you, Diana," Eddie hissed.

"Be my guest," she retorted, not missing a beat. "But alas, I can see you're already taken." She glanced at his wedding band. "Twice taken, in fact." Diana walked to my desk and picked up a manila folder. "For your information, this is what I came for. Your monthly report. You know today's the deadline." She shrugged her shoulders. "I knocked and knocked but no one answered. I figured you were out and let myself in. I didn't think you'd mind. I didn't realize I'd be . . . interrupting." She looked at Eddie, letting her eyes linger on his zipper. A tiny smile curled at the corners of her mouth. There was nothing to see. Any evidence of Eddy's desire had faded the moment we heard her open the door.

Diana started toward the door, then stopped. "By the way, did Roger mention that I'm taking him to lunch next week?"

I felt my stomach flip–flop. I said nothing.

"I'm *really* looking forward to it. We have *so* much catching up to do." She giggled. "Oh, baby, don't look so worried. It gives you wrinkles, you know." The door closed behind her. Eddie tried to put his arms around me but I stepped away from his embrace. I couldn't touch him. I wanted to throw up. "Don't let that bitch get to you."

"Why shouldn't I? Don't you realize what's happening here? She's out to destroy my marriage!"

"And what if she does?" Eddie looked at me. Then,

softly, "It could be the best thing that's ever happened to you . . . to us."

'Til next time,

$\mathcal{V}$

April 10

This morning at breakfast Roger violated the tacit rules of our cold war and actually initiated a conversation. I was hopeful until I realized that the topic was Diana Pierce. I had just dipped my spoon into a bowl of corn flakes when he mentioned his upcoming lunch. "Diana says she has something important to tell me," he said, eyes on the sports section. "Something about the office. Something big. Have any idea what she's referring to?"

What could I possibly say? Sure, Roger. She wants to tell you all about the day she broke into my office and found me with the office gardener. Oh, and the fact that my lipstick was smeared all over my face.

"I'm not sure . . ." I began, my appetite quickly draining away. Incapable of swallowing even a spoonful of cereal, I began clearing the table. If there was ever a time to broach the subject, this was it. Petey was still asleep and my first appointment wasn't until 1 P.M. I wasn't ready to confess any wrongdoing, but if Roger was going to hear about Eddie, I wanted him to hear it from me first.

"I have a theory, though. There's this guy in the office. I think he has the hots for me." I moved quickly around the kitchen, keeping my back to Roger as I spoke. "Diana—who's not my biggest fan, if you haven't already figured that out, by the way—has it in her head that I'm having an affair with this guy. A *gardener*, for

Christ's sake. Can you *believe* that? You'd think Diana would have a better imagination than that!" I forced a laugh. I was talking too much, gesturing too wildly.

The more I talked, the more I began to believe my own story, and this belief enabled me to continue in earnest. It was a testament to the profound power of human denial. In that tiny pause between "I don't know" and "I have a theory," I managed to convince myself that Eddie was nothing more than a dumb lug with a schoolboy crush, a pest, a triviality. Denial allows teenagers to move through all nine months of pregnancy and never acknowledge that they are carrying a baby. It's probably what keeps O. J. Simpson sane. Bolstered by denial, I continued: "He's always coming around to water my plants. They're practically dead from all the water they're getting. The guy has an IQ of 40! Vinnie, Tony, whatever his name is."

"Eddie."

"What?" I was stunned.

"I believe his name is Eddie." Roger was no longer reading the sports section. He pushed his plate away and folded his arms across his chest.

"How do you know his name?" I tried not to stammer but my face flushed with blood and heat.

Roger let out a humorless chuckle. "I know more than you realize."

'Til next time,

𝒱

April 17

Suddenly everything seemed to move in slow motion. How could Roger know about Eddie? Did I whisper his

name in my sleep? Had Diana revealed her suspicions?
Was my husband, a man who virtually sleepwalks
through our marriage, more aware than I realized?

"Eddie's the guy who called you a while back. About
the plants."

"Huh?" I tried to appear clueless. Of course I knew
what Roger was referring to. Eddie had called me at
home, at night, under the pretext of choosing plants
for the office—a ridiculous ruse. Roger had picked up
the phone first and seemed to suspect nothing. Now I
checked his face for any hint of awareness. It was hard
to tell.

"Sure. You remember. He called about plants. At
night."

"I guess. I really don't remember." I shrugged and
reached for the last plate in the dishwasher. It clattered
to the floor and broke into three neat pieces, like a preschooler's puzzle. I bent to pick it up and cut myself on
an edge.

"Nervous?"

Now I knew Roger suspected something. Damn
him—he was playing with me. I pretended not to hear.
Some therapist. The woman who urges communication
can't even talk honestly with her own husband. I
couldn't. I knew that speaking the truth now could lead
to the rapid dissolution of my marriage, and as miserable as I may be, I'm not prepared to be single.

Neither is Roger. He could have pursued it but instead he let the subject drop. He picked up the newspaper and poured himself another cup of coffee. "I'll be
home late tonight," he said. "Student conferences." My
mind leaped to the image of Roger and Alyssa outside
the Learning Attic, her hands adjusting his scarf. And
their stupid smiling faces.

Roger had one-upped me. He knew I was in no position to say a word about her. If Roger was the black-
ened kettle, I was most certainly the pot. "Should I keep
dinner warm for you?" I asked, shamed and contrite.
In context, the question made a mockery of a real marriage.

"Don't bother. I'll grab something on the way home."
That's precisely what I was afraid of.

I feel like I'm in a kind of purgatory, a limbo land
where I have neither the affections of my husband nor
a full-fledged relationship with a lover. I have never felt
more completely alone. Next week is Roger's lunch
with Diana. I'm scared.

'Til next time,

V

April 24

It has been forty-eight hours since Roger had lunch
with Diana, and I have absolutely no idea what tran-
spired. Based on Roger's behavior, however, I fear that
Diana has told him everything she knows about Eddie
and me. Roger has been silent as a monk. When I walk
into a room, he leaves. When I sit down at the table, he
clears his plate. When I ask a question, he responds as
minimally as possible; instead of speaking he nods or
gestures or grunts. He wasn't in bed when I went to
sleep, nor was he there when I woke up. I found him
in the study last night, whispering conspiratorially into
the phone. I had to know who he was talking to. Later
that night I hit the redial button on the cordless phone.
A young woman picked up. I heard myself say, "Is
Alyssa there?"

"That's me," she answered perkily. "Who's this?"

I felt my chest clench. I fumbled for a response then said, idiotically, "Sorry. Wrong number." I pushed the flash button to disconnect the line, then stood there in the dark, phone in hand, shaking.

So why aren't I rejoicing? Isn't this exactly what I'd wanted, a reason to leave my cold-as-a-fish husband and leap into Eddie's eager arms? If this were a soap opera, that's exactly what I'd be doing now. I'd hop in my car, call Eddie from the highway on my cell phone, and arrange to meet him at a motel, where we'd screw our brains out. He leaves Patty, I leave Roger, and we live happily ever after. But this isn't a soap opera. It's my very real life. I'm too introspective, too *guilt ridden* to dispose of my marriage like a used coffee filter. To what extent am I responsible for whatever may be going on between Roger and Alyssa? Do I really want to start over with someone new? (It gives me a headache just imagining what it would be like to establish the kind of familiarity I have with Roger. Do I really want to pick up Eddie's dirty underwear? Do I really want him to see my stretch marks?) What if the only thing attracting me to Eddie is the fact that he's attracted to me at a time when I'm most vulnerable? Could I really spend the rest of my life (or even a year) with a man who would abandon a wife and three young daughters? Even more painful to contemplate: What if he has no intention of leaving them? And why can't I forget the taste of Eddie's mouth, the fleeting sensation of his body sinking into mine on the couch?

As I replayed that scene in my head this morning, my secretary buzzed me on the intercom. "There's a Mrs. DeLuca here to see you. She says it's important." I opened the door to find a tiny, scowling woman in my waiting area. "Can I help you?" I asked.

"You don't know me, but I know you," she said, shaking a finger at me.

"Excuse me?" I was truly mystified. We get all sorts of borderline cases in our office, and I figured she was one of them.

I was wrong. This was no borderline. It was Eddie's mother-in-law! She pointed an arthritic finger at me and spoke in a voice loud enough for everyone in the office to hear: "Leave my daughter's husband alone!"

She was standing in the anteroom to my office, four feet of finger-wagging fury. Eddie's mother-in-law.

"I'm telling you," she growled, "you got no business bothering with a married man." She clutched a black vinyl purse in one hand and pointed with the other. "And I ain't leaving until you promise me, missy. Hands off."

I felt a rapid flush rise from neck to scalp as I searched for an appropriate response.

"I'm sorry," I said, hoping to appear confused yet kindly. "Do I know you?" The woman cocked her head, arched an eyebrow, and hissed: "No. But I know all about you. Oh-ho, I sure do. I know what you're trying to do to a good man." She glared at me disdainfully. "A *married* man. A man with three little girls and a wife who loves him." Now she was yelling at me. "But you'll do it over my dead body. You hear me? OVER MY DEAD BODY!"

At this point I noticed that the office has come to a standstill. The secretaries and several of the social workers are watching intently. Gail, my secretary, gestured toward the phone and mouthed the words:

"Should I call security?" I nodded my head and she began punching in the number. "I'm sorry, ma'am," I told her. "I'm going to have to ask you to leave."

I heard the chime of the elevator and I'm relieved to see Mark, the building security guard. He looks at the woman, then at me, clearly confused. He's obviously thinking: You call *this* a security threat? "Please escort this woman from the building." He puts a gentle hand on her elbow and begins leading her toward the elevator. "Come this way, please," he says. She will not go quietly, though. "Listen here, you slut! Stay away from my son-in-law! I'm warning you! Stay away!" I can still hear as the elevator descends. As I turn toward my office I see a figure leaning against the water fountain. It's Diana, and she's staring straight at me. Laughing.

That cow! Who else but Diana would be venal enough to call Eddie's mother-in-law? I phone Eddie at work and tell him everything, sobbing into the receiver. "Jeez," he whispers, momentarily stunned. But he doesn't appear particularly worried that Patty might know about us. Right now he seems to care only about me. "Awww, honey," he coos softly. "You shouldn't have had to go through that. I'm so sorry." After a pause, he says, "Listen, I've been saving this for later but maybe now's a good time to tell you." I stopped crying. "What?"

"I think I've got something on Diana that will shut her up once and for all. But I don't think we should discuss it on the phone. Meet me at Jim Dandy's tomorrow at five."

'Til next time,

V

April 25

"STAY AWAY FROM MY SON-IN-LAW!" Mrs. DeLuca's furious warning is clanging in my head as I make my way uptown to Jim Dandy's. I will never forget the look of pure contempt on her face, the disgust. Nor can I forget the sight of Diana, self-satisfied and laughing as I trembled. As comptroller, Diana has records on every employee, even the contracted service workers like Eddie. She knew his last name—Bennedetto—and could easily have found his number in the phone book.

I feel such despair. How is it that other people manage to have these torrid and clandestine affairs while I can't even manage a kiss, let alone a relationship, without everyone knowing about it? Who will be next to drop in unannounced—my minister? My sister Teresa? The gods must be conspiring against me.

Eddie was waiting outside Jim Dandy's. He started to kiss me but I pulled away. (With my luck, my mother was shopping next door. Can anyone blame me for being paranoid?) He led me to a booth in the back room, a place normally reserved for the restaurant's owners and friends. The maitre d' greeted him warmly and bowed elegantly toward me. A young waiter made a tentative approach but Eddie waved him away. "Give us a few minutes alone." The waiter retreated. Eddie leaned toward me and whispered: "Diana's a thief."

"Huh?"

"Listen. A buddy of mine happened to be at a party where Diana had gotten herself stewed. I mean, flat-out drunk. She decided she wanted to take him home and was blabbering about all kinds of nonsense. The next thing he knows, Diana pulls out her wallet and flashes these bills. He never saw so many hundreds. So he says, 'How'd you get so rich?' And she says, 'Creative accounting,' and starts laughing."

"What happened next?" I asked, stunned.

"She threw up on his jacket." Eddie howled. "Anyway, I nosed around her desk after hours on Wednesday and came across this." He pulled a slip of paper from his shirt pocket and waved it at me. A deposit slip. I stared at it blankly. "So?"

"It's a dummy account. She's scamming the center." A triumphant smile spread across Eddie's face and he thumped a fist on the deposit slip. "She's as good as gone." He pulled out an envelope with photocopies of records he "borrowed" from Diana's office.

For the next twenty minutes, Eddie reconstructed Diana's scheme. Apparently she had applied for state and corporate grants to cover a program in which AIDS patients get free and confidential treatment for depression. Because patients remain anonymous, she can construct as many fictitious clients as she pleases, bill the granting agency, then pocket the cash in a dummy account. Eddie called his brother, a tax lawyer, to test his theory. It checks out. Diana may have embezzled hundreds of thousands of dollars or more from the Center.

"So what do we do now?" I felt thrilled and terrified.

"What do you think we do? We bust her." Eddie slid around to my side of the booth and put his face close to mine. He clinked his beer bottle against my water glass. "To us," he said, his eyes locked on mine.

I whispered, "To us."

'Til next time,

𝒱

May 15

This is how my day begins. The phone rings. I pick up. Roger, in another room, picks up simultaneously. I let him answer first while I listen.

"Hullo?" he says.

"It's me." It's Alyssa.

"Yeah?"

"Uh. I think I left my diaphragm in your van."

"You what?" Long silence. "Jesus God. What were you thinking?"

No answer. Then, a childish: "I'm sorry . . . Roger?"

"Yeah."

"I said I'm sorry."

"Okay. I'll take care of it."

"Roger? I love you."

"Yeah." Click.

I didn't know whether to scream or cry. My husband was screwing this girl. I heard his racing steps down the stairs but I beat him to the door leading from the mud room to the garage. I told him: "I think I'll take the van today. My Jeep's out of gas."

Roger looked as if he had swallowed a grenade. For once, he couldn't seem to muster his usual smug retort. "No!" he practically shouted, stepping into my path toward the door. "You can't."

"Why not?"

"The brakes," he blurted out. "I think they're mal-functioning."

"I know how concerned you are about my well-being, Roger, but I'll be fine," I told him, pulling the door open. "I'll just drive to the mechanic's and get it fixed. See ya."

He stood there helplessly while I backed out of the garage. I drove with my hands clamped to the wheel, my skull literally buzzing. I pulled into a shopping center at an intersection and allowed myself finally to look. There it was on the passenger seat, the ultimate emblem of my marriage's demise: a plastic case, violet and smooth, bearing an embossed daisy on the cover. I picked it up. It smelled of perfume and spermicide. I traced a finger along the daisy. I didn't open it. I slipped it into my bag.

I finally have my proof but I'm hardly victorious. I feel sick. I always suspected that Roger and Alyssa had some sort of relationship but never believed he would actually make love to her. Yet . . . as I drive to the office, even in my dazed grief, I know I am not ready to abandon my marriage. It's odd: when I was a teenager, I believed (with the kind of unwavering righteousness and certainty that comes with youth) that if my husband ever cheated, I'd boot him out the door.

But things aren't so simple now. I know that I've been as instrumental as Roger in fouling things up. By the time I reach the office, in an uncharacteristic moment of maturity and grace, I have resolved to salvage my marriage.

But this is how my day ends: Eddie slipped into the elevator as I was leaving for the day. I thought he wanted to talk about Diana but I was wrong. His eyes gave my body a hot, raking gaze. "Be with me now," he said, pressing me against the wall. Then he did something I'd only seen in movies. He pushed the red button and the elevator abruptly ground to a stop between floors. He put his lips on my neck. I could feel his breath, warm and moist, and I pulled his head toward mine. I was propelled by an energy that had no conscience. My lips met his as he slipped his hands under my blouse, then my bra. I could feel his arousal as he pushed slowly, rhythmically against me. "Let's get a room," he whispers, "at the Roundtree."

Like someone who must have one last hot fudge sundae before starting a diet in earnest, I decide that before Roger and I begin counselling, I must have Eddie.

'Til next time,

$\mathcal{V}$

May 22

The Roundtree Hotel was four and a half blocks from the office. We practically sprinted there, yet I felt as if I was moving through Jell-O. The anticipation was unbearable, painful.

Could this really be happening, after all these months of fantasy and flirtation and contemplation? The animal instinct I'd felt in the elevator had subsided, replaced by a stream of self-rationalizations: After over six sexless months, I deserve this. I need this. Just this once. I can handle it. Roger's doing it, why can't I? My marriage had collapsed like the Berlin Wall, how much worse could it get?

I remembered couples I'd seen on TV who had "open" marriages, and thought, that's not such a bad idea. I recalled scientists who said humans weren't built for monogamy. I thought of a client of mine who had unselfconsciously nurtured a twelve-year affair after her husband was stricken with multiple sclerosis.

Then I remembered my prim neighbor, a forty-year-old named Ann who admitted (after a few too many tequilas at a Labor Day block party) that a brief fling with her dentist literally saved her life; her marriage wasn't just dead, it was in rigor mortis. She found herself weeping in supermarket checkout aisles. She despaired at the notion that she might spend another forty years in this airless chamber of a marriage. It took a scant three months with the dentist to revive her—a faster turnaround than any therapy could offer. She saw herself through her lover's lens as a sexy, vivacious woman, and now, from this position of strength and security, was able to resuscitate her marriage. I held fast to Ann's story as Eddie slid his credit card across the counter and signed for our room. When he put his hand in the small of my back to gently guide me toward the elevator, I suddenly remembered, with astonishing lucidity, the summer of my sixth year when, after much hestitation, I finally plunged off the diving board into a swimming pool. There is this moment when fear and reason are simply overwhelmed by irrational desire, when one must stop thinking and *move*.

And now I sit here, alone in my office, staring at the hand that holds this pen, and know I must write about the two hours I spent with Eddie in Room 1040 at the Roundtree Hotel. How can I possibly give language to what happened between us? If it had been a disappointment, if he didn't know how to move me from arousal to climax, if he'd been selfish or hasty or lazy or clumsy . . . I'd be relieved now. I could say, I tried it, and it is over, and I can turn my attention once more to the man who shares my bed night after night.

But I would be lying.

The Roundtree is the only really nice hotel in town, the kind of place you send out-of-town guests if your goal is to impress. The closets are filled with good wooden hangers, the kind that could actually function in your closet if you chose to swipe them, and there are always two large wicker baskets in the bathroom, one to hold a pair of soft terry cloth robes, and another for toiletries, and not just the usual shampoo and shower cap, but peppermint foot cream, a wooden rolling back massager, and a small plastic case filled with sixteen sewing needles already threaded in sixteen different colors.

Our suite was done up in shades of peach and creamy yellow, and there was a large arrangement of silk flowers on the narrow table in the foyer, and I remember thinking that someone had taken great care to arrange this room but the only thing of any value right now was the expansive bed against the wall. It really didn't matter whether it had a sheet, let alone this lovely bedspread with its brocade trim and its swirls of peach and creamy yellow.

And then, after Eddie had pulled me urgently toward him, and pushed me up against the wall, I knew that even the bed wouldn't be necessary. As Eddie ripped down my zippers and yanked up my bra, he was more beast than man, lapping me up greedily, kissing my mouth with savage insistence. He still had his clothes on, which intensified my arousal, but when I tried to reach for his belt buckle he pulled my hand away. "Not yet," he whispered hotly into the nape of my neck.

I slid his pants off and we fell upon the bed, and with fingers and tongue he explored and savored each part of me. He seemed to know intuitively how to please me, softly here, a bit harder there, quickly then slowly. His rhythms matched mine, his mouth tasted like honey. He stared at me as he brought us both to the peak, and he sighed into my neck as he collapsed beside me, exhausted and elated. We both dozed off—it couldn't have been more than ten minutes—but when I opened my eyes and saw him snuggled beside me, slaked, comfortable as a cat, I felt a terrible surge of adrenaline streak through me. What had I done? What, really, do I know about the man whose body fit mine so perfectly only moments ago? What does he know about me? And where do I go from here?

'Til next time,

V

May 28

We spent the evening at my in-laws' last night. It was a bon voyage party for Roger's sister Lori, who has decided, rather suddenly, to teach English to peasant children in Peru.

I'd never felt so joyless. There I was, sitting next to Roger on the patio, picking at my skewered vegetables, trying to make small talk, pretending to be a real wife. Everyone was so festive, so engaged in the celebration, while I felt more and more isolated, as if I were watching the scene from a corner of the room.

Then someone put an old Paul McCartney song on the stereo and I remembered how it felt to lie beside Eddie in our bed at the Roundtree. He had traced a finger over my stretch marks—the crinkly skin I'd been almost too embarrassed to reveal to him—and said softly, "I love these." He slid down and pressed his lips against my soft belly. "You're a beautiful woman," he told me. The only comment Roger ever made about my stretch marks was, "What the hell are those?"

I watched Roger cross his legs and I saw his little foot in his little leather loafer and felt like killing myself. I excused myself, locked myself in the bathroom, and cried until my eyes swelled.

I had to call Eddie. I'd written his number on a drinking straw wrapper and had stuffed it behind the credit cards in my wallet. I fished through my purse and retrieved the tiny paper wad, unrolled it, and pulled out my cell phone. Patty answered. I hung up on her. My mother-in-law was standing outside the door when I opened it, took one look at my face, and knew I'd been crying. "Is everything okay, dear?" she asked me. I assured her I was fine. Allergies, I said.

When I rejoined Roger on the patio I felt as if someone had slipped a plastic bag over my head and tightened it around my neck. I literally could not breathe. My heart fluttered erratically and I thought I might be having a heart attack. I felt claustrophobic, but no space was large enough to contain me—I wanted to crawl out of my own skin. I staggered away from the table (Roger, characteristically, did not notice I was in distress) and paced the front porch waiting for the terror to subside. Roger's father appeared beside me. He slipped an arm around my shoulders, under the pretext of comforting me. I wriggled away and went back inside.

It wasn't until later that I realized I'd had a genuine panic attack. Several of my patients suffered from panic disorder, but I never realized how harrowing panic attacks are until last night.

When I got home I took some antihistamines, as much for the sedation as the relief from congestion. I was fairly doped up by the time Roger slid into bed beside me. Unbelievably, he wrapped his body around me from behind. He was aroused. I felt repelled at first, but I was too drowsy (and curious) to resist him. He traversed my body with a skill and ferocity I'd never seen before, and as long as I didn't dwell on the origins of his newfound abilities—his forays with Alyssa, no doubt—I actually managed to enjoy myself.

But here it is, the morning after, and I feel only remorse. I know it's crazy. He is still my husband, after all.

'Til next time,

V

June 5

That night of lovemaking could have been an opening for Roger and me; once we had bridged the chasm between us physically, maybe we were ready to reconnect emotionally. But the following day, it was business as usual. Roger acted as if he had no memory of what happened in bed, like a drunk who blacks out after a bender. After sex, we slept in our traditional back-to-back position. When I woke up in the morning, he was already gone.

If sex couldn't provide a starting point for discussion, then Alyssa's diaphragm would. All week I planned how I'd confront Roger with the plastic case I've carried in my bag every day since I found it in the van. I thought I might put it on his dinner plate and announce, "We're having the chef's special tonight. I call it 'adultery souffle.' " I could leave it on his computer keyboard with a note: "Is this yours?" I even considered dangling it from the rearview mirror.

But none of these are realistic options, of course. First of all, they're entirely too immature for two adults (one of whom is a licensed therapist!). Second, who am I to cast stones? Now I'm not sure I know what to do with this stupid diaphragm. It's really kind of gross to think that another woman's birth control is rattling around in my bag, next to my lipstick and keys and pictures of Petey.

In the meantime, I can't stay away from Eddie. We had lunch at the Parthenon and Eddie actually got up and *danced* while the waiters shouted, "Oppa! Oppa!" Eddie, it turns out, is a full-blooded Greek (he changed his named from Pappas to Bennedetto after his mother remarried and he was adopted by his stepfather). I became virtually intoxicated by the whirling music, the baklava that dripped with honey, the cheering of the rowdy waiters.

A veiled bellydancer coaxed me onto the dance floor, and against my better judgment I found myself mimicking her undulating steps while Eddie watched, amused at first, then transfixed. As we walked back to the office he pulled me into an alley between stores and pushed me up against the wall, then kissed me long and hard until I couldn't breathe. I wanted to have him right there, but quickly imagined the headlines: Local Therapist Caught in Public Sex Act!

Eddie mentioned, casually, that he'd be going to his eldest daughter's softball game, and for the first time I felt jealous of his family. I imagined Patty (a short, bouncy blond is how I picture her) sitting thigh-against-thigh with Eddie in the bleachers, sharing a bag of chips, cheering their girl on. What if she hit a home run? Would they embrace?

What am I saying? Only a week ago I'd resolved to repair my marriage, and now I'm having masochistic fantasies of Eddie and his wife? This is nuts.

To do this week

1. Make an appointment with a good therapist (Sue Bridges? Alex Wellman?) and go—with or without Roger.

2. Tell Eddie I've decided to work on my marriage and can't see him anymore. Really.

3. Send Petey to in-laws for the weekend and start talking to Roger.

'Til next time,

♉

June 8

My period is two days late. I'm normally as regular as the morning paper. I'm sure it's just stress. I'm not going to think about it.

'Til next time,

♉

June 10

I'm now four days late. I'm looking for clues: the metallic taste on the tongue, the queasiness, a heaviness in my breasts, the fatigue. I seem to have them all. Or maybe I'm just imagining it.

'Til next time,

♉

June 11

Five days late. I'm sure I'm pregnant. I can't believe this is happening to me. Oh God. I don't know if it's Eddie's baby or Roger's! And I'm frantically trying to remember what I've put into my body in the last few weeks. When I was pregnant with Pete—even before I got pregnant—I was neurotically careful. I didn't take aspirin or cough medicine. I stopped spraying the rose bushes, stopped painting my nails, stopped tinting my hair. I stood twelve feet from the microwave, never used an electric heating pad, stopped going to the dry cleaners, steered clear of cigarette smoke, hired someone to paint the nursery, and took a hotel room overnight to avoid the fumes.

But now I'm just living life, exposing myself to all the usual hazards. And I've been drinking. Oh God, what have I done? What if this baby is born with a tail, or some other hideous reminder of my negligence?

I have to go throw up now.

'Til next time,

𝒱

June 12

It is 1:15 in the morning and I'm in the grip of another panic attack. A half hour after falling asleep I was awake again, heart pounding in my ears. My mind would not rest. I felt like my brain was channel-surfing, restlessly clicking through surreal images, fragments of conversations, irrational thoughts. I felt nauseated.

By the time I slipped out of bed, the panic had fully taken hold. I tried to distract myself, but every thought led to an intensification of the panic. The upcoming conference in Washington, my parents' visit next month, Petey's preschool picnic—events I'd normally anticipate with at least some measure of enthusiasm—

now filled me with terror. And then there was the possibility—no, *likelihood*—that I'm pregnant!

No doubt some of what I'm feeling is related to pregnancy hormones. But that can't be the only reason why I'm awake now while everyone else sleeps. It's also because my world is in turmoil.

I've never been much of an adventurer. When I was in college an astrologer told me that I craved the security of a stable family and home, that the key to my happiness would be rooted in the everyday routines and simple pleasures of a well-run household built on a strong foundation. Though she offended my feminist sensibility, I knew she was right. When all is right with my family, all is right with the world. Now our little trio teeters on the precipice.

Maybe it will help to unload some of what's gnawing at me now . . .

1. Petey has been wetting his bed, after almost two years of wearing his "big boy" underwear. He's so ashamed of himself, it just breaks my heart. What's worse, of course, is knowing (and I do know it) that the bed-wetting is a reaction to the tension in the household. He's a bright kid. Even if he doesn't understand what's happening, I'm sure he knows intuitively that his parents are headed for disaster. I feel so guilty.

2. I might be carrying another child. But whose child is it—Roger's or Eddie's? What will they say when they find out? What will Roger say if this baby turns out to be dark and Mediterranean-looking? How do I *really* feel about having another baby?

3. After weeks of assembling the evidence against Diana, I plan to share my information with the clinic's CEO next Tuesday at 2 P.M. As much as I revile that

woman, I'm not as excited about turning her in as I thought I'd be. I'm actually scared. After all, I'm about to destroy her career, her life. She may even wind up in jail! So what am I afraid of? I have this horrible idea that she might show up with an automatic machine gun and blow my head off. Or hurt Petey.

4. I finally confronted Roger with Alyssa's diaphragm. I couldn't muster the kind of self-righteous outrage I'd originally envisioned when I first suspected he was sleeping with her. Now that I've been with Eddie, and in light of Petey's bed-wetting, all I could do was pass it across the kitchen table and ask, quietly, "Do you want to talk about this?" Roger stared at the plastic case for a long time as his face flushed, then drained of all color. In silence, he reached feebly for it, unable to meet my eyes. All he could manage to say was, "She's my student. I was holding it for her. She didn't want her parents to find it." Another long pause. I could almost hear his brain riffling for an alibi. Finally: "She has a boyfriend. She uses it with her boyfriend."

Did I believe him? Of course not. (What kind of student gives her teacher a diaphragm to hold for her? And what kind of teacher takes it? Besides, I heard them on the phone. I know what's going on.) But tonight, in my panic, I thought: what if my impetus for plunging into bed with Eddie—Roger's affair—never existed in the first place? And now I'm the only true sinner?

I'm going to try to go back to sleep now.

'Til next time,

V

June 13

I'm beginning to warm to the idea of having a baby. A BABY! I've missed the delicious smell of baby skin, the warm, soft, milky breath, the adoring gaze as she (I'm sure it's a girl) suckles at the breast. I see young mothers wheeling their babies to the park and think, I will be among them once more. My childbearing days aren't over after all. I, too, can be a young mother again. I can wear maternity clothes again. I will feel the heft of a swelling belly again and I will know the profound joy of pushing a new human being through my loins and into the world. I, too, will have a sweet new baby to stroll down the street, to swing at the playground, to nurse and cuddle and kiss. This nostalgia is so powerful that, at least for a moment, it doesn't seem to matter who the father is.

'Til next time,

V

June 19

When I got to my desk this morning, I found this quotation, generated by my screen saver, scrolling across the computer screen: "Revenge is a luscious fruit which you must leave to ripen."

By the time my appointment with Dick Popavitchi rolled around, I had no misgivings about busting Diana. My PMS had subsided and, with it, so had my neurotic fear that she would murder me or take Pete hostage.

As I studied the photocopies of her dummy accounts and fabricated AIDS patients one last time before my appointment with Dick, I remembered everything she'd said and done to torment and humiliate me, going as far as to call Eddie's house and send Mrs. DeLuca after me. (Eddie told me later that when Mrs. DeLuca answered the phone, Diana began prattling at once, unaware that she was talking to the mother, not the daughter. Mrs. DeLuca set her straight, told her she had no intention of sharing Diana's suspicions with Patty, but planned to "discuss" the issue with me directly. Later that evening, Mrs. DeLuca confronted Eddie privately, and he promptly denied everything. To this day, Patty still knows nothing about Diana's call or her mother's visit to my office.)

The truth is that when Diana first started teasing me about Eddie, shortly before I'd seriously considered sleeping with him, I thought divine providence had sent her my way. I stupidly imagined that Diana, like Jiminy Cricket, would give voice to my higher self, keep me on the straight path, remind me of my moral obligation to remain faithful to my husband.

I soon came to realize that there was nothing divine or moral about Diana. God hadn't sent her, the devil had. Like a grade school bully, Diana's only goal—her mission—was to make my life miserable. But by 2 P.M. on Tuesday, her reign of terror had finally come to an end. And no *Melrose Place* writer could have scripted it more beautifully.

A half hour before I was scheduled to meet with Dick, Diana strolled by my office and, seeing I had no client, walked right in. She asked me something like, "How's your boy?" For a moment I thought she was talking about Petey, but then she said, "You know, *Gar-*

den Boy." She plopped down on my desk (actually put her fat ass on the file I compiled against her!) and told me that she was planning to cancel the Center's contract with Eddie's company. She said she was sick of seeing him around the office. "Surely you can find some other place to meet your loverboy."

Then, in a moment so perfectly timed it felt like someone else's life, I looked into Diana's eyes, straight through to her rotten core, and said, "It's over." I even managed a genuine chuckle, the purest indication that, at last, I had the advantage.

"I know about the grant you've been draining, the fake AIDS patients, the dummy account at First Liberty." Diana suddenly had the panicked, wild-eyed look of a trapped animal. It was a beautiful sight. She insisted I couldn't prove a thing. I didn't tell her about the photocopied bank statements and fabricated client files—I was afraid she'd disappear before I had the pleasure of seeing her escorted from the building.

Which is exactly what happened, at 3 P.M. the following day, in front of the entire staff.

I plucked the fruit of revenge. It was, as promised, luscious.

'Til next time,

V

June 21

I got my period this morning. I stared in disbelief at the dark stain in my underwear. I canceled my first appointment. I'll be fine if I can just stop crying.

'Til next time,

V

June 26

A horrible week. Petey has regressed so much that I'm considering putting him in Pull-Ups (the only thing stopping me is knowing how humiliated he would be to go back to diapers). The preschool teacher, who seemed so patient and understanding only two weeks ago, is obviously at the end of her rope. When I stopped by to bring yet another set of dry clothes, Linda reminded me of the school's policy of admitting only toilet-trained children, and told me that if things didn't change we might have to find another preschool for Petey. I cried all the way back to the office.

Eddie sent me an e-mail today that read: "Can't stop thinking about you. Noticed a beauty mark on your inner thigh. Would like to see it again sometime soon. Roundtree next week?"

As lousy as I'd felt when I got to the office, the message sent a flare through my body. Eddie's attention is like a drug. I am an addict. I know it's destroying my family but I cannot seem to turn away. I wrote back, "Mmmmmm. Yes."

I have no idea whether Roger is still seeing Alyssa. Someone called the house on Sunday during dinner and hung up when I answered. The Caller ID read, "anonymous call," so whoever it was knew how to circumvent the system. I immediately suspected it was Alyssa and impulsively said, "Your girlfriend, no doubt." Petey said, "You have a girlfriend, Daddy?" He knew the word—Roger's father is always teasing him about the cute girls in his class—and now looked confused. Somewhere in his four-year-old brain he knew that a daddy can't have a girlfriend when he already has a wife. His question made me sick to my stomach.

Roger said something like, "Of course Daddy doesn't

have a girlfriend, silly boy." Then he went on babbling about how you can have girls who are friends but that doesn't make them girlfriends, and that girlfriends were different. I was hoping Petey would lose interest in the subject but he pressed on. Next he asked, "Is Mommy your girlfriend?" I started clearing the plates. I was afraid to hear what might come next. "No, Mommy's my wife. She used to be my girlfriend, though."

I looked at Roger across the kitchen and his eyes met mine. His eyebrows were raised and there was the slightest hint of a smile. Was that a wistful look flickering across his face? Did I detect a trace of love? It was hard to know. But just then I remembered that yes, I was his girlfriend once. And we were deeply in love.

After getting Roger's reluctant consent, I called Bonita Loeb and arranged an appointment. Bonita specializes in what she calls "triage therapy," counseling couples on the brink of divorce. Her success rate is about 60 percent—although she has told me that she considers it equally successful when couples realize they cannot remain happily married. I wonder which kind of "success" is in store for Roger and me.

That's all for now.

'Til next time,

V

July 2

Roger and I had our first appointment with Bonita Loeb yesterday. It did not go well. At first, Roger sat slumped in his chair like a sullen teenager, arms across his chest. I wasn't surprised. Seeing a therapist was my idea, not his. And even though he's married to one, he has never held the profession in particularly high regard. He says psychology is not a science but an ideology based purely on theory.

Bonita started with the standard question: "Why are you here today?" I waited to see whether Roger would offer an explanation, but he stared intently at the floor, as if he were watching a parade of ants move across the tile. I've seen him do this before; he once admitted that he counts floor tiles when he's in uncomfortable situations. Finally, I said, "We're here because our marriage is deteriorating and we have a little boy who seems to be . . ." I stopped myself. Maybe it was too soon to draw conclusions about Petey. The truth is, I felt so deeply remorseful about the possibility that I've caused Petey's bed-wetting that I simply couldn't bring myself to articulate the situation. I wasn't ready. Bonita asked Roger whether he thought the marriage was deteriorating. He shrugged.

So there we were, in Bonita's lavishly decorated, sun-lit office, and Roger wasn't talking. I've confronted this situation in my own practice. Men can be notoriously recalcitrant, especially if they suspect that the therapist and wife are in cahoots. I have gone to great lengths to engage the husband, which is probably what Bonita was attempting to do when she playfully nudged Roger's leg with the tip of her high-heeled shoe and, later, tugged at his shirt sleeve. ("Talk to me, Roger," she said, laughing. "This is your dime. Make the most of it.")

And it sure did work. Roger sat taller in his chair and turned to face her as he spoke. He became animated as he described his career as a playwright and the success of his first play. Bonita looked fascinated (although I suspect she wanted him to describe his feelings, not his resume). Suddenly the two of them were talking and laughing like old friends, and though the playful repartee was strategic on her part, I was beginning to feel left out. Soon I was convinced she was flirting with my husband. And by the end of the session, I decided she reminded me too much of Diana. I can't go back to her.

I did, however, make a minuscule step toward repairing my marriage by starting a gratitude journal. I know it sounds New Agey, but I've heard it can work miracles, so I gave it a try. I forced myself to think of one thing about Roger for which I'm grateful. This is what I came up with:

1. I am grateful that Roger does not beat me.

Eddie and I never did make it to the Roundtree this week. He has a pinched nerve and is flat on his back at home. It kills me to imagine Patty tending him. Somehow he manages to find time to send daily e-mails from his laptop. Today's message:

"Can't believe I'm stuck here in bed. Would rather be with you (in bed). Are you wearing the black bra today?"

I blushed and quickly turned off my monitor. How can I ever hope to work on my marriage with Eddie constantly enticing me like this?

'Til next time,

V

July 9

Last month the senior partners at the center voted to establish a phone tree so staff could be quickly notified in the event of an emergency. Today the tree was informally put to the test: At 7:30 I got a call from Filomena

Perez: Diana Pierce was sentenced to nine months in a minimum security women's prison.

'Til next time,

V

July 10

Eddie's back is still bothering him and he's considering surgery. I don't want to think of him as frail, vulnerable. That's not a lover, that's a husband. I like having him back in the office, but knowing that he's within fifty feet of my desk makes it impossible to concentrate. I find myself daydreaming about him while I'm in session with clients and they're beginning to notice. Today my client Louis interrupted my reverie by telling me I seemed "distracted." And now I feel guilty, because instead of apologizing and admitting he was right, I turned it into a therapeutic moment and asked, detachedly, "Why do you feel that way?"

Petey has had a few dry days. The day care center isn't going to eject him—at least not this week.

Decided to give Bonita Loeb a second chance. I can see why people call her work "guerrilla marriage counseling." Some of her ideas are so unorthodox I wonder if they're even ethical. She said she sometimes has couples invite their lovers to therapy. *Can you imagine?* Me, Roger, Alyssa, and Eddie in group therapy? Another technique: Roger and I are supposed to treat each other as if we're happily married, even though our relationship is on the verge of collapse. "Imagine you're actors!" she exhorted. "Go for an Academy Award! Make it a winning performance!" Roger slumped a little lower in his chair. I felt myself stiffen. Can't imagine what she'll come up with next week. Maybe she'll have us dress in costume. Or bring boxing gloves. God only knows.

Saw an article in the paper last week about infidelity. Very amusing. These experts claim to understand why men have affairs—it's all evolutionary, they say. Males are programmed to ensure the survival of the species by mating with as many females as possible. But the social straitjacket of monogamy stops them from dispersing their seed hither and yon. Those married men who get a little on the side are simply obeying a deeply rooted biological mandate. Or so the theory goes.

Now here's what has the pundits stumped: *Women who stray*. It just doesn't make sense, evolutionarily speaking. Mothers are naturally inclined to seek the stability of pairing with one male. Female infidelity goes against the evolutionary logic.

Give me a break. These (male) researchers should spend less time in the stacks and more time talking with real women. They got one thing right, though. It's all about survival. I'd tell them how it feels to be brought back from the dead by another man's touch, gaze, mouth. I'd tell them what it's like to have him trace his finger along my neck and ignite every cell in my body. A man who listens without arguing or judging. This isn't about evolution, it's about *attention*.

Last night I lay in bed beside Roger as he relentlessly clicked through the channels, his face pasty and pale in the blue glare from the Zenith. He'd start with the Christian network on 3, make his way to the shopping channel on 46, then back to 3 again. Again and again and again until I thought I would scream. I rolled over, closed my eyes, and remembered Eddie's reaction when I'd told him about Roger's TV fixation. "If I had you in my bed, I wouldn't have time to watch television." He was sitting on the edge of my desk, legs splayed. He pulled me against him, and I could feel his arousal. He smiled and pulled me even closer. I knew he wanted to have me there, in my office, on the desk. We could have. It was late. Even the cleaning ladies had gone for the night. I wanted to. But then I recalled something Bonita Loeb had said: "Screwing around while you're in marriage counseling is like smoking during heart surgery."

Oops, almost forgot about my gratitude list.

2. I'm grateful that Roger isn't a crack addict.

'Til next time,

V

July 17

I'm afraid Roger and I did not fulfill Bonita's homework assignment. For one week we were to behave as if we were happily married. That meant engaging in respectful conversation, behaving cooperatively, touching affectionately, going out together. "Does it also mean we're supposed to have sex?" Roger had asked suspiciously.

"Sure!" Bonita exclaimed, silver hair bobbing, oblivious to the fact that Roger hoped to avoid sex, not invite it. "If the spirit moves you, why not? Remember, you're pretending to be happy. And happy couples have sex."

Who remembers? It's been so long since Roger and I could be classified as a happily married couple, I can't recall the last time our lovemaking was prompted by genuine happiness or mutual attraction. Our motivations were more utilitarian: procreation, duty. Sometimes we would do it after we'd had too much wine. Or after he'd surfed the porn sites on the Web. Or after he'd read some survey on the statistical frequency of sex among married couples (Roger hates to feel as if he's not keeping apace with the norm).

More often than not, sex would happen after he had exhausted all the TV channels. It never began with a kiss or a stroke, or even sexy words. He would reluctantly switch off the set, stare at the ceiling, and mumble, "I guess we should have sex. It's been a while, huh?"

And I would say, "Yeah. Guess so." Ten minutes later it was over. Roger would check the TV one more time, just in case there was something worth watching on ESPN.

So when Bonita Loeb encouraged us to act as if we were happily married, I'm not sure either of us knew what to do. At one point I greeted Roger at the door with a kiss and a cold beer (always the teacher-pleaser, I felt compelled to do as told). Roger reached for the beer and kissed me quickly, then headed for Petey's bedroom. I called after him, "That's it? Aren't you going to ask about my day? Remember our assignment? We're supposed to be happy!" I know I sounded shrill, whiney. He came back into the hallway and harshly whispered: "The assignment's bullshit. I'm no friggin' actor, and neither are you."

Damn him. I felt like an ass, having stood there with the beer, ready to kiss his cold lips. But I couldn't just blow off the assignment. Why couldn't he have at least tried? But maybe Bonita's strategies can't work for a marriage that's already dead. It's like the time I told a depressed patient to force herself to smile three times a day. The advice was based on a study that showed that the act of smiling actually tricks the brain into thinking it's happy. Maybe that's all it takes for someone who's a little grumpy now and then, but my patient was clinically depressed, suicidal. She needed medication, not some silly trick.

Silly tricks won't help our marriage, either. Bonita, however, was undeterred. "Try again. Give it another week." She grasped our hands in hers. "You two can *do* this."

Then she went into a little spiel I'm sure she's recited a thousand times. She walked over to her door and opened it with a flourish. "Imagine you're on a rocket ship. You're about to take off. Everybody's buckled in, the engines are rumbling. Now comes the countdown, and the rocket is launched." Bonita slammed the door dramatically. "No exit. You're stuck on this rocket and you're not going anywhere. No matter how bad it gets, you're staying."

She sat down with us again. "I want you to think of your marriage like that. You've decided that you must stay together, if only for Petey's sake. There are no exits. So let's work through this mess and maybe you'll discover that your journey together ain't half bad."

Inspiring? Sure. But rockets also explode in midflight sometimes.

As for my gratitude list, I think I'll have to pass this week.

'Til next time,

V

July 24

I told Eddie that Roger and I had started marriage counseling. He responded with something like, "Good for you. You should try to make it work, I mean, with Petey and all."

But he looked stricken. Wednesday morning, over coffee at McDonald's, he wanted to know more about the counseling. "So how's it going? You know. The therapy." He seemed anxious, bordering on needy. I'd never seen him that way. It was pathetic. I wanted to tell him the truth and say: "Counseling is a farce. We're supposed to do all these dumb homework assignments as if that's all it takes to put this mess of a marriage back together. I'm trying, but Roger's acting like a jack-ass, and I'd rather jump out of the rocket now and spend the rest of my life orbiting Pluto than stay stuck in a burning marriage with no exits."

I couldn't say it. Now that Roger and I are in therapy together, there's a protective veil between us and the rest of the world. To reveal the details of the process would be like sabotage, a betrayal of all three of us—me, Roger, and Bonita—and while I'm no stranger to betrayal, I can't explain it. There's something different now.

So all I said was, "It's going okay." Eddie cocked his head back and looked into my eyes, as if seeing me from another angle would elicit more information. It was hard, but I managed to keep my mouth shut. I know he's worried and wants me to reassure him that we can still be together. I wish I could. I literally hunger for him. Even if Bonita manages to patch up our mar-riage, could I ever have this kind of passion with Roger? Is he capable of lusting for me the way Eddie does? Would he call me in the middle of the day just to say the memory of my body is so distracting he can't con-centrate on work?

So I told Eddie about the counseling. But I never told him to leave me alone, which would have been the right thing to do now. I'm not an idiot; I know that my marriage doesn't have a fighting chance until I end my relationship with Eddie. But damn it, I just can't do it. Call it sordid, immoral, and cheap, but what I have with Eddie is real and it makes me feel good (when I'm not feeling guilty and panicky and remorseful).

I am not ready to give this up. And Eddie seems to be doing everything in his power to see that I don't. We were in the back of the elevator this morning, jammed against the wall in the 9 A.M. crush, Eddie standing behind me in the corner. As we ascended I felt his hand slip under my shift, then between my thighs. With his other hand he pulled me back against him. When the elevator reached my floor I moved toward the doors but Eddie held me tighter. I felt powerless to escape his grip and the idea excited me. He took away his hands as the elevator got less crowded, but put them back when it emptied. We rode this way until we reached the top floor. He said, "Let's take the stairs down." We made out in the stairwell like a couple of teenagers. God, it felt so good, it took all my strength to pull away.

Next week Roger and I are meeting separately with Bonita, presumably to discuss our respective affairs. From that point on, I figure we'll be either moving toward true reconciliation or divorce.

'Til next time,

V

August 3

Last night I ran into the K-Mart on the west side to pick up sunblock and I heard a man say: "Nicole, I *told* you to leave that crap alone. Now quit before I smack your heinie." He sounded loud, rough.

My first thought: What a lowlife. Then I realized that I *knew* that voice. I peeked into the next aisle. Eddie! My lover—it still feels weird to use that word, but that's what he is—screaming at his preschool daughter. And using a word like "heinie"! I felt sick.

I was too embarrassed to approach him, too stunned to sneak away. Hiding behind a stack of electric fans, I watched him. It was impossible to discern the sleek, carnal man who has occupied my heart and mind and daydreams for months. What I observed instead was a harried and exasperated father who used a word like "crap" when addressing a preschooler. And threatened to smack her heinie. (I can't get that word out of my head!) I also saw that the cart was filled with every form of junk food known to humanity, stuff I wouldn't let Petey eat if it was the last thing in the house (well, maybe if it was the last thing . . . but you know what I mean). And then I noticed his potbelly. Where did *that* come from?

A woman rounded the corner with her own cart. Could this be Patty? I waited. She pulled out an aqua blue housedress and held it up. I heard her say, "For Mom. What do you think?" It *was* Patty! She looked nothing like the round, bleached-blond woman I'd envisioned. She had brown hair straight as pins, cut bluntly at the jaw line, and looked like a kindergarten teacher. A mean one.

Eddie glanced at the dress and answered, "Whatever." I was relieved. Part of me was terrified that he'd embrace her in the analgesics aisle and say, "It's a lovely dress, darling. And you're a lovely woman. Let's have sex tonight." Ridiculous, isn't it? Truth is, I didn't want to see anything to suggest that their marriage was happy and stable. And I didn't. They even shopped with separate carts! (In her cart, a package of something for yeast infections, I was delighted to observe.)

Interestingly, I was able to put that entire K-Mart scene out of my head when Eddie called me at the office on Thursday. His back is better and he wants to meet at the Roundtree next week. I told him I'm scheduled to go to Washington for a conference, and now he wants to come with me. The idea of spending three days with him is so exciting and scary I can hardly breathe when I imagine it.

This morning I found a manila envelope on my desk. Inside, wrapped in pale violet tissue, was a *teeny*-tiny black teddy from Heavens To Betsy. The moment I found it, I heard my computer ding. An e-mail from Eddie. It said only: Washington.

Now for the big news. Alyssa left a message on my voice mail at work. Sounding like a spoiled, spiteful child, she said she had something to tell me about Roger. "You need to know something about me and your husband," is how she phrased it. She said she'd call back next week. Of course, my imagination has devised every imaginable scenario: She and Roger are running away together. And they're taking Petey. They're having a baby. They're collaborating on a play about their sexual escapades.

If I don't stop this I will lose my mind.

'Til next time,

$\mathcal{V}$

August 11

Taken together, the events of the week have a kind of magnificent order, as if a master puppeteer (God?) has led me toward the only decision I can make now: I must stop seeing Eddie.

The Washington trip was a disaster. Eddie and I actually had a fight! It started in a cafe near Dupont Circle. He was incredibly hostile toward the waitress, a frail little college girl who was obviously trying her best. At one point she forgot to bring a soupspoon and he said, "Do you expect me to eat this with my teaspoon? Or maybe I should just slurp it out of the bowl?" The waitress started to cry. I told Eddie to cut the poor kid some slack and he went into this long harangue about the eroding work ethic in young people and how "when I pay good money for a meal, I expect good service." I told him I'd be happy to pay for the meal if he would just be nicer to the waitress, and he threw me such a chilling look that for a moment I was almost afraid of him.

"This isn't how it's supposed to go," Eddie said. "We're not supposed to be fighting like an old married couple, we're supposed to be back in the room, screwing our brains out."

"Oh? Is that what we're supposed to be doing?" I asked, hearing my voice sharpen and arch like an eyebrow. "So, I guess you've done this before?"

Eddie contorted his lips to suppress a guilty smile. "Well, you know how it is," he said, shrugging his shoulders.

"No, Eddie, I don't. Why don't you tell me?"

He wiped his mouth as if to rub the smile away. "You know. You're away on business and you're lonely. It happens. What can I say?"

"Don't say anything, Eddie," I said. I left the table.

When we got to the hotel, I just told him I'd rather not have sex. He packed his bag and left. I haven't heard from him since.

On Wednesday, during a private session, Bonita Loeb told me point-blank that as long as I was having an affair, I couldn't remain in therapy. (I wonder whether she said the same thing to Roger.)

Thursday I received this letter from Petey's school:

Dear Ms. Ryan and Mr. Tisdale:

With tremendous regret we must inform you that Petey can no longer continue at the Acorn Early Education Center. As you know, the school policy mandates that students be toilet-trained. In this way, we can maintain a sanitary environment, as well as keep teachers in the classroom. I know that you have tried hard to remedy the situation, but unfortunately Petey continues to wet and soil himself, and it has become a distraction to the other children as well as a strain on our teachers.

It is also terribly embarrassing for your child. When Petey began at Acorn, he was an outgoing little boy, but in the past few months we have noticed dramatic changes, not only in his toileting habits, but also regarding his behavior. He has been withdrawn and weepy, and rarely exhibits the joie de vivre he had when he began here. I don't mean to intrude, but I wonder if there is something in Petey's home life that is causing his distress, and if there is anything you can do to ease the situation for him.

Again, we are sorry to lose Petey. On behalf of the staff here at Acorn, we wish your family the best of luck.

Most sincerely,
Emma Burgins
Director, Acorn Early Education Center

I cried after I read that letter (I'm crying again just thinking about it). Roger looked ashen, as though he might cry too. I've canceled my appointments for next week so I can be with Petey. I feel so responsible, so guilty. This sweet little boy has been the receptacle for all the unhappiness in my marriage, all the sneaking around, all the shame. Oh God, how I desperately wish I could go back in time to reverse all the damage that's been done. But how far back would I have to go? To the day I met Eddie? Or the day I met Roger?

'Til next time,

𝒱

August 14

I haven't wanted to write about Alyssa's phone call. But I managed to tape the whole thing (my phone is rigged to record since I occasionally do phone sessions with clients), and this morning I transcribed the tape. It gave me stomach pains to hear it again.

ALYSSA: I need to speak to Roger's wife. Are you his wife?

ME: Speaking. Who's this? (I knew exactly who it was. Her voice is high and soft, like one of my babysitters.)

ALYSSA: This is Alyssa.

ME: Who? (Playing dumb, heart racing.)

ALYSSA: I'm Alyssa. Roger's student. You know? *Alyssa.*

ME: Okay. And . . . ?

ALYSSA: Look. I just called . . . I mean, I called to let you know that this therapy thing isn't going to work.

ME: (Silent, waiting.)

ALYSSA: Are you there? Did you hear me?

ME: I'm sorry, but I don't know what you're talking about.

ALYSSA: Give me a break. You know Roger and I are together.

ME: What, exactly, do you want from me?

ALYSSA: I want you to give up. He's done with you. So just let him go and get on with his life. (She sounded petulant, like a little girl. Part of me wanted to send her to her room for a nice long time-out.)

ME: Give what up?

ALYSSA: Huh?

ME: You said you want me to give it up. What do you mean?

ALYSSA: Don't play games with me. You know what I mean. Roger told me how you dragged him to see that loony lady, that counselor. What a joke. Roger loves me. And I love him. So just give it up. (Now it hit me. Roger must have broken up with her. She's panicking.)

ME: (Determined to sound detached.) Okay. Anything else you'd like to say before I hang up the phone?

ALYSSA: Yeah. He told me you're as stiff as a board in bed. You just lie there, like you're dead.

ME: (Silence. I felt like crying.)

ALYSSA: And he said I'm the best lover he's ever had. You don't know what you're missing. He's a total hotty. (Pause.) It's a shame you couldn't appreciate that. When you still had him, I mean.

Alyssa has tried to reach me three times since that call. She's left sick messages for me at work and has even sent me an e-mail message. In one voice mail message she said, giggling, "Roger told me about the way your breasts flop to the sides when you're flat on your back, like he'd need a forklift to get them to stand upright." In another message she said something like, "It's really a pity that you never loved your husband enough to give him what he wanted in bed. He told me what a prude you are." And then the e-mail: "Greetings. I'm wearing the black lace lingerie your husband bought me for my birthday. It's exactly the kind he got you two years ago except it's probably a few sizes smaller. Have a great day!"

I saved all the messages in case I'd need them some-day (divorce court? custody hearings?). It kills me to replay them, but I find myself masochistically going back again and again. It's bad enough that Roger had an affair with his student, but how could he talk about me that way? And how could he be attracted to this demented little girl? I played the messages for Roger but he refused to admit that he is, or was, sleeping with Alyssa. I could tell by the way his lips trembled that he was lying. All he would say is that she's a crazy girl with a wild imagination. He even managed to feign con-cern for me, and suggested I change my phone number and e-mail account.

That made me lose all control. I threw my Rolodex at him (missed), then pummeled him with my fists, screaming, crying. He watched me, terrified. At one point he pulled me toward him, as if to hug me, but I fell to the floor, limp, spent. He backed away from me, slowly and scared, as if trying to elude a cobra. I begged him, "Please, tell me the truth about Alyssa." Again, he insisted that she was infatuated and that she was lying.

I played the messages for Betsy. She says I should get a restraining order against Alyssa. I'm not at that point yet, and anyway, I'm not even sure I have a case. But if the calls continue, I may have to involve the police. In the meantime, Eddie sent me flowers with a note that said, "I was a jerk in D.C. Forgive me?"

'Til next time,

V

August 23

This week Bonita had us describe on paper our parents' marriages, which we would then exchange at our next session. Here's what I wrote:

My parents were deeply in love. Any fool could see that. But having directed all their affection toward each other, there was almost nothing left over for their children. Except for a rare peck on the top of my head, my parents did not hug or kiss me, nor did they offer tender words. I felt like an interloper on their honeymoon. Nearly every night I would hear the *crawk-crawking* of the floorboards above me; the whole house seemed to rock with their passion, and I would wrap my pillow around my head to muffle the sounds. They were so absorbed with one another that once, when I was four years old, they actually left me at the curb as they obliviously sauntered ahead, arm in arm like two teenagers. I remember standing there, watching them cross the street, and in a little voice crying out, "Isn't anybody going to hold my hand?"

So I grew up looking forward to the time when I would have a husband who would give me his undivided attention and adore me and love me. To be married to someone who neither notices nor wants me has been a tortuous but also profoundly familiar experience, as if this is my lot in life, to be invisible and unloved.

I was surprised by this assignment at first, since most therapists would prefer to have couples *talking* to each other rather than writing. But given how reticent Roger has been in her office, I guess Bonita figured this would loosen him up. We'll see next week whether she's right.

Alyssa continues to torment me, and it's gotten to the point that I don't even pick up the phone anymore. In one message she listed all the places where she and Roger had had sex, including the rest room at Jim Dandy's, the supply closet at the Learning Attic, and the gazebo at Ellis Park. As angry as I am with Roger for bringing this woman into our lives, I have to admit I'm starting to wonder how far things really went between them. I just can't picture Roger doing these things—this is a guy who wouldn't even kiss me in public, let alone have sex with me in a gazebo!

As for Eddie, he is doing his level best to get back in my life. He knows I collect mermaids and left a tiny ceramic one on my keyboard Wednesday morning. I'm rapidly losing interest in him. In fact, he is starting to make me a little nauseated. But a part of me—the part that's been listening to Alyssa's messages—wouldn't mind running into him . . .

'Til next time,

V

August 28

I've gained five pounds since the last time I weighed myself. I can't seem to stay away from sweets. I started the day with a Kit Kat bar for breakfast, and last night after everyone was asleep, I plowed through half a chocolate cake. What's happening to me?

Betsy called me yesterday, insisting that I start a new life with Petey somewhere far away from here. I've often fantasized about that, but it's simply not an option. I could never do that to Petey. Yeah, yeah, I know, I'm not doing Petey any favors by staying with Roger. It's not good for children to live with miserable parents.

I've heard that theory a million times. And you know what? I don't believe it. I've counseled enough children of divorce to know that most of them want two parents under the same roof. Whether the parents are happily married isn't important. Unless Roger starts beating me, I cannot justify walking out on him. And as horrible as things are right now, I have a little hope left in me yet.

Here's Roger's response to Bonita's question:

DESCRIBE YOUR PARENTS' MARRIAGE
   Withholding. Rejecting. Stable. Funereal.

James and Beatrice Tisdale, upright as wedding cake figurines, and just as plastic, immovable, and silent. Father, buttoned-up in shades of gray, unsmiling and unyielding. Mother, nervous as a parakeet, a handwringer, bone thin and perpetually fatigued. Both were miserly with affection, as if there were a limited supply that somehow required storage for some future date, for emergency use only. Made a bundle in the stock market, but lived like ascetics for most of their lives.

Never saw them kiss, spent most of my childhood convinced my siblings and I had been conceived immaculately. Still convinced. Realize only

now that there were great cauldrons of anger roil-
ing under the silence. James has carried on an affair with his secretary for twenty-seven years.
Found them on the floor of his workshop when I
was fourteen. Didn't recognize Father at first, had
never seen him so full of life. Never told Mother.
Suspect she has always known.

Roger's straight-arrow, fussy father an adulterer? Big
surprise. The old goat once tried to play footsy with me
before Roger and I were married. The Tisdales had
taken us out to dinner to celebrate our engagement.
The next thing I know, I feel his stocking feet crawling
up my pants leg. I thought it was Roger being playful,
until I noticed the wicked glint in my future father-in-
law's eye—and felt his hot dry hand on my thigh. I
left the table and sequestered myself in the rest room,
shaking and gagging. When I got back, he acted as if
nothing had happened. I called him at work the next
day and demanded that he never touch me again. He
promised he wouldn't, and except for the occasional
hug, he has remained true to his word.

I really pity my mother-in-law, living all those years
with a man whose heart belonged to another woman. I
can't imagine what that must feel like. What am I saying? Of course I can.

I haven't heard from Alyssa at all this week and now
I feel vaguely worried, wondering what she's cooking
up next. I thought I caught a glimpse of her in the
parking garage under my office building, but when I
looked again she was gone. Either I imagined it or the
girl is stalking me. I had to resist the urge to check my
car for explosives.

Roger has been on a retreat at an artist's colony in

the mountains, which is wonderful because I cannot stand to be in the same room with him. After Alyssa's last phone message I asked him again, point-blank, "Did you have sex with this girl?" Again, he denied it.

'Til next time,

V

September 4

Roger phoned to say he was extending his stay at the artist's colony. When I asked him for how long, he said something like, "A week, maybe more." I wonder if he plans on coming back at all. This feels more and more like a separation, and I'm scared. Yes, I want to strangle him, but I'm not ready to lose him. I don't like being alone.

Had quite a day yesterday. Started off with me not being able to find anything in my closet that fit, as I've become enormously quaggy. Spent so much time searching for something not totally horrible that I had no time to wash my hair and walked in late for a first appointment with a new client. Finally found those khaki stretch pants I got at the Gap, thinking: stretch has to fit, right? They stretched all right, all over my fat ass. By lunch I couldn't bear it a minute longer and ran out to find something—anything—that fit. I was in the dressing room, struggling to pull up the zipper on a black skirt, when this girl asked me to button her. She had her back to me, holding her long, curly hair away from her neck, smelling of Estee Lauder's Pleasures, my personal favorite. I was happy to help, but then she turned around to thank me and I saw who she was.

Alyssa! I actually let out a little scream. I thought she recognized me, too, but apparently not. Looking concerned but also a little scared, she asked, "Are you okay?" in that *voice*, the voice that has tormented me for weeks. I wanted to confront her—claw her eyes out—but she was wearing a size four nothing of a dress and I felt like a giant upholstered couch. I couldn't possibly reveal myself.

I left the store immediately, but instead of going back to the office, I waited in the car, then followed Alyssa back to her house. I expected her to live downtown in one of those singles condos near the health club, but it turns out she lives in the dowdy Windsor Acres subdivision, which can mean only one thing: she's still living at home with her parents. I decided that I must return to her house (thinner) and nail her once and for all, in front of her parents. With enough Slim-Fast, maybe next week.

Now for the big news. I hadn't talked to Eddie all week, though he'd e-mailed me several times and continues to leave little gifts on my desk. This morning he asked me to lunch, said he had something really important to tell me. As soon as we sat down at a table, he reached for my hand and dropped the bomb, "I'm leaving Patty. I want to make a life with you." I couldn't believe it. I honestly thought it was some kind of joke. I started to laugh, then saw the tears in his eyes. I tried to talk him out of it, told him I was committed to keeping my marriage together for Petey's sake. He said he told Patty all about me, about us, and she wanted him out by Monday! Now what?!?

'Til next time,

V

September 9

After five days of Slim-Fast I am down only three pounds. My thighs are still chafing. I spent an hour on makeup and hair, determined to look entirely different from the frazzled behemoth Alyssa encountered in the dressing room. I changed my side part from left to right, even tried a new deep purple lipstick—too bride-of-Frankensteiny, so I frantically wiped it off. I pulled on black jeans and a white tank top. My arms looked like twin dolphins, so I tore off the tank top and put on a T-shirt. I decided that if Alyssa recognized me from the dressing room I would insist it was my fat look-alike cousin.

I dropped Petey off at my mother's and drove back to Windsor Acres, determined to finally confront Alyssa, ideally in the presence of her parents. In case her parents had any doubt about their daughter's involvement, I'd brought along copies of her e-mail messages and a tape of the phone messages. I drove maniacally, almost rear-ended a cyclist. I rehearsed what I would say and narrowed my opening line down to three possibilities:

1. "Alyssa: Whatever is going on between you and my husband has got to stop." (No. This assumes I'm sure there is something going on. Not sure.)

2. "Listen, you little bitch. Keep your filthy hooks out of my husband." (Better not. It makes Roger look like innocent victim. Plus, I don't want to appear vulgar in front of parents.)

3. "I'm Roger's wife. I think we need to talk." At this point I will gesture toward her parents and ask them to sit down. "I'd like you to stay, please. I believe you'll

want to know what your daughter's been up to." (Yes. I'll say this. It sounds poised, in control.)

As I pull up to the curb across the street and begin walking toward Alyssa's house, I see her parents on the porch and my heart sinks. Her mother is in a wheel-chair and her father looks as if he could use one. They both appear old enough to be her grandparents, and I wonder if that's the case until I hear Alyssa's voice from the backyard, "Daddy, should I pick the rest of the to-matoes?" The old man calls back, "Sure, darling. We'll have them with supper."

What can I say? I simply lost my nerve. I just didn't have the heart to plunge these two kindly, geriatric people into crisis. At least not today.

'Til next time,

V

September 11

Eddie e-mailed me his new address. Apparently he's renting a place near the university, in the student hous-ing area. He wrote: "Come check out my new crib." I read this and immediately became nauseated. I did not e-mail back.

'Til next time,

V

September 14

Roger finally came home. He seemed serene, happy. He looked good (dare I say . . . sexy?). He offered me a small box, and I opened it to find a tiny silver armadillo (an inside joke: it was our pet name for each other when we were dating). He tumbled with Petey on the family room floor (Pete was overjoyed), and for a moment I thought, "We're a family. This is how it should be."

Then Roger opened his mail and everything changed.

He held a letter and his whole body trembled. He backed into a chair and stared at the piece of paper. "Jeez," I heard him say softly. I'd never seen him look so unnerved.

"What is it?" I asked. "Please tell me."

"Apparently," he rasped, "I'm being charged with sexual harassment. One of my students." He passed the paper across the table.

Alyssa had brought charges against him. "I guess you need a lawyer," I told him, my mind scrambling to comprehend. I was scared but knew I had to ask: "Roger, did you harass that girl?"

He leaned toward me and reached for my hand. I pulled it away. "I think it's time you knew exactly what's been going on. You deserve to know the truth."

I'll fill in the rest later, when I have more time to write.

'Til next time,

V

September 25

What compels a man to tell the truth, even when the truth will stain his name, shame his family, and threaten to shatter the foundation on which his life and career are built? Does the man confess because he has found his moral center? Or is he motivated by fear of protracted legal action and the loss of a job he holds dear?

After months of evasion and deceit, and faced with the terrifying reality of Alyssa's sexual harassment suit, Roger finally admitted that he and Alyssa had been lovers. It began, he said, with playful flirtation. (Even this small and relatively benign point makes me ill. How could my sullen, brooding husband play and flirt with another woman?)

Alyssa had invited him for coffee after class and he agreed, under the tacit but mutually understood pretext of improving her dialogue-writing skills. Coffee at Starbucks led to wine at Bernardo's, and wine led to a first kiss by the pay phone as he dialed home to tell me he would be late. "I knew it was wrong," he told me, "but at some level I honestly believed that I was entitled to this. Our marriage . . . held nothing for me. I felt you had lost interest." (Lost interest?! I thought of the times I'd paraded like a fool in that stupid teddy or reached for his zipper and was rebuffed. I wanted to strangle him.)

After several weeks of making out and petting (always at her initiation, he insisted), she asked for a ride home. They parked by the lake and had sex. Just to spite myself, I asked Roger if that was the night she left the diaphragm in the van. He looked away and I watched the color rise to the tips of his ears. He wasn't sure. "Maybe. Maybe not. I can't remember."

They'd had sex five or six times over the following months, but once we began therapy, Roger insists he told Alyssa their relationship was over. Apparently Bonita had explained that she would not accept him as a client if he continued to play around. "I'll be honest," he said. "It wasn't easy letting go. The affair was so . . .

invigorating. I was like a god to her, and yes, she made me feel young." He looked at me directly for the first time since he had started talking. "Can you understand how hard it was to give that up?" And, of course, I could.

Ultimately it was Roger's concern for Petey that pushed him to end it with Alyssa. I wasn't surprised. Roger may have been a negligent husband, but he would lay down his life for our little boy. Roger called Alyssa, made it clear that the relationship must end. But she wouldn't hear of it. And that's why we've got real trouble on our hands.

This moment was so profoundly serious, so dramatic, so horribly *real,* yet I found myself slipping in and out of a disembodied state. A small and distant voice whispered, "This is really happening. Pay attention!" But I wanted to go to sleep. And there were moments when I felt the total impact of Roger's confession as though I were standing on the beach in winter, taking the ice-cold waves head on, feeling the force of every painful shard. I took the confession like a lashing, retribution for my affair with Eddie. Yes, I was hurt. But any impulse to play the aggrieved wife was quickly smothered by the memory of Eddie's body heaving above mine in our bed at the Roundtree.

I found myself doing the math. I flirted, I kissed, I fondled. But I only had sex with Eddie once. In this contorted comparative analysis of infidelity, I ranked my transgressions against Roger's. Is he the bigger sinner because he went between the sheets with his lover more often than I did with mine?

One thing I never felt, not even fleetingly, was compassion for Roger. Every detail he proffered stirred jealousy and antipathy. I felt capable of murdering them both. Yet I felt driven to know every detail. What did she wear that first night? How did her tongue feel in his mouth? Was she better than me?

Once Bonita laid down the ground rules, Roger says he dropped Alyssa cold. (On this point, he was more honorable than I was; I have yet to make a clean break with Eddie.) But Roger's withdrawal only intensified Alyssa's obsession. "She started with e-mails, then progressed to phone calls," he said. "Then she started showing up here while you were at work." I felt my whole body constrict as I imagined Alyssa rifling through my things, laughing. "I never let her in," Roger said. "Not once." By the time Alyssa started harassing me, Roger knew his scorned lover had completely lost it. "It killed me when she began involving you," he said. "Involving?" I snapped back. "How about tormenting?"

Roger grabbed my hands. "I am sorry. I am so sorry." He made a little choked noise in his throat, and I knew he was about to cry. "I need you now. I can't get through this alone," he said. I pulled my hands away.

'Til next time,

$\mathcal{V}$

October 9

It's been two weeks since Roger moved into the guest room. After his confession, I told him, "I can't stand having you in bed next to me, knowing you had an affair." He was relieved I didn't kick him out of the house and was happy to oblige. "Separate rooms? Of course. I understand. Completely," he said, nodding uncontrollably like one of those dashboard dogs. "Anything. Anything you want. Whatever you want." Of course, I still haven't told him about Eddie.

Roger has kept a respectful distance—I hardly see him—but he has also made all sorts of conciliatory gestures (cleaned the house, bought flowers for the table, had my Jeep detailed). Whenever I do see him he practically bows and scrapes at my feet. I was at first disoriented by his sudden obsequiousness. Smug is an affectation he mastered long ago; acquiescence is uncharted territory.

But, I have to tell him about Eddie. I sent Petey to his grandparents' house for the weekend and now wait for Roger to come home from playing racquetball. There's so much I want to say, and I am afraid I'll forget—or start blubbering. So I decided to write it in a letter:

Roger,

I never thought it was possible to be both married and lonely, yet I've learned over the years that it is, indeed, possible. I have a husband, yet for most of my marriage I have felt entirely alone. I have sat on the edge of the bed, undressed, inches away from you, waiting for some sign that you wanted me. You rarely wanted me. Do you remember when the Realtor showed us the house and how she winked when we got to the Jacuzzi? "Plenty of room for two in there," she said. Do you realize that we have never taken a bath together? First me, then you. It's always like that. Even when I'd invite you in, you'd say, "I'd rather wait until you're done."

I suppose all this is my way of justifying what I'm about to tell you. I, too, had an affair. Unlike you and your student, we had sex only once. But I must be hon-

*est: my affair started long before that. It started the mo-
ment this man turned his attention toward me. I had
such longing. He filled it. Was he my soul mate? No.
Was the sex good? Absolutely. The sad truth is that I
probably would have had sex with anyone who showed
an interest in me, and perhaps that's my problem, not
yours. But I also believe with all my heart that if you
had paid as much attention to me as you do that
damned TV, I never would have done it.*

*We've both been entangled by our misdeeds. You
have this lawsuit. And I am burdened by the knowledge
that a family has been ripped apart because of my affair
(he moved out last month and has tried to convince me
to join him).*

*Roger, I don't know where we go from here, but I'm
willing to talk about it. I'll be waiting upstairs.*

—V.

I stood at the top of the stairs and listened as Roger
walked toward the kitchen, opened the letter. I waited
a few minutes, expecting him to come up the stairs. But
the next sound I heard were his footsteps moving back
toward the door. I called out to him, but he ignored me
and slammed the door behind him. I ran to the window
and watched him pull out of the driveway.

That bastard! After everything he's done with Alyssa,
how dare he walk out on me? I waited in the kitchen
as long as I could, inhaling half a frozen mousse cake
before finally collapsing on the couch, doped up from
all the sugar. I heard a key in the door, checked the
clock—4:30 A.M. Roger sat on the edge of the couch. I
thought I was dreaming.

"I know I've got no right to feel this way," he began.

I propped myself up on my elbows. My head throbbed. Sugar hangover. "But I can't help it."

"Can't help what?" I asked.

"I cannot help the fact that I'm very angry with you." He gripped his head in his hands. "How could you sleep with another man? How could you?"

Now I was certain I was dreaming and actually reached out to feel his sleeve to confirm it. No, Roger really was sitting there, and this was really happening. My cheating, lying husband had the gall to say that he was angry at me. I rolled off the couch. "Are you out of your mind? You sleep with this, this *child* for months, lie your ass off about having an affair, treat me like shit, drag our family into a sexual harassment lawsuit that our lawyers say you have little hope of winning, and now you have the balls to say you're angry? Screw you! If I slept with Eddie it's because you've behaved more like a roommate than a husband for years and the only thing you've wanted to hump in this house is the frigging TV set!"

All of a sudden I hear this low hissing sound and for a moment think it's the teakettle even though I haven't made tea since last winter. Then I realize it's Roger, crying. I'm still angry. "What the hell is wrong with *you?*" Now he's sobbing like a child.

"We've made such a mess of things." He sniffles loudly and wipes his eyes with the back of his hand. He peers up at me. It's now 5 A.M. My alarm clock is set to go off in an hour. I'm in no shape to see clients. "You're going to leave me, aren't you?"

Until he mentioned it, I hadn't seriously considered leaving as an option. But once Roger had actually uttered the words, it was as if he'd broken some kind of spell, and suddenly the prospect of leaving didn't seem quite so forbidding. For now I've decided to simply live with these feelings. I don't have to make any decisions right away.

'Til next time,

𝒱

October 23

Crazy week. It began with my new client Claire, and I'm still reeling. On the surface, Claire is a model wife and mother, a pillar of her church and a hardworking PTA volunteer. She's petite and rather plain-looking, wears no discernible makeup, and speaks with a flat midwestern accent. Underneath her bland surface, though, is a woman I thought only existed in the pages of Nancy Friday sex fantasy books.

Clarie's husband, a respected endocrinologist, simply has no interest in sex. So in 1995, sweet little Claire decided quite consciously that if her husband wouldn't give her what she craved, she would find it elsewhere. And not with one lover, but almost fifty. A different lover every month for the last four years. "I never wanted love," she told me. "I already get that from my husband. He's a good man, a wonderful father, a friend. I never wanted another husband. That's not what I need."

At first I didn't understand why she came to me. She doesn't seem particularly troubled. While I'm so wracked with guilt I'm ready to disembowel myself, Claire feels perfectly justified and appears amazingly guilt-free. But after our second session, I understood. She simply needed to share her stories. She'd had no one to talk to. So now she talks to me. I'm dying to tell someone, but obviously I can't. All I can do is write.

Her first affair wasn't planned. "We had new neighbors, and I'd baked some cranberry muffins for them," she told me. "I rang the bell but no one answered. I opened the door and walked in on a housepainter. Apparently the new neighbors were having work done on the house before moving in. He was reading a dirty magazine and playing with himself in the dining room." She paused. "He didn't stop when he saw me, and I didn't leave. I just watched. After a while I helped him and before I knew it, we were on the floor. I don't know what possessed me, but it was the most fun I'd had in years. We kept it going for three weeks, until he was done painting the house."

I tried to remain expressionless, but I wanted to scream, "Are you *nuts?*" At the same time, frankly, I find this woman absolutely fascinating.

Now here's how my crazy week ended: The phone rang as I was leaving the office. "Hi, Sweetie." The tone was spry, playful. I felt my adrenaline surge as I realized who it was. "Don't hang up. Please."

"Diana." I had to grip the phone with two hands to keep from dropping the receiver.

"The one and only," she responded, in a voice that seemed, unbelievably, to be more kind than cocky. "I need to see you to make amends."

"Please, no, that's okay," I told her. "Just live your life. You don't need to make amends to me."

"But I do. I must." There was a long pause, and then: "Don't be afraid of me. I won't hurt you. I really need to see you." She explained that she gets a day pass from prison next week and wants to stop by my office.

Against all instincts I agreed. "Fine. But I'll only have a few minutes."

"That's all I'll need," she assured me.

Is she really coming to make amends, or is she going to blow my head off?

'Til next time,

V

October 30

I've been having my white cottage fantasy a lot lately. In this reverie I'm living alone in a small and simple white cottage on the south side of town and everything is exactly the way I want it to be. I've got a Maine coon cat, a few apples in the refrigerator, creaky wood floors, and no TV. I'm sickened by the excesses of my suburban life—the Weber grill on the deck, the overstuffed closets, five TV sets, the flood of junk mail, the mess. For as long as I've been married, every decision— choosing carpets, appliances, vehicles, wallpaper—has been made by committee. I want to be alone.

Of course, this is only a fantasy. I'm superstitious. God, if you're reading this, please don't punish me by killing my kid (you can do whatever you want with Roger, however). I have this fantasy when I'm feeling totally overwhelmed. Do I really want to live alone? Not if it means giving up Petey. He is still the love of my life. And I'm thrilled to report that he hasn't had an accident in weeks and he's back in preschool!

As for Halloween, it's a toss-up between a pirate and Barney (I vote for the pirate).

As planned, Diana came by the office today. I still can't believe she had the nerve to show her face, but she insisted it was part of her "recovery." Apparently, she joined Alcoholics Anonymous when she was in jail. One of the twelve steps is to "make amends" to everyone she has harmed. She looked smaller than I remembered her, but also happier. She hiked up one trouser leg and showed me the electronic device strapped to her ankle. "My personal Big Brother," she said, rolling her eyes. "What can I say? It's the least I deserve."

Diana explained that her only purpose in visiting was to apologize. "I'm an alcoholic," she said, looking straight at me. "I'm not making excuses. I tried to wreck my life, and everyone else's too. I was awful to you. And I'm very, very sorry." She looked so earnest it was almost spooky. "I've been sober for thirty-two days," she said.

I stared at her. Was she for real? I waited for the snide remark, and eventually, it came, although in retrospect I believe she was trying to be helpful, in her own twisted Diana-esque way. "There are twelve-step programs for overeaters, too, you know," she said, eyeing my expanded waistline, then gesturing toward the two-pound bag of M&M's on my desk, already half empty.

She was quiet for a moment, then said, "I knew about Alyssa. And I guess I'm also sorry I never told you. I mean, I assume you would have wanted to know." I could feel my jaws clench. "I actually walked in on them together in his office," she continued. "I'd stopped by for a quick hello. They were on the floor." She stopped and checked my reaction. I turned away. "I told him he was being a pig." Diana stood up and straightened her pants. "It was a rare moment of clarity. I knew he was wrong, even if you had your own thing going with Eddie." I knew it. The old Diana had reared her ugly head. It didn't take long.

"Don't start with that," I warned her.

After Diana left, I took the bag of M&M's and dumped the whole thing in the garbage. Then, on impulse, I looked for Overeaters Anonymous in the phone book. I jotted down the phone number, then threw that in the trash, too. Before I left, I dug out the bag of M&M's. And the phone number.

One last thing: Today we met with Roger's attorney and learned that Alyssa claims she can prove that she wasn't the first student my husband "harassed." Roger denied having any other involvements, but I'm suspicious. If it turns out this man has had other affairs, my marriage is over. I swear it.

'Til next time,

V

November 6

Publicly I am a success; my practice is stronger than ever. I've been invited to present papers at two different conferences next year and to moderate a panel discussion at another. From all appearances, I lead a charmed life. A dashing blond husband, an adorable child, a lovely home. Privately, I am dying inside. I am eating my way through the week, from Kit Kat bars to dry cocoa mix. My marriage is a farce.

I saw Claire again this week. She shared another of her escapades, and I listened, captivated. (I must say, this client makes up for all the ones who have nearly put me to sleep.) She had been called in to audit a law firm in Headley (she's a CPA) and was working closely with the firm's accountant, Dave. "He was married and geeky," she recalled, "but there was something else there, something almost animal. I imagined he was like me. You know, quiet on the outside but capable of great passion. I also thought . . ." She trailed off.

"Go on," I told her.

"Well, he seemed lonely. Like me. And I thought maybe I'd be doing him a favor." After a week on the job, Claire made her move. "It was easy," she said. "I told him he smelled good—and he did. Royal Copenhagen, I think. He blushed, and I said it again, whispered it this time: 'God, you smell good.' He looked at me and I just knew. I knew he was interested. I was up all night, thinking about that look. Pure desire. I need that more than food, I think."

Apparently, Claire wasted no time in making her next move. The following evening, she and Dave were working overtime, bleary-eyed from all the number crunching. She ran a finger lightly across his hand and suggested they take a break. Over coffee she told him, simply, that she was attracted to him. "I thought he was going to have a heart attack. His eyes bugged out and he started sweating. Then I saw . . . you know . . . movement . . . in his trousers." They were the only ones left in the office. They had sex in the conference room.

I knew that Claire belonged to the Sweet Valley Christian Church, one of the most conservative fundamentalist churches in the city. I wanted her to explain how she reconciled her sexual behavior with her faith. "Don't you think it's a sin?" I asked her.

"Yes, it's a sin," she said, leaning forward. "But I'll tell you what's a greater sin. When a man won't love his wife, body and soul. That's a sin." She fell back in her chair. "Yes, I'm a sinner. But I sin out of necessity, like a starving person stealing food to stay alive. I truly believe that."

I was going over my notes from that session when I heard a soft rap on the door. It was Eddie. I hadn't seen or spoken to him since that icky e-mail about his "crib." He was extremely polite and seemed to be using all the big words he knew. He was nervous. He admitted that he thinks about our afternoon at the Roundtree every single day, and he asked—no, begged—me to be with him again. I felt a mixture of revulsion and searing arousal. "No strings," he said. "I won't pester you, I won't ask you to leave your family. Just a little mutual pleasure between two consenting adults. Come on, what do you say?"

I told him I needed to think about it. Like Claire, I am so lonely.

'Til next time,

V

November 13

It's been a hell of a week. On Monday I ran into Eddie's wife, Patty, at the supermarket. There she was looking like death with no makeup and an ugly yellow-green bruise on her cheek. She had two kids in tow. No, make that *three* kids. She is pregnant! I don't know if Eddie's the father but I wouldn't put it past him to screw her while they're separated. On the other hand, she looks like she's about five months along, so maybe this happened when he was still living with her. But Eddie had claimed he'd stopped having sex with Patty soon after we became involved. I don't know what to think. This has clearly put a damper on any feelings he may have stirred in me. It makes me absolutely sick to my stomach to think he may have knocked her up. It also makes me a little sad to realize that I could have been five months pregnant by now.

I literally cannot remember the last time I had sex. I'm still too angry at Roger to feel amorous, and all our meetings with the lawyer make me even angrier. Privately, I told his lawyer I had an eyewitness to his affair (Diana) and asked whether that might weaken Alyssa's case against Roger. He doesn't think so.

If her lawyer is crafty enough, it's possible to prove that she had sex only to placate him, and, above all, he abused his authority. As for the tapes I'd made of her phone call and messages: I cannot find them anywhere. I thought I'd stashed them safely away in my dresser drawer, but they're gone. If I were a more fastidious and organized housekeeper, I'd assume someone had stolen them, but I'm so damned disorganized it's quite possible that they're sitting at the bottom of a heap of crap in my closet. I must locate those tapes!

I've now confided in three people regarding this mess (a.k.a. my life), and the consensus is that I must leave Roger. Betsy, who has heard only snippets of this saga when I have the energy and nerve to share them, is adamant. "You've suffered long enough," she told me. "Stop being such a martyr. Make a new life for yourself." Elaine, a woman in my cardio-spin class, insists that I'm actually damaging my child by exposing him to my rotten marriage. "What kind of life are you modeling for him?" she exhorted between gasps for air. "Do you want him to replicate your marriage in his own life?" (A budding family dynamics therapist, no doubt.)

And then there is my own mother. Over drinks at Pico's, I poured out the whole sorry tale and she surprised me by grabbing my hand and saying, "You know your father and I don't approve of divorce, but if you have no other alternative, we will always be here for you." She even offered to help pay my attorney expenses! (The truth is, she never liked Roger anyway and probably wouldn't mind if she didn't have to spend another Thanksgiving with him.)

So now my best friend, my mother, and an objective outsider are all urging me to leave my husband. I'd probably offer the same advice to any one of them if they were in my position.

But there is one thing I've learned as I've matured: life isn't all black-and-white. There's plenty of gray. In fact, maybe it's all gray. I cannot be convinced that my leaving Roger will be better for Petey, and frankly I simply don't believe those who say I'd be doing him a favor.

First of all, it's not at all clear that I'd get full, or even partial, custody. Roger has been the more involved parent since he works from home, and the kind of lawyer he can afford could easily make the case that Roger's the better choice for a stable, loving environment. Secondly, more and more judges in our state are ruling *against* shared custody, pointing to recent studies suggesting that it actually may be detrimental to children to divide their lives between two different households. So the possibility that I might actually *lose* Petey is so sobering, so very horrifying, that I refuse divorce.

Call me stubborn, crazy, stupid, whatever. The day I see someone like Alyssa playing with *my kid* in the park is the day I shoot myself in the head. And if Betsy or Mom or cardio-spin girl has a problem with that, she can mind her own damn business.

'Til next time,

V

November 20

It's a miracle I haven't been institutionalized by now. I'm so stressed, so miserable, so conflicted—I feel as if I could spontaneously combust. A quick rundown of my god-awful week:

On Monday, Roger's attorney informed us that Alyssa had apparently turned up a former student, as well as a secretary at the Writers Guild, who claim they were coerced into "sexual contact" with Roger. He played dumb during the meeting, then later that night told me he had some "involvements" with other women several years ago, but wouldn't offer further details except to insist that he never had sex. My reaction to all this? I was too fatigued and disgusted to get angry. For the first time in my marriage I looked at Roger and saw a total stranger. A pathetic, troubled loser.

I told him he had to pack his things and get out. I haven't heard from him since.

Petey woke up Tuesday morning and asked, "Why isn't Daddy having breakfast with us?" I said, "Pete, something's happening with your Dad and me." He sighed and rolled his eyes. "I know, I know. You're getting a divorce, aren't you? Just like Patrick's parents and Sabrina's parents and Emily's parents. Right?"

I took a deep breath. I wasn't ready for this. I looked at my little man sitting there, bracing himself for the bad news, and at that moment all I wanted to do was hold him and rock him. "Well, sweetie, we don't know about that yet. We're having some trouble getting along, and Dad needed some time to be by himself."

I watched Petey digest this bit of information. "Mommy?"

"Yes, honey?" (I wanted to cry.)

"If you and Dad get a divorce, will you buy me a Power Wheels Jeep? 'Cause that's what Patrick's mom did when she got a divorce."

On Wednesday, my mother called to say that my father has been diagnosed with prostate cancer. In the meantime, I haven't been able to get the picture of Patty—pregnant with their fourth child and looking like a bruised banana—out of my head all week. I know it is none of my business. After all, I'm the one who told Eddie to go back to his wife. I told him I was sticking with Roger. I had rebuffed his most recent attempts to reach out to me. Do I have the right to complain? Of course not! But I just can't let it go.

Dinner last night: a loaf of bread, six Reese's peanut butter cups, and a beer. I fell asleep on the floor next to Petey's bed. I know I should feel happy that Roger's gone. This could be the start of a new life, a happy life. Why aren't I celebrating?

'Til next time,

$\mathcal{V}$

November 25

Roger showed up Sunday morning looking like he'd slept in the gutter. His clothes were rumpled and he smelled bad. He said he'd been sleeping in the van, parked by the lake. He begged me to talk to him.

"Not a chance, you philandering little shit," I told him.

He laughed derisively. "Some therapist. All that money I spent on your doctorate, and that's your response? Tell me, Doctor, clinically speaking, is this really the best way to handle a spouse who seems to be making an effort toward reconciliation?" The supercilious bastard! I wanted to kick him. He tried another approach: "Look. It's not as if you haven't had your dalliances. Face it. We've both screwed up."

I considered this reasoning for a moment. On some level he was right, of course. But I didn't have the energy to start weighing his affair with Alyssa—and now his "involvements" with two other women—against my relatively sexless relationship with Eddie. I also suspected that there might be even more "involvements" with even more women. I didn't want to talk to him. I told him I needed more time to be alone. And I told him he wasn't welcome in the house.

He could have forced his way in. It is, after all, his home too—generously financed by his family's trust fund. But Roger was apparently remorseful enough to back off. "Fine. Whatever you say. Just let me get some of my things." When he came back downstairs with his clothes stuffed in a Hefty bag, he asked, "So what do we call this? A separation?"

"Yeah, Roger. A separation. For now, let's just call it that."

I watched him slouch his way back to the van, looking for all the world like a panhandler. He turned and waved. I realized he wasn't waving to me, but to Petey, who must have been watching from his window upstairs. Roger heaved himself into the van, slumped over the wheel, and appeared to be crying.

I raced upstairs to Petey, who was now curled in the fetal position on bed, sucking his thumb. "Is Dad coming back?" he mumbled. I felt I had to be honest with him. "Not for a while, sweetie." His little body curled more tightly. I hate myself and I hate Roger for what we're putting this child through.

Other news: I obsessed all week about pregnant Patty, then finally decided to confront Eddie. I e-mailed him today at EdBennedettoPlants@hotmail.com.

Eddie:
Had a cancellation. My Monday is now totally open. How would you feel about me coming by to check out your new place? Are you free?
Val

Literally forty seconds later, I got this reply:

Val:
Are you serious? If so, you are most welcome to check out my new place. How about if I get some carrot soup and fresh bread from Water Lily? (Is carrot soup still your favorite?) Write back to confirm, please.
Eddie

I felt guilty when I read that. He was already gearing up for a cozy afternoon of soup-slurping and sex, while I was planning my attack. He even remembered that I love carrot soup. In just this brief e-mail I could sense his urgency. God, what am I doing? What, exactly, do I want from this man? Why stir things up when it would be far more responsible, ethical, moral, and mature to just leave him alone? Then I remembered Patty, bulging with child number four, and I felt my chest tighten. I e-mailed back:

Eddie:
Yes, I'm serious. But let's skip the food. I have to talk to you.
Val

And again, seconds later, I received this:

Val:
Okay. Whatever you want. But now I'm in suspense. I
can't wait to see you.
Eddie

Today I started a high-protein, low- (make that *no-*) carbohydrate diet. I think I already lost a pound, if that's possible. I am determined to lose weight! I wonder if it's possible to lose eleven pounds by Monday.

'Til next time,

V

December 4

The bad news is that on Monday I discovered that, not only had I failed to lose eleven pounds, but I had actually gained three. I couldn't face Eddie. I e-mailed him to let him know something had come up (it's called flubber, I believe). He e-mailed me back right away: "Damn."

The good news is that another Thanksgiving has come and gone and we've all apparently survived. I'd planned to host, but my sister Teresa knew I'd kicked Roger out and mercifully invited everyone to Milwaukee for Thanksgiving at her house.

I suppose it doesn't matter where we gather because every Thanksgiving replicates itself year after year. Some of us are a little grayer, some a little fatter. There's Mom lounging on the sofa, gorgeous as always in a sleek cat suit and blazer, halfheartedly offering to help in the kitchen. Normally we'd insist she relax (everyone knows Mom is no worker bee), but this time Teresa calls her bluff and actually asks her to monitor and baste the turkey. Mom becomes so flustered, and approaches the task so spastically, that my sister finally grabs the baster and snaps, "Oh, just forget it!" Mom feigns indignation, but we all know she is relieved to be off the job.

Over there on the couch is my brother-in-law, alone and scowling at nothing and everything. In the middle of the dessert, Ted stands up and declares that it's time to put up the Christmas lights. We don't see him again for the rest of the evening until we're backing out of the driveway and notice him teetering on a ladder outside.

And here, scuttling between the kitchen and dining room, is my other sister, Julia, skinny, earnest, dutiful. Julia and her husband, Luke, drove in this morning from Connecticut. Both are fussing over the seven-year-old twins, Michael and David, who won't touch any of the ninety-seven offerings on the table. Julia whips up peanut butter sandwiches, pasta, and hot dogs in rapid succession, none of which they eat. (They finally settle on tomato Cup-A-Soup.)

My father looks remarkably hardy for someone with cancer. As one would expect, given my family's natural aversion to open communication, no one mentions his illness or the upcoming surgery. I talk to him privately in the basement. I ask him if he is scared. He smiles bravely and says, "Princess, your old dad is prepared for anything." I hug him, and he whispers, "Sorry about Roger. I always suspected the guy was a loser, and this just confirms it." At that point my mother materializes (predictably), Dad quickly extricates himself from our hug, and the conversation comes to an end.

Finally, we have Grandma Anna (ninety-seven and

still ticking), propped up at the table, clicking her dentures. She stops every so often to ask, "Where's Elizabeth? Where's Elizabeth?" (Elizabeth is her sister, dead since 1977.) Toward the end of the night she shifts her query to "Where's Roger? Where's Roger?" I heard my mother whisper something, to which my grandmother responded with a low, "Oh. I see." When she came back to the table she leaned over, winked, and squeezed my hand approvingly.

Everyone else is careful not to mention Roger, which makes his absence as palpable as if he were in the room, behaving as he normally does when he's among my family, bored and indifferent. At one point I was almost tempted to set a place for him, the way Jews set out a cup of wine for the prophet Elijah during Passover. I kept expecting Roger to show up at the door, reeking and forlorn.

Spoke to Betsy last night. She insists on driving out here next weekend from Iowa for a "girls' night out." She's got it all planned: a day of beauty and relaxation at the Bella! day spa and a night of debauchery at Swingfellows, where guys do the lap dancing (how's that for a switch?). I don't know if I'm ready for this. Or maybe I am.

'Til next time,

V

December 11

As promised, Betsy came down this weekend, determined to minister to her newly separated best friend. Tabitha sat for Petey (under the circumstances, I didn't think it would be appropriate to ask my in-laws to watch him), and Betsy and I tore out of the driveway like a couple of teenagers. First stop was Bella!, where I treated myself to an incredible massage (she spent fifteen minutes just on my hands—sublime!), a haircut, and a manicure (silk wrap and French tips—looks amazing).

Then we stopped at Starbucks for a cup of coffee. No sooner had we perched at the counter when Eddie appeared. He leaned close enough for me to feel his breath on my face and cocked his head toward Betsy. "Who's this?" He appraised her quickly in that hot testosterone way of his, and Betsy must have felt it, judging from the sudden crimson in her cheeks.

"This is Betsy, my good friend and old college roommate," I said. "And Betsy, this is Eddie, my . . ."

"Whatever," Eddie cut in, grinning. He clasped his hands behind his head and gave us a perfect view of his flexed biceps. I wanted to bury my face in his chest hair. I could feel my face flush with pleasure at the sight of him.

"I gotta run," he said. "You ladies have a nice time." He pointed a finger at me. "And I'll see *you* later." As he sauntered off, Betsy grabbed my arm and pulled me toward her.

"Oh my God, Valerie. You've got to be kidding." She shook her head incredulously. "He's tough, he's coarse, he obviously spends more time in the weight room than in the library." Betsy grinned. "He's perfect."

"I know! I know!" I was squealing like a seventh-grader. "Isn't he gorgeous? Isn't he just delicious?"

"Yes! Oh my God, yes!" Betsy squealed back, squeezing my arm. She was wild-eyed and giddy. "Oh, please, you've got to get this guy back into bed, Valerie. Please, promise me you will, promise!"

"Okay, okay," I said, giggling. "I promise."

The next stop was Nordstrom, where I bought three new silver rings for my elegant new fingers. Then I got myself a—drumroll, please—Wonderbra! I'm laughing as I write this, because (a) I remember my scornful re-action when the Wonderbra debuted, and (b) I abso-lutely *love* this bra!

The minute I put it on I knew my life would never be the same. Okay, maybe that's a bit of an exaggera-tion. But not too much. The cleavage! The lift! I haven't looked like this since high school (of course, that was without assistance, but after one pregnancy and eleven months of breast-feeding, I'll take all the help I can get). All of a sudden, men are looking at me, truly star-ing—something that would have bothered me ten years ago, but now feels like a gift from God.

Swingfellows was our next stop and it was absolutely unreal—magnificent men, ice-cold beer, grinding music, and a hundred sixty horny surburban wives stuffing dollar bills into magnificent men's G-strings. Even the waiters were part of the scene, each one dressed in some macho fantasy getup: construction workers in nothing but boots and tool belts, shirtless cowboys in leather chaps, cops and firemen in various stages of undress.

And, yes, I did indulge in a lap dance. I was com-pletely swept up in the Swingfellows subculture, and the men were so damn good-looking and friendly, I simply could not resist. At first I giggled self-consciously, then managed to relax and genuinely enjoy it. When he was done, though, I had nowhere to go with all that desire; I felt what must be the female version of blue balls. I literally ached. That was the sad part.

This weekend I felt like I did when I was a child, after I had my tonsils removed: for three days, nothing but ice cream, toys, and treats, and what a sense of *entitlement!* If I feel guilty about anything right now, it's that I don't feel guilty enough.

As for the rest of my week, I have so much to say but so little time: I've discovered something absolutely scandalous about Alyssa. Details to follow.

'Til next time,

V

December 18

I am out to lunch with Dale Miller, a social worker from the office, when Alyssa walks into the restaurant. The minute we see her, Dale and I both say, out loud and simultaneously, "Oh my God."

He looks at me. "You know her?" he says.

"Unfortunately, I do. My husband was . . . involved with her. She's one of the big reasons we're separated now." Dale knew that Roger and I were having problems.

He gives my arm a squeeze. "Oh, God, I'm sorry." Then he shoots Alyssa daggers. "Bitch." Dale can be a real sweetheart.

"And how do *you* know her?" I know it couldn't have been through a sexual liaison; Dale's gay. He grabs my arm and whispers, "You'll never believe this." He wipes his mouth with the napkin and leans in closer. "About two years ago, I was at a CD release party for one of Eric's clients." Eric, Dale's partner, is an entertainment lawyer. "This girl is there with Leroy Michaels from accounting, a real toad, total nerd. She was hanging all over him. I'm telling you, Leroy couldn't get a date with Godzilla, let alone a cutie pie like that." He covers his mouth with a hand. "Sorry." We both look at Alyssa, who is alone at a small table reading a paperback, apparently unaware of us.

"So?"

"So . . . it turns out she was an escort." Dale puts his fingers up to indicate quotation marks around *escort*. "You know, a professional."

I almost choke on my linguine. "Dale, what are you saying?"

"I'm saying, dear heart, that the girl is a hooker. A couple of guys in Eric's office had . . . uh . . . partaken of her services."

It didn't seem possible. "Are you sure she's the same girl? Can you be absolutely sure?"

Dale looked at her again. "Positive. Her name's Melissa something."

"Alyssa?" I offered, the linguine still caught in my esophagus.

Dale wiped his mouth and considered it for a moment. "Alyssa, Marissa, Melissa, something like that. All I remember is she said she was getting her degree in elementary education and she was doing the escort gig to pay her way through school."

I still had my doubts until Dale remembered one last detail. "She wasn't thrilled about going into teaching, though. Admitted that she didn't really like little kids all that much. She said her big dream was to write a screenplay."

"Incredible," I whispered. "Absolutely incredible."

I don't know what, exactly, to do with this tantalizing bit of information. But I know I've got to do something.

'Til next time,

$\mathcal{V}$

December 23

On Wednesday, I'm grinding away on the StairMaster at the club, grooving to the Deep Forest *Comparsa* CD, when a man gets on the machine next to mine. He's looking at me, and his mouth is moving, but I can't hear him because I've got the volume cranked up to eight. I pull my earphones out. He's fumbling with the buttons, asking me how to get the machine started, and I oblige. He's truly befuddled. He calls himself a techno-spaz, says that he's intimidated by gadgets. He says he doesn't even know how to turn the machine on.

I help him get started and figure he's finished talking to me. I put the earphones back in. I see his mouth moving again. I pull out the earplugs. Now he wants to know how fast he should go. He is engagingly self-deprecating. Tells me that he feels like such a spaz around heavy machinery like treadmills and Stairmasters. He's about forty-three, graying, and though his legs are strong, I can see that he's on the tender cusp between youth and decrepitude. He is reading a chemistry journal.

"Looks like fascinating reading," I say teasingly. "Bet that keeps you motivated."

"Talking to you is a lot more motivating," he says. "Why don't I just put my journal away, and you stay here."

I realize with a jolt that he is flirting with me. He's trying hard to keep me on the machine, even though my time has expired. Like a magician pulling an endless variety of objects from his sleeve—a bouquet! a rabbit! a dove!—he swiftly moves from one conversational topic to another, each one fertile and enticing.

What this man does not realize is that I know his wife. Her name is Leslie, and she was in my stained-glass-making class years ago, and though we're not friends (I don't even know her last name), we always exchange greetings and pleasantries when we run into each other. Leslie is tall and slender, with aquamarine blue eyes and long, honey blond hair she wears in a single, thick braid. I recall the times I've seen him with Leslie, and he was like any other husband: cold and sullen, tense, or half asleep. A blob. If only he knew that I've already seen him as he really is, a husband! And if poor Leslie could only see her blob-husband now, so witty and animated.

He wants to keep talking, but I've got to get to work. I feel as if I'm extricating myself from a bear hug. He seems genuinely unwilling to let me go. I tell him to enjoy his workout, grab my water bottle, and walk away.

Was he my type? No. And the last thing I needed was another married man in my life. So why did I feel so . . . well, happy? Because he showed an interest in me, and we'd made a connection, and it felt wonderful.

In the meantime, Roger has come by to see Petey twice this week, which is fine with me. Pete needs his father, even if I don't. Last week, I invited him to help us decorate the tree and spend Christmas Eve with us. He's already given me a gift: a picture of the two of us in Hilton Head on the beach at dawn, circa 1991. He'd rigged the self-timer on the camera, then raced back to my side and posed like a muscle man. I'd cracked up, the camera clicked, and the moment was preserved. Roger has also asked for an "appointment" with me, presumably to talk about his "involvements" with those other women. I'm caught in the push-pull of wanting and not wanting to know. He says that the sexual harassment suit is forging ahead, and things look bleak for him. I didn't tell him what I'd learned about Alyssa, although I realize that sharing this information could be the best Christmas gift he'll ever get.

The strange thing is, in the little time we've been separated, I've seen him changing. He is, in a word, kinder. Almost courtly. I don't know what to make of all this. I don't want to be sucked in again. I'm not ready. I may never be ready.

'Til next time,

𝒱

December 31

I met with Roger Tuesday after work to discuss his "involvements." He told me that he had given several casual neck rubs to a tense secretary at the Learning Attic. (Assuming he's not lying, I don't have a problem with that. I have given and received neck rubs from colleagues and male friends and, while finding them pleasurable, didn't consider them particularly sexual.) He also mentioned that he'd kissed someone at a Christmas party many years ago but couldn't remember her name. They were both somewhat drunk. Yes, on the lips. No, tongues were not involved. I listened and just shrugged. It's amazing what a little separation can do for the spirit. I was in a forgiving mood. Besides, now that I've had some male attention of my own, I feel more grounded, more tolerant.

Once again, techno-spaz hopped onto the stepper next to mine at the gym and, once again, charmed me into pulling my earplugs out (bye-bye Los Van Van, hello blabbermouth). As he fumbled with the most basic controls ("How do I turn this darn thing on?"), it occurred to me that he might actually be faking ignorance. His hapless, helpless routine seemed implausible; he was a chemistry professor, after all, surely capable of switching on a StairMaster.

I indulged him again, walked him through the protocol until his speed matched my own. I must admit, I enjoyed his company. My time on the machine—which normally drags interminably—went swiftly as we covered great expanses of conversational terrain, from the estrogenic effects of pesticides on the environment, to the tragedy of puppy mills, to the comic genius of Abbot and Costello.

He asked for my name, and in return I asked for his, though I already knew it: Ben Murphy. This time I noticed the absence of a wedding band, which confirmed what I'd suspected. He and Leslie are either divorced or separated. I had seen her earlier in the week at a neighborhood party and had made a point of examining her lovely, slender fingers. ("What gorgeous nails!" I exclaimed, grasping her hands in mine.) No rings, not one.

I don't know why I even bother to write about this man. I'm not looking to trade one set of husband problems for another; if someone as fabulous as Leslie didn't want him, why would I? Anyway, it's too soon to think about dating. This is, after all, a trial separation, and I continue to hold out the hope that somehow Roger and I can piece our relationship back together.

Yesterday I did something I haven't done since I was in sixth grade: I prayed. I'd given up prayer after my grandfather died. He'd had lung cancer and every night for two months I asked God to make him well. I had an elaborate ritual that required at least fourteen "amens" (I was convinced that if I stopped at unlucky thirteen, the prayer would be null and void). When my grandfather finally died, I decided that God didn't listen to prayers, at least not mine.

But last week, after I'd visited one of the social workers who had just had a baby, I felt drawn to the hospital's chapel. It was empty. I sat in the first row and stared at the wall sculpture, an abstract wood-and-brass ordeal designed, I suppose, to represent all faiths. I stared and waited for divine inspiration. When that didn't arrive, I closed my eyes and simply asked God, "What next?"

I listened to my breath, felt my heart pumping, and waited. Gradually, two words emerged like headlights through fog. *Give love.* I don't know whether I just invented the message, the way kids do when they play with Ouija boards, or whether God, in fact, had spoken to me. But those two simple words have been with me every day since then. I don't quite know what it all means, but I'm willing to find out. And I pray that next year will be better.

Happy New Year.

'Til next time,

𝒱

January 8

I made the mistake of renting *You've Got Mail* last night. My colleague Dale and his partner Eric suggested it, convinced that a romantic comedy would be an ideal way to begin the new year. Yes, it was charming, adorable, enchanting, two thumbs up and all that. But I'm sick of movies perpetuating the romantic ideal. *When Harry Met Sally, Sleepless in Seattle, You've Got Mail* . . . it's all the same. And it's all bullshit. Fast forward five, ten years. Let's see how our love-struck couple is doing now, shall we? He's a workaholic who's still busting up independent bookstores along the eastern seaboard, she's drinking a little too much these days and back to cruising the chat rooms. And they fight. Constantly.

I'm awful, I know. But I'm just so damn sick of the whole notion of romantic love. It's like buying a St. Bernard: As a puppy, it's absolutely irresistible, but be stupid enough to buy one based on your initial impulse, and in ten months you've got a shedding, slobbering monster that eats like an elephant and poops like one too.

Three years ago, when my parents still lived near my sister Teresa in Milwaukee, their surburb was rocked when a dental hygienist marched into an orthodontist's office and shot him at point-blank range. It didn't make sense. The meek Miss Linda Sheppard couldn't hurt anyone, let alone Dr. Mel Neary, Milwaukee's favorite orthodontist.

It turns out that Sheppard and Neary were involved. They began their relationship at a dental convention, and Sheppard, thirty-seven and hurtling toward spinsterhood, was bewitched by Neary. For five days he wooed her: he recited Shakespeare sonnets, arranged for a single rose on her pillow, rented a rowboat, and sang to her under the thin light of a half-moon. By the last night, Neary had convinced Sheppard to surrender her virginity, assuring her that he loved her with a full and devoted heart.

Six months later, he had lost interest. He stopped calling. He was remote and inaccessible. Sheppard confronted him at the office, but he put her off, day after day. She finally learned that her "intended," the man who'd won her heart and body, was now seeing the first soprano in his church choir. Sheppard was numb, despondent. She stopped eating, showering, brushing her hair. She continued working but seemed disoriented.

One gorgeous spring morning, the kind of morning that satisfies all the senses and makes you glad to be alive, Miss Sheppard marched into Mr. Neary's office as he consulted with a new patient, and she blew his face away. Sheppard is in prison, serving a life sentence. I asked my mother, who knows virtually everyone in her town, for her interpretation of the events.

"From what I hear, the orthodontist had never intended to marry the girl," she explained. "She was just one in a long trail of broken hearts. People say he really did care about her, at first. He really did. I hear he was really good at beginnings. He loved beginnings."

Every now and then, it resounds in my head: a man who loved beginnings. And I realize with a chill that I, too, am in love with beginnings: new puppies, new gardens, new jobs, new projects . . . I love those early moments when everything is fresh and full of promise. And, yes, I love the romance of new relationships. I am loath to accept that relationships must lose passion, urgency, and affection.

As for the men in my life:

Roger continues to call and visit almost daily, and I've encouraged him to do so—although Petey still doesn't understand why his daddy has to sleep somewhere else.

Eddie is back together with Patty; I saw them at Taco Bell on Tuesday night, and she is definitely pregnant. I haven't seen or heard from Eddie since I canceled out on him.

And Ben Murphy is still my unofficial StairMaster partner.

'Til next time,

$\mathcal{V}$

January 15

I went to get my nails done and brought Pete with me, a move that probably qualifies as child abuse given the toxic stench of the place, but he really wanted to come along. I made him duck outside periodically for fresh-air breaks. I decided to ask him about one of his buddies, a cherub named Aaron, whose parents split up last summer.

Petey was rummaging through a dirty basket of old toys designed to keep kids busy (good idea, bad execution). He finally settled on a worn Fisher-Price farm set, minus the farm animals. He improvised with a Matchbox race car and headless Barbie.

"So . . . Petey . . . how's Aaron doing?" I started. I watched him push the small, metallic blue car into the hayloft and close the shutters as best he could. The hinges were busted, and the doors kept swinging open.

"He's good."

"Is he happy?"

"Yeah." Pete looked up. "Aaron has two rooms now," he told me, eyes widening. "He gets to see his mom and dad all the time. He likes it."

I checked my son's face for traces of apprehension. There were none. I ventured further.

"Does he ever talk about his parents' divorce?" At that, the young Vietnamese woman doing my nails exclaimed from beneath her pale green paper mask, "Divorce? Divorce no good for kids!" She pulled the mask off her face and filed my nails more ferociously. "A little boy in my son's Bible school cry all time." *Grind, grind, grind.* "Poor boy, he cries 'cause his mama and papa are getting divorced. He pray every day—every *day*—for mama and papa to get back again." *Grind, grind, grind.* "He's sick. Don't get any sleep. Cry all night. Poor boy!" She looked at me and arched an eyebrow.

I had to remind myself that this woman was a manicurist, not a mind reader. "Sure, of course."

I didn't want to engage her in a deep philosophical discussion of domestic strife. I glanced at Petey. He was now stuffing headless Barbie into the hayloft. Every hopeful contemplation of divorce—this morning in the shower, for instance, I lathered my hair and thought, *I could actually be happy someday*—is matched by a sense of apocalyptic foreboding, visions of Petey still wetting his bed at thirteen.

I've been thinking about Eddie. It's a form of self-torture, really, and not only because I'm thinking about a married man who has returned to his pregnant wife, but because I can't seem to conjure his face. Always, the nose is too long, or flat like a boxer's, or he's got a sleazy Don Ameche mustache. It's a kind of cruel, subconscious sabotage. Already his image is fading from memory, like a deteriorating old newspaper clipping. And even though I'm glad it's over, I miss those big arms and the warmth of his solid body, the sweet smell of his thick, black hair.

One last note:

At the club last night I watched Ben Murphy climb onto a StairMaster and program it expertly. I checked later and saw him switch to an elliptical trainer. Again, he programmed it without hesitation and moved like a pro. Now I know for certain that Ben's flustered Stair-Master confusion was a con! And it gives me the willies! I feel like I was in one of those scary Valerie Bertinelli made-for-TV movies on Lifetime where she discovers the one chilling clue that proves beyond a shadow of a doubt that her mild-mannered husband is really the crazed maniac murderer.

Betsy thinks I'm crazy. "Aw, come on," she insisted on the phone this morning. "It's not scary, it's *sweet!* Any guy who's willing to make himself look stupid to win a girl's attention . . . I think that's romantic!" I'm not so sure.

'Til next time,

𝒱

January 20

I saw an infomercial today for something called Elastal-ift, a nonsurgical face-lift. The celebrity spokesper-son—a soap opera actress, I think—said it changed her life. She said she wasn't ready to surrender to gravity, but she didn't want the risk of cosmetic surgery either. I hate the flubber under my chin. The Elastalift is only $19.95 plus six dollars for shipping and handling. It couldn't hurt to try it, could it?

'Til next time,

𝒱

January 27

Yay! The Elastalift came today! I can't wait to try it.

𝒱

January 28

When I opened the box from the Elastalift people, I was surprised to find a dozen black elastic straps (like the kind that come attached to party hats) and twenty-four squares of clear adhesive tape. It also came with an instructional video which explains how to give your-self a nonsurgical face-lift and promises that "it's as easy as putting on your makeup." First you attach the tape to each end of the strap. Then you stick one end under your ear, hide it with your hair, snake it around the back of your head, and stick it to the other side of your head. After a few tries, I got it to work. My flubber-neck disappeared. And once I became accustomed to the tugging sensation, it actually looked pretty good. A little cumbersome, perhaps, but what did I expect for $19.95? I'm going to try it next week when I hope to go out with Ben for coffee. I really do want to look my best.

'Til next time,

V

January 22

My parents are back from three weeks in Cancun (three weeks! I'm so jealous!). On Wednesday, I met them for dinner at Cafe Rouge and am pleased to report that Dad is making an astounding recovery. After the diagnosis, Mom took a class in macrobiotic cooking, put Dad on a million vitamins and herbs, taught him creative visualization (apparently he imagined that the cancer cells were Chicago Bulls players), and even found a yoga instructor who makes house calls.

The effect of the surgery and Mom's holistic steamroller is that Dad looks ten years younger and better than ever. He's lost sixteen pounds and his face is full of color and light, aglow like a Chinese lantern. I know that it's too early to make firm predictions, but Dad's oncologist believes he'll make a full recovery! (Thank you, God.) I watched my parents share a single plate of strawberry sorbet, and my father stroked my mother's slender back while she traced a finger across his knuckles. I was happy for her—she wouldn't be alone, not yet. My mother would be rootless without him.

Over espresso, my parents told me that Roger had phoned their house. The first time he called, Mom impulsively slammed down the phone the moment she recognized his voice. Now they check Caller ID first—if it's him, they let the answering machine pick up. I'm not surprised; it's almost an ideology for them, always leaving me and my sisters to face our opponents alone, whether it's a cruel math teacher, nasty playmate, or philandering husband (although I still don't know if their detachment was a carefully conceived parenting technique or just laziness).

I mustered the courage to ask, "Why didn't you talk to him, Dad? You might have told him how you really feel, you know."

"It's none of our business, dear," said Dad, firmly but not without compassion. "Besides, if he wants to win you back, he needs to deal directly with you, not your old folks." (My mother visibly bristled at Dad's mention of "old." Vain and beautiful still, she thinks of herself as the woman who defied time.)

Dad is right. Roger is clearly trying to wheedle his way into my heart by playing the good son-in-law, but it's a role he's never mastered—or even attempted. He always thought my parents were superficial and often retired to his study when they came to visit.

I asked Roger why he's been calling my parents, and he said, "Just to stay connected. You know I care about them, especially your dad." (At this, I had to suppress a snort.) "But they won't talk to me. Your mother actually hung up on me!" Then, as an afterthought, he asked, "How's your dad doing?"

"Fine. Recovering." I added, superstitiously, "We're keeping our fingers crossed." I didn't want to sound too cocky, in case the gods were eavesdropping. "Don't bother calling. They've told me they don't want to talk to you." (Not quite accurate, but it sounds better than the complicated truth about their anti-interventionist philosophy.) "Besides, can you blame them for hanging up on you?"

I noticed that Roger had also lost a few pounds dur-

ing our separation. Is he eating enough? Or is he working out more? I couldn't tell, and didn't want to ask . . .
didn't want to appear more nurturing than would be
appropriate under the circumstances. Thinking of exer-
cise reminded me of Ben, and a shimmery feeling
passed through me. I pictured his strong legs pumping
the StairMaster.

"Roger, while we're separated, have you thought
about the ground rules?"

He knew what I was getting at. "In other words, you
want to see other men."

I could have said, "No, I want to know if you're
seeing other women," but what would be the point of
being disingenuous now?

"Yes," I answered.

"My love," he said, resting both hands on my shoulders and searching my eyes, "you may see anyone you
want, but you need to know that I'm saving myself . . .
for you. I want us to be a family again."

I disentangled myself from his grip. This is not what
I'd wanted to hear, especially since I'd already resolved
to invite Ben for coffee. I stepped backward. "I don't
know if we can be a family again," I finally mumbled.
"And to be perfectly frank, Roger, I'm not sure monogamy is in your future. Speaking as a therapist and as a
woman, patterns of infidelity aren't easily altered."

"You sound like a textbook," he said, scowling. "Give
me a chance." He smiled suddenly, as if he held a happy
secret from me like a gift in his coat pocket, the secret
of his miraculous psychological transformation.

I could only think of Ben, the man who liked me so
much that he was willing to make an idiot of himself
(Betsy's interpretation) to win my attention. I was

warming to the idea of Ben and have decided that he's not a homicidal maniac after all.

And tomorrow I will ask him out for coffee.

'Til next time,

V

January 29

This week I pulled all my bills together and tried to figure out if I could survive on my salary alone. The good news is, yes, I can.

The bad news is, I'll need to work full-time, something I've been determined to avoid until Petey started kindergarten in the fall.

With Roger's monthly check—a sizeable one, at that—I never have to worry about my billing hours. I can be selective about accepting new clients, and I can always shuffle my schedule if Petey gets sick, or whenever his preschool needs a room mother in a pinch. Except for the occasional late night (and the time I'd spent with Eddie, I must add, guiltily), I am one of the few women I know who is routinely done with work by two or three o'clock; while the others labor in offices, I am already home with my son, making play dough or sharing a chocolate peanut butter cone at Sweety Todd's. It hurts my heart to think about it. Losing the freedom to spend time with Petey is, in itself, a compelling incentive to stay with Roger.

Then I got this letter from him, and all the doubts came flooding back. The letter begins with his whining, again, about the fact that my parents won't talk to him: "Promise me that the next time you see Weezy and JR, you'll send them my best. Tell them that this is a separation, not a divorce, and they are still in my heart."

I was mystified by Roger's sudden attachment to my parents. (It was never Weezy—a nickname only her closest friends use, short for Louise—or JR, just "your parents." I was always amazed, in fact, at the syntactical contortions he would undergo just to avoid addressing them by name.) Betsy speculates that he's careening toward more depression or a real breakdown, since he seems to be yearning for all his old connections, even the most tenuous ones. I read further:

"Even my own parents and siblings have cut me off. My mother says I'm a screwup (can you imagine those words coming out of her mouth?), and my father is diplomatically silent on the matter. You know how much they adore you."

And I believe they do in their own reserved way. The letter ends with Roger's version of an apology: "I know I've been less than attentive. But please realize that when I was depressed, it felt like you were giving up on me. Not that I blame you. I was a lump, a vegetable. At the same time your career accelerated. But even after my Prozac kicked in, you continued to turn away from me. You took to wearing those hideous sweatpants and my black socks to bed. You'd undress in the bathroom. So I eventually lost interest too. You see, you're not the only one whose sense of self-worth hinges on another's desire. I needed to know you were still attracted to me. By the time you started making your moves—and I'll never know what motivated this resuscitation of desire—there was too much distance between us. Only now, with real geography separating us, do I feel true hope—no, confidence—that we can be together again."

And then, at the bottom of the page, this postscript:

"I wish I could be in bed with you right now. I still fantasize about our night in Antigua. I love you." I folded the letter up into a tiny square, shoved it into my underwear drawer, and tried not to think about the night in Antigua. It was right after Roger's success with his first play, *Basic Black*. We'd burned musky incense, anointed ourselves with almond oil, and, by the light of forty flickering candles, my husband brought me to orgasm once, then again, and again. Just when I thought I was completely spent, Roger pulled a black velvet rope from a drawer. "Turn over," he commanded. My inhibitions now fully evaporated thanks to the potent island moonshine we'd imbibed, I complied without reluctance, and he proceeded to bind my wrists to the bedposts. "I'm going to have my way with you," he whispered in my ear. And he did.

I felt a pulsing between my legs as I recalled that night. Damn him for bringing it up. I felt manipulated.

As I'd vowed, I asked Ben out to coffee. We had been commiserating about the lack of good Chinese food in town, and it seemed natural to suggest that we continue the conversation over coffee. He was so thrilled and shocked that he nearly fell off the StairMaster.

"Yes, I'd love to, I mean, wow . . . really? I'd love to." I did it!

"But I can't," he said, a moment later. My heart sank. "I promised my son I'd go with him to check out a used truck he has his eye on."

It was classic divorced dad behavior. If he'd been married, it would have been easy to reschedule the truck-hunting, but now that he's divorced, he must continually prove his fatherly devotion. "I understand,"

I said, feeling my cheeks flush. I felt rejected and embarrassed.

"How about next week, same time, after we work
out?" he suggested, smiling.

"Fine," I heard myself say. "Next week, then."

'Til next time,

V

February 5

My big "date" with Ben had finally arrived.

We'd done a half hour on the StairMaster, then left
to shower. As I soaped up, I imagined what he looked
like, naked and dripping, on the other side of the wall
that divided the two locker rooms. I applied my
makeup carefully, dried my hair, and dressed quickly
(jeans, green chenille sweater, cowboy boots). I waited
by the pay phone. From the corner of my eye, I saw
him coming toward me, smiling, and I thought, God,
please don't let this be him.

What I saw was a man who looked like he'd been
dressed by an overprotective, possibly lunatic mother.
He wore a giant furry white hat with the ear flaps down,
a coat that appeared two sizes too big, knee-high rubber boots, and baggy pants of some strange material—
not Polarfleece, exactly, more like felt?

I considered backing out. I could cough phlegmati-
cally in his direction, claim to have been suddenly over-
taken by the flu. He looked shorter than he did in the
gym, and older. I'd only seen him in wrinkled blue
nylon shorts and a faded T-shirt; given the wide range
of what's considered acceptable clothing at the club, his

rumpled getup was no cause for concern. The wrinkled shorts I attributed to life minus wife.

But this? My stomach churned. Yes, it was only coffee, but even so . . . this was the kid in second grade math who picked his nose and ate it. This wasn't at all what I'd envisioned for my (okay, I'll say it) lover. It was too late to run. He beamed at me. "As they say down South, you clean up real nice."

"Thanks," I managed.

"Why don't we take one car?" he suggested. I wondered why he suggested this, had a quick vision of him throwing me into his trunk, and shivered.

"Any particular reason?"

"The parking lot at Starbucks is impossible. We'll have an easier go of it in one car."

He was right. Last time, I'd parked so far away I might as well have walked from my house. "Okay, then. Uh, let's take my Jeep."

"Dandy!"

As we walked to my car, I almost slipped on a patch of ice. He reflexively reached out with both hands, grasped my waist. "Whoa, there. I gotcha." His grip was firm, his arm strong. I liked it.

"Thanks."

We found an empty table in the back. Once Ben had peeled off his sixty-three layers of outerwear, and we were finally face-to-face, I could see he had:

1. A deep cleft above his upper lip (very nice)
2. Sparkly blue eyes rimmed by dark lashes (also nice)
3. A really great haircut
4. Lovely curly chest hair

He asked me about my work, and I found myself talking about Pete, how I've never loved another person as much as I love him, and how the intensity of that love made me feel vulnerable and, sometimes, frightened.

"I hate to tell you this, but it doesn't get any easier as they get older," he said. "Even now, just as I'm drifting off to sleep, I'll sometimes get these horrible images in my head. My son running his car off a bridge, trapped, drowning." He stopped, then forced himself to brighten. "What's your diagnosis, Doctor? Crazy, huh?"

"Not at all," I said quietly. "I've had those same awful visions about my son. When my brain's in overdrive and I can't sleep. I hate that. So I'll go in to check and make sure he's okay."

"Yeah, and sometimes they're not okay." Ben told me about another son, Matthew, who had died of leukemia when he was almost five. Petey's age. "Pure hell. Burying your own kid. It was fifteen years ago, and I still have nightmares. I'll wake up in the middle of the night and just cry like a baby." He left to get a refill. When he returned, he had a piece of baklava on a plate. "Share this with me," he said. Then, "I see you're married." He eyed my wedding band.

"Separated, actually."

"Ohhhhhh," he said, a tiny smile flickering across his mouth. "I see."

"And you?" I ventured, feeling guilty since I already knew more about his life than he would have ever imagined.

"Divorced," he said, wiggling his bandless ring finger. "Since June. It was mutual. Things fell apart years ago, but we'd agreed to stay together until the youngest was in high school. And now he is." Ben sipped his coffee. "Going through Matthew's illness, and then his death . . . well . . . it's just not good for a marriage.

Especially when your marriage is on shaky ground to begin with."

He gestured as if to put the whole topic aside, then asked, "I know this is a horribly rude question, and you don't have to answer it, and please, by all means, tell me if I'm out of line here, but I'm just wondering . . ."

My mind raced with possibilities: How much money do you make? Do you like oral sex? Can I feel your boobs?

"What?"

"Why did you and your husband separate?"

Is that all? Whew! "We both made some mistakes," I said, surprised by my self-restraint, which didn't last long, though. "Actually, he'd been messing around. You know. With other women." (I wasn't going to tell him about Eddie. Apparently I knew him well enough to let him know that my husband was a philanderer, but not so well that I could tell him about my own misdeeds.)

"I must say, in my humble opinion"—Ben touched his hand to his heart—"the man must be a fool." I resisted the urge to say, "Damn right," and shrugged. "Things happen."

As we said good night, he asked, "May I kiss you?" I found the question charmingly old-fashioned, though it was difficult to find him appealing in his bizarre winterwear.

"Yes, you may." I turned my head and let him move toward me.

Holy mother of God. The man could kiss. I felt my whole body respond, and wanted more, but decided that this kiss would have to be enough. For now.

He kept his face very close to mine. "Thank you. That was very, very nice. May I kiss you again?" he asked, and my heart did a little flip-flop. This time he reached out to gently draw my face toward his. Suddenly I heard a *boing,* a springy sound that reverberated through my head. Ben yelped. I pulled back and saw him rubbing an angry red mark on his cheek. "What the heck was that?" he asked, looking bewildered.

"I don't know," I said, wondering if perhaps I'd bitten him without knowing it. Then I felt something hanging at the side of my face and realized that it was my Elasta-lift. I'd assaulted him with my nonsurgical face-lift. Ben didn't seem to notice the black elastic strap dangling from my head, and for this small blessing I am grateful!

'Til next time,

V

February 14

I don't care what the poet says: *February* is the cruelest month. Sunless, joyless, and there, in the midst of all the dirty snow and gloom, comes, incongruously, a celebration of love contrived by confectioners and as dreaded by lonely hearts as New Year's Eve.

I actually had plans for Valentine's Day, but under the circumstances, didn't think they were substantial enough to exempt me from the lonely hearts club. Roger had called earlier today. "I know it's short notice but I want you to find a sitter," he said in a low voice. "I'm taking you out on a date."

"Roger, we're separated. Remember?"

"Yes, of course I remember. How could I possibly forget?" He sounded playful and light, as if the separation were a folly that he was willing to indulge, like my sudden interest in breeding canaries, my insistence on learning to play the tuba. He played along bemusedly, assuming that this interest, like the others, would eventually run its course. "What harm would there be in having dinner with me at our favorite restaurant? What do you say? Bellamy's at eight o'clock?"

"Fine," I agreed with a sigh. "Bellamy's at eight." I smiled as I hung up the phone, secretly pleased to have Roger wooing me but also skeptical. I couldn't believe he'd changed that dramatically in three months, while I feel as if I've been transmogrified. It couldn't possibly work.

He arrived at 5, before the sitter, so he could give Pete a bath and ready him for bed. I noticed that Roger wore the jeans he knew I favored most, because of the way they hung low on his hips. He caught me looking and asked, "How about we make this a conjugal visit?" I folded my arms across my chest and shook my head. He flicked the bath water at me. "Well," he said, "maybe next time." He tucked Pete in and straightened the kitchen (insisting above my protestations), and told me about his new play, about a group of fraternity brothers who reunite after twenty years. It sounded intriguing.

We drove to Bellamy's in my Jeep. He looked natural behind the wheel again, but there was something unnatural about his magnanimity. He asked me to choose the music (he normally seizes control over the CD player, claiming it's "driver's prerogative"). When we arrived at the restaurant, he trotted around the Jeep and opened my door with a flourish. The old Roger was too stingy to splurge on an appetizer, but this one insisted on two: tapenade with fresh baguette and a plate of chevre tarts. The old Roger would have steered me toward the least expensive entree, but this one encouraged me to order the pheasant with leek and pecan stuffing, one of the priciest items on the menu.

He laughed and motioned for the sommelier. "A bottle of your tete de cuve, please." I thought I was hallucinating. My Roger? Ordering champagne?

I stared at him. "Hey. Who are you . . . and what have you done to Roger Tisdale?"

He sipped his water and smiled serenely. "I'm not entirely beyond rehabilitation, you know."

We spent the rest of the evening reminiscing about the early years of our marriage, our upstairs apartment in a house owned by a quirky sculptor and her husband. "What was her name again?" Roger asked.

"Lola something," I said, trying to recall her last name. "Jacobson. Lola Jacobson."

"Right!" Roger slapped the table. "What a nut!"

Lola was a bit odd, but I loved that apartment. It had wide-plank wood floors and sunny rooms, and an attic that always smelled of warmed cedar. When we returned to the house, Roger kissed me lightly on the lips but didn't push his luck. I watched him pull away from the house, and for the first time in months, I felt hopeful.

'Til next time,

𝒱

February 19

I woke up with a messy cold and my period. I called Roger's lawyer to get a progress report on Alyssa's lawsuit (I'm anxious to get this resolved one way or the other) and learned that the case is still in discovery. It could be months before it even goes to trial. I can't imagine that there are that many people worth questioning.

I was pulling into the lot at work, listening to a talk show on AM radio, when this divorced guy phoned in. He started talking about how he met this fantastic woman—the only problem is that she's still legally married.

The psychologist said, "Uh-oh. Sounds like trouble. Run to the nearest exit!"

"But she's separated," he protested.

"I don't care if her husband lives in Timbuktu," the radio doc shot back. "If she's married, she's off-limits. Do yourself a favor and forget her. You sound like a nice guy. You don't need this kind of nonsense."

"Well," he said, "I guess you're right."

"Sure I am," she cackled. "That's why they pay me the big bucks. Listen, hon. If she gets divorced, give her at least a year—hear me? a year!—and if you're still sweet on her, *then* ask her out. But promise me that you'll wait a year from her divorce. Got it?"

"You have my word," he said.

As he was talking, I was thinking . . . jeez, that voice sounds awfully familiar! Oh God, could it be . . . Ben? It's a nationally broadcast show. Of the hundreds of calls that this woman gets, what were the chances that she picked one from this little town? What were the chances that Ben Murphy had called a radio pop psychologist for advice? What were the chances that I'd be listening at the precise moment that the man I kissed two weeks ago called in to talk about *me?* It just didn't seem possible! On the other hand, Ben did not show up at the club this morning.

Hmmm . . .

So now I'm wondering, should I ask Ben if that was him on the radio?

'Til next time,

V

February 26

What a week. Roger came for dinner Tuesday night, bearing the *Blue's Clues* dog in one hand, a bouquet of pink tulips in the other. Petey raced through the living room, then slid through the hallway across the wood floor like Derek Jeter. He grabbed the stuffed animal from Roger's hand.

I frowned at Petey. "Is that how we behave when someone has a gift for us?" I had a queer feeling in my stomach as my words echoed back to me. My formality was meant to dig a moat between my son and his father. I felt as if I'd just appointed myself the One True Parent, and Roger was simply a visitor bearing gifts. In the old days I wouldn't have thought twice about Pete's grabbing it—he's a kid, kids grab.

Roger quickly shot me a hard look. "Is that who I am, now? Just another someone?" He dropped to the floor and tickled Pete on the belly, sending him into instant hysteria. "If you want to grab something out of my hands, boy, go right ahead." He kept tickling Pete, who was now doubled over. "Of course, it's terribly ill mannered to grab"—tickle, tickle—"and I'll have to think twice"—more tickling—"about letting you join me for tea with the queen." Then he put his hand over his mouth and, in a stage whisper, said, "Don't mind the old lady, kid. She's just a tight-ass." I expected a wink, but Roger wasn't even looking at me. The two

boys had shut me out, and I stood there above them feeling gangly and unwelcome.

I knew I deserved it—I'd started the whole thing by treating Roger like a guest in his own home. But this! Countermanding my instructions! Telling my son I'm a tight-ass! Screw you! I screamed to myself. I felt my jaw lock. I was amazed at how quickly he ignited my rage. He'd been here only moments, and already I was cursing him.

Roger stood up and brushed off his pants. He remembered the tulips and shoved them at me. Looking away, he mumbled, "Got these for you." I wanted to throw them at him. They flopped to one side in the wrapping paper. Pink tulips always remind me of ballerinas. I was too angry to appreciate their exquisite beauty. I took the flowers and snipped off the bottoms, in the open air, not under water. Even as I cut through the smooth, green stems I knew I was destroying them; the air would block the water and they'd be wilted within an hour. I hadn't given them half a chance.

I noticed that Roger had dressed in just-cleaned chinos and a faded-to-perfection blue workshirt and smelled of my all-time favorite cologne. Now I felt terrible. He clearly had expected a nice dinner—and who knows what else—but I'd ruined it. I served up the salad and spooned carrot soup into two ceramic bowls.

I'd lost my appetite.

"Not eating?" Roger asked. He wouldn't look at me.

"I don't think so," I told him, trying to sound conciliatory. "I've got some paperwork to catch up on. Why don't you two just have a nice meal without me." It came off as spiteful.

Petey twisted around in his chair, soup dripping down his chin. "Eat with us, Mommy. Please?"

Roger kept his eyes on the soup bowl. I ached to be with Pete, but said, "No, sweetie. You guys have a boys' night, okay? I'll be up to help tuck you in bed later."

I know I need to decide whether I should stay with Roger. Let me sort it out:

The pros

1. It's better for Pete if Roger and I can work it out and stay together.

2. Roger is a great dad.

3. We have years invested in the marriage—can I really just throw it all away?

4. Financial stability. I'd be dishonest if I didn't list this as a factor. Before my marriage started to fall apart, I never really understood women (including some of my clients) who refused to leave lousy husbands just because they paid the bills. *Now* I understand. I don't want to have to work full-time. I don't want to rent a crappy little apartment on the south side of town. I don't want to have to choose between dry cleaning and eating out. Yes, I know I sound like a spoiled little brat, but I've grown accustomed to the creature comforts of a dual income, and I don't want to give it up. There, I've said it.

5. Fear. I'm afraid to put myself back on the singles market. I don't mind a light, sex-based relationship; but I'm terrified of making a commitment to a man. I've messed up one relationship, how can I be trusted with another? What if I never really loved Roger? Do I have the capacity to love? Blah, blah, blah.

The cons

1. What if Roger cheats on me again? What if he's incapable of being faithful?

2. Can I trust him? Can we ever get back to where we used to be?

3. What if he's not sexually attracted to me (again)?

4. What if there's a wonderful man somewhere out there for me, but I won't ever find him because I'm stuck with Roger? (I know how awful that sounds.)

Instead of obsessing about men, I should be focusing on me, my life, what I want. Can I help it if my vision of a life *always* includes a man? I love men, love sex, love companionship, love being in love.

Speaking of men, I hadn't seen Ben in weeks and convinced myself that it was him on the radio, but Betsy said I was crazy. "He probably has the flu like everyone else in America," she said. "Why don't you call him to see how he's doing?" (A part of me resented Betsy's suggestion. I felt like she was egging me on from the comfort and security of her happy home. She's got four kids, a good husband, a stable marriage. Maybe she gets some vicarious satisfaction from my suddenly single life.)

Yet I felt emboldened by her encouragement. I looked in the phone book and found Ben's number. I felt giddy and flushed just looking at his name in print. I dialed. He picked up on the second ring.

"Hello?"

"Ben Murphy?"

"Yes?" His voice was warm, easy. I could see that cleft above his lip, the glittery eyes. "And this is . . . ?"

I told him my name. "You know, from the club? Starbucks?" He didn't say anything for a long while. Surely he didn't have that many women to sort through.

"Ah, yes," he said finally. "Of course I remember. How can I help you?"

God, I felt like such an idiot. *How can I help you?!* Was this the guy who'd kissed me in my car, or some salesman behind the counter at Radio Shack? I wished I'd never called. I wanted to hang up.

"Uh, is this a bad time?"

"No, not at all." Silence, again.

"Have you been sick?"

"No. Why?"

Now I felt more than foolish. I felt ill. "Oh, just wondering. With the flu and all going around. You know." I had to ask him if he'd called in to that radio show. Now. Just ask! But I couldn't. I felt like such a gutless, spineless, wimped-out jackass! "Ooops. There goes my doorbell. Hope you feel better! Bye!" I slammed down the phone. Hope you feel better? How lame! He already said he wasn't sick. I was such a wuss! Then, continuing my self torture, I sat by the phone and sent desperate brain waves, waiting for him to dial *69, get my number, and call me back.

He didn't. But I saw him at the club this morning, and he seemed to gaze longingly at me. He *wanted* me. I just knew it.

My inner seventh-grader doesn't want to give up. Here is Ben, being reasonable, mature, smart. Here's me, wanting to seduce him into bed, all the more enticed by his desire to pull away. Now, tell me, how screwed up is *that*?

This time it was *me* who grabbed the StairMaster next to his, and though I didn't say anything besides "hi," I pulled off my tank top so that I was wearing only my sports bra, something I rarely do. I could see him watching me as I pulled off the top, then again as I wiped the sweat from my chest, letting the towel linger at my cleavage. I felt so manipulative, so raunchy! Why did I do that?

'Til next time,

V

March 26

I'm still in that odd and unfamiliar state of not knowing where I stand with my husband. Even the phrase "my husband" is beginning to feel like an ill-fitting jacket. He's part of my life—I see him almost every day—but he's more like a brother, a roommate, a friend. Can I remain married to him under those circumstances? Should we aim for an "arrangement," in which we share a home but not our bed?

I've been checking up on my old friend Alyssa. Her lawsuit against Roger seems to be in a holding pattern while her lawyer rounds up more witnesses to depose. At the supermarket I ran into Letha Harris, an acquaintance of mine from Lamaze class who teaches first grade at Oak Hills Elementary, where Alyssa works. I asked about kindergarten teachers there, under the pretext of preparing Pete for starting school next year (as if I'd ever let him in Alyssa's class—over my dead body!).

Letha's take on lovely Ms. Elkins: What she lacks in experience, she makes up in energy and creativity. The kids love her, parents are divided (fathers like her, moms are wary), and colleagues have yet to accept her into the fold ("My guess is she's too damn sexy for them," Letha observed). As for the principal, "She's got him under her thumb. She managed to get a $1,000 grant to establish a saltwater aquarium when everyone else is still struggling just to get Lego tables."

I hadn't heard from my client Claire in about two months and had written her off until this week, when she called to say that she was in "big trouble." Claire is usually unflappable, and it was weird to hear her sound so shaken. I've arranged to meet with her first thing Monday morning. I wonder what's up?

'Til next time,

cV

March 19

"What, precisely, are we?"

The question took me by surprise, but shouldn't have. I'd been wondering the same thing myself. It was Friday night, and Roger and I were stretched out before a fierce and magnificent fire, probably the last until next fall. He'd brought a bucket of chicken, and I'd made his favorite salad: wild greens, toasted walnuts, Gorgonzola cheese, and mandarin oranges. He refilled my wineglass, slipped off my clogs, and rubbed my feet with more care and skill than he'd ever demonstrated even in our happiest years. I lolled my head back and felt the fire's dry heat against my face. He pulled my little toe. "So? What are we?"

I knew we needed to have this sorting-out discussion, but with my full belly and warm feet, I was too content to get into it. Pete was finally asleep, the workweek was behind me, and except for the fact that my marriage was in limbo and my romantic life confused, it was a truly perfect moment. But I owed him an answer, if only an abridged one. "Well . . . we're Pete's parents, and we're . . ." He watched me, hopefully. ". . . figuring things out."

"I guess I can accept that for now."

"Good. Now keep rubbing," I commanded, flicking his nose with the tip of my sock, hoping a playful tone would derail a serious discussion.

He bit his lower lip, an expression I always took as a vestige of childhood—his signal that he was gearing up to ask a favor. "Now that you're putty in my hands," he said, wiggling his eyebrows, "it's probably a good time to ask you something." He topped off my glass again.

Uh-oh. I wasn't prepared for sex, mentally or physically. Now that I was in hot pursuit of Ben, I didn't want to muddy things by falling into bed with—horrors!—my own husband. Besides, the Merlot he had brought had made me too drowsy. I half considered pulling a cushion off the sofa and falling asleep by the fire.

"What did you have in mind?" I asked, certain of what he'd say next. But he surprised me.

"I want to move back in."

I sat straight up. He stopped rubbing my feet.

"I thought I'd camp out in the guest room, at least for now."

I looked at him, absorbing his sweet and somber face. Maybe it was the wine, or maybe it was the foot massage, or maybe I've lost my mind, but there seemed to be only one right answer. "Yes, of course. Petey will be thrilled." At that moment, I had no reservations. I was ready.

"Thank you." Roger crawled toward me, brushed the hair away from my face, lifted my chin with his finger, and put his lips on mine. He smelled of wine and soap and, well, a uniquely Roger scent that hasn't changed since the day I met him. I let him kiss me, then kissed him back. The only sound I could hear was the dull groan of the fire, my breath as it escaped my parted lips, the pendulum of the grandfather clock in the dining room. He kissed me harder, and I arched my back to fill the space between our bodies. He slipped a hand beneath my sweater and began trying to unhook my bra, until he realized it was the kind that fastened in the front. Before his fingers could change direction, I'd already changed my mind.

"No," I whispered, pulling his hand away like a chaste schoolgirl. "Let's not."

He persisted.

"We can't do this," I tried again. His lips were still on mine, muffling my protests. He tasted as sweet as berries. His tongue explored my mouth as if for the first time. My body responded. I could feel him reach down to unbuckle his belt. "Roger," I said, "not now. Really."

But I was swept along by a force as strong as an undertow, I was woozy and slow, incapable of resisting. Now he was on top of me, and I could feel his tumescence against my belly. "Remember this?" he said with a low chuckle. "We've missed you." He pulled my flannel skirt above my waist and now was inside me. My hips met his urgent thrusts as I was enveloped in his heat. I opened my eyes to find him staring at me. "We're still married," he grunted. "This isn't a sin."

He came. I did not. I could not. Just as I felt ready to climax, my brain snapped the shades wide open and the cold glare of reality came flooding in. I hadn't asked for this.

Roger pulled out of me, then flopped on the blanket beside me, gasping. "Oh. God. That was incredible."

In the meantime, I felt stricken. I lay beside him,

silent and motionless, my heart trembling. Roger moves in tomorrow.

'Til next time,

𝒱

March 26

I woke up the next day—almost noon—head throbbing, eyes aching, tongue furry. I rolled off the sofa and found my underwear on the floor, then remembered. I stuffed the panties into my skirt pocket and slurped water out of the faucet, convinced that pulling a clean glass from the dishwasher would create an unbearable clatter. I staggered to Pete's room and pulled the covers off his bed, thinking, stupidly, that he had also overslept. He was not in bed. I looked in his closet, under his bed, in the bathroom, my anxiety intensifying as it became clear that he was nowhere upstairs.

"Come on out, you rascal," I called, and the words sounded strangled. I checked the basement, the garage, even the kitchen cabinets. Pete wasn't exactly skilled at hide-and-seek; he always revealed himself giddily before I finished counting. Now the fear rose to my throat like an express elevator, and I felt ready to throw up. I ran out the front door and found a handful of broken colored chalk on the driveway, and the words, "Love you, Mommy," scrawled on the blacktop, every letter a different hue. I ran back into the kitchen and grabbed the phone. Whom would I call? What would I say?

Then my eye caught the hot pink Post-it note on the cabinet above the phone. "Took Petey out for breakfast to celebrate Daddy's homecoming. Don't eat. Will bring back fresh bagels. Love you."

"P.S. You were great last night." Relief washed over me as I felt my terror ebb and my pulse slow. I put the phone back in its cradle and reread the note. "You were great last night."

Was I? Great as in, a masterful lover? Or great as in, too drunk to stop him? I remembered his tongue pressing into my mouth as I tried to speak. The sound of a belt unbuckling. The fingers unhooking my bra. I remembered how he felt slipping inside me. He did not have to push. My body was not dry and unwelcoming but ready and supple, even as my mind and mouth tried to stop him. I remembered, too, how quickly the wine had taken effect, hastened by the antihistamines I'd swallowed only moments earlier to quell a sudden eruption of hives.

The house shook gently as the garage door rumbled open. I splashed some water on my face, gulped down a couple of aspirin, and waited. Petey burst through the side door first, his whole body joyful as a puppy's.

"Happy days are here again, Mom!" he yelled.

"Where did you get that, you little nut?" I let him climb on my lap even as my skull pounded.

"Got it from Daddy. He was singing it the whole way in the van." Pete slid off my lap and ran to the door to wait for Roger. "Dad, Dad, Daddy, Dad, Dad. Hurry up. Tell Mom what you told me before." I could hear Roger call back from the garage. "She already knows, punkin. She's in on the whole thing."

I watched Roger pop off his sneakers and slip into the moccasins he'd apparently repositioned by the side door. He was holding a big bag of steaming bagels. I could smell them from the kitchen, and I felt nauseated. I waited for Pete to switch on the TV in the family room, then said, "I think we need to talk."

Roger busied himself with the bagels. He sliced a salt bagel, smeared it with cream cheese, put it on the porcelain dish I'd saved since childhood, and set it before me. "Madame? Your bagel." The fake French accent. The hidden rose, pulled from his sleeve and now placed beside the plate. I didn't say anything. "What? You no like?"

"No. I mean, yes. It's very nice. But, Roger . . ." Part of me wondered, should I say anything about last night?

"*Oui?*"

"Enough with the French waiter routine. Please. It's just that . . . well . . . what we did last night . . ."

Roger put a finger to my lips. "Shhhhh. Don't ruin it with words. Just let it be."

I pushed his finger away. "No. I can't 'just let it be.' You see, I don't actually recall giving you permission to have sex with me."

"Excuse me? Per-*mission?*"

"It's just that I remember asking you to stop," I went on, ignoring his tone, trying to keep things conversational. "I mean, that's just how I remember it. But I know I'd had a lot to drink."

Roger pulled back and stared at me. "As *I* recall, dearest, you were extremely receptive. In every way."

I was now more confused. Yes, I received him. I could have clamped shut my legs, rolled aside, pulled myself out from under him. Instead, at some point my hips met his, my rhythm matched his. I felt myself retrenching, felt my indignation fuzz and blur.

"Furthermore, dearest," Roger continued, "I seem to recall this coy game of cat and mouse being a standard act in our repertoire. That's what made it so much"—he

lifted a finger to trace my nipple through the blouse—
"fun."

I felt myself harden against his touch. I didn't know
what to believe. I had cotton-head and a parched throat
and the *Rug Rats* theme song from the TV in the other
room was somehow resonating in my sinuses. Roger
pulled a chair up to mine, and I winced as it scraped
across the tile. "Love. Don't ruin things. I'm back, and
we're together. Pete's happy, I'm happy and . . . can't
you try to be happy too?"

I wanted to pull away, clear the dishes, ignore his
question. But that was too much like the way it used to
be, the sullen dysfunctional kitchen scene. Talk about a
standard act in our repertoire. I looked out the kitchen
window to the backyard and could see the crocuses
pushing through the hard earth, the pale green buds on
the linden trees. Now is the time for new beginnings.
Couldn't I, now, make a new beginning here in my own
kitchen?

"What do you say?" Roger was asking me, drawing
an imaginary smile across my face with his finger.

I stared ahead. I asked him to be patient with me. I
said I would try to be happy with our new arrangement,
but he had to be patient. He puts his hands up, palms
toward me, an expression of his willingness to back off.
"I can wait."

Having my work is a real blessing now, if only because some of my clients are dealing with a lot worse
problems than I am. Claire, for instance. Someone had
written on her daughter's locker in middle school,
"Your mother's a slut." The girl has been shut out by
friends, haunted by gossip and graffiti. This happened
the same week that Claire's current plaything—a thug
from the health club—had started calling on her at

home in the evening, when her husband was in the house!!! Now she's piling lie upon lie to keep her husband in the dark, but how long can her ruse possibly last?

I've got to run. More later.

'Til next time,

V

April 2

Roger finally moved the last of his things into the house, and I'm aware of how cramped and put-upon I suddenly feel. I had gotten used to having things a certain way (*my* way) and now I have to share, compromise, discuss, negotiate almost everything again. I have to contort my body to get out of the Jeep now that his van is back in the garage. Meals are now planned by committee, as are Pete's playdates and new shoe purchases. Roger has reorganized the pantry, and once again the peanut butter is in the fridge, even though I've told him that it belongs in the cabinet. He has also tried to sneak into bed with me—I woke up to find his hand stroking my butt—but I told him I wasn't ready (for sex or a permanent bed partner), and he reluctantly retreated to the guest room. The only consolation is seeing the joy in Petey's face when he wakes up in the morning to find Roger at his bedside.

Today's session with Claire was riveting, devastating, draining.

Her story starts three months ago at the health club (where everything seems to start these days). She was there in the middle of the day, a time when the club draws the oddest assortment of people. There are suburban housewives, college professors, real estate agents, therapists, and everyone else with pliable schedules. And there are the Hulks, brawny men with questionable work histories and enormous, tattooed arms, men who never run the track or use the Cybex machines, swim in the pool, or take classes, but restrict themselves to the weight room, a dimly lit place that is silent except for the grunting and occasional cry as great barbells are lifted. The one essential truth about this room is its maleness. And it is here that Claire wanted most to be.

She had fixed her crosshairs on one Hulk in particular, Kevin, the strongest, gruffest, most heavily tattooed of them all. "I don't know," she told me. It was like my endocrine system was activated in his presence. It's a primitive thing, I think. Like my body somehow knew that he was built for sex." She paused. "There was something else. He was so serious, almost mean. I can't explain it. It turned me on."

Claire pretended to know nothing about weight lifting, and the Hulk was polite enough to show her how to use some of the lighter free weights, assuming the role of unofficial personal trainer. She loved feeling the heat radiating off his thick arms, loved the sight of his black T-shirt stretched tight across his rock-hard chest. She took every opportunity to inch closer to him, wanted to fold herself into his arms. (Having felt precisely those impulses around Eddie, I knew just what she meant.)

It took her three weeks to rouse Kevin's interest, longer than any other man she's pulled into bed (or onto a conference table). She wasn't his type, she found out later, and hadn't even registered on his radar screen. He preferred leggy blonds, not plain accountant/

mother types. "But he was still a man, and when I made my intentions clear, he wasn't about to turn down the opportunity."

"How, exactly, did you make your intentions clear?" I asked her.

Her lips curled slyly. "Some of the guys were talking about Monica Lewinsky. At some point I mentioned that I thought pleasuring a man was an art form."

"You didn't."

"I sure did. I mean, it's true, isn't it?" I said nothing, but secretly agreed. "Anyway, then I told him I felt I'd mastered that particular art form. And that's when I hooked him. He just stared at me. I mean, really stared. Up and down. Wouldn't take his eyes off me. And I could see he was breathing a little faster. And I knew I had him."

Kevin hung drywall, and as luck would have it, he was working on a new and as yet unoccupied house across the cul-de-sac from Claire's in her plush subdivision, The Pines. She gave him her number, and he would call from the new house and command her to present herself. "It was the hottest experience I'd ever had. I still get hot just thinking about it, even now. Even after everything that's happened."

Sometimes he'd tell her what to wear (short black skirt). And what not to wear (underwear). It was a thrilling game, and Claire became more daring with every episode. At first she visited only when she knew he was alone, or when her kids were in school. Then she showed up when other workers were in the house, or on weekends when the kids were home or playing in the street.

One day he called her and told her to stand by her

bedroom window. She took the cordless phone to the window.

"Now raise the blinds."

She did, and gazed out. He was standing in an upstairs room in the new house, facing her squarely, only a few yards away. She could see him clearly.

"Now lift up your top."

Claire could hear her family downstairs, the TV, the clattering in the kitchen, her husband's voice. She slowly pulled her blouse over her breasts, and watched him.

"Good. Now pull up the bra."

Claire looked at me. "I thought I was going to die. It was so naughty, so risky. And I was so unbelievably horny." I have to admit, as screwed-up as Claire was, her story was starting to turn *me* on. I tried to stay impassive. "So I pulled up my bra," she continued. "Then he asked me to press myself against the window. I did. And that's when I heard the doorknob turn."

Just as alcohol slows the reflexes, so did the crazed, flaming lust that consumed Claire as she pushed her breasts against the huge picture window in her bedroom (recently Windexed, crystal clear). Otherwise she could have reacted, would have escaped.

"Do you like what you see?" she said into the phone, breathlessly.

"Mmm. Yes. Yes." She was frozen against the glass, head lolling, one hand raised high, the other between her legs. It's a kind of lunacy, really, that kind of heat, wild and mindless. And in the grip of this lunacy, Claire heard her husband open the door, heard the soft squeak of the knob as if it were a million miles away. She heard him say, "What the—" but even his voice was not enough to jar her into real time.

She turned toward the door and saw him there, wearing—of all things—a striped apron that the kids had bought him for Father's Day last year and a real chef's toque he'd found in Quebec but never had the guts to wear. Then she heard her ten-year-old behind him, heard him say, "Get the camera, Mom! Dad's wearing the hat. Take a picture!" All this in a half second, no time to pull away from the window, no time to yank down the blouse.

Her husband had enough sense to close the door between him and their son, and, through the thick oak, instruct the child to go back downstairs. It's not clear whether Casey had seen his mother splayed across the window like one of those decals meant to deter birds from smashing into glass.

Claire backed away, said nothing, pulled her blouse down, feeling like a complete ass. What had seemed so sexy just moments ago now felt tawdry, shameful, disgusting. She felt the wetness between her legs and was sickened by it. The phone dropped from her hand. Calmly, her husband picked it up, moved toward the window, gazed out.

Kevin was still there. He must have witnessed the whole scene but was firmly rooted to the spot. Claire could see him actually smirking, still holding the phone. Then she heard him say, "Your wife's hot."

Her husband pulled down the blinds and returned the phone to its cradle. Claire watched him in the ridiculous hat and dowdy apron and thought, "It's over." She expected an explosion but there was none.

"The kids are waiting for us downstairs. They decorated the dining room. Pull yourself together." He opened the door and turned around. "And do me a favor. Act surprised."

Surprised? Why? Claire's head ached, felt stuffed with goosefeathers. Then she remembered. It was their anniversary.

Later that night, after she had endured the farce of an anniversary party and smiled for the Polaroid pictures and opened the handmade presents her youngest (the sentimental one) had made, her husband told her he had known. "Maybe not everything or everyone. But I knew plenty. How could I not know? Don't you realize you're the town whore?"

The words stung like a slap. She recoiled. He switched on the reading lamp by the bed. "Don't look away. You need to hear this. You need to hear about your kids, who've been hearing all about *you* from the other kids in school. They know about the painter you screwed in the new house down the street. The math teacher you jerked off in the teacher's lounge, and God knows who else. And in case you're wondering, they probably know about this guy, too." He gestured toward the window. "Brandy Johnson is in Cara's homeroom. Her father's doing the electrical work on the house. So you can assume the whole middle school knows by now."

Claire wanted him to stop, but knew he was entitled. What she couldn't understand was his chilling lack of emotion. Why wasn't he screaming? Why hadn't he thrown something at her, or slammed his fist into the wall?

"You don't think the kids know? You think you can live in a town this size and carry on the way you've been carrying on, and keep it a secret? Do you realize that there's a rumor going around that Casey's not even my son? Everyone says he's the spitting image of Pastor

Michaels. Is there something you want to tell me? Did you make it with the pastor, too?"

Claire shook her head slowly, too stunned to respond. All this time, he knew. He *knew*. And he never let on. "Why didn't you say something?" she said feebly. "Why didn't you just leave my clothes on the lawn and change the locks?" There was something in her voice then, a simmering blend of awe, confusion, and something else: anger. Claire had waited her whole marriage for her husband to show some signs of life, and even now, confronted with his wife's raging infidelity, he remained calm. A model citizen. That's what she'd thought the day she met him. A Boy Scout.

"I would never kick you out," he told her. "You just don't get it, do you?"

Claire stared at him. "Get what?"

"I love you. I have always loved you. I just . . ."

"What?"

"I always thought of you as sick. And I prayed that you might get well someday. I never stopped praying."

Even as Claire realized what a saint she had for a husband, she also knew it was more complicated than that. They'd made a tacit arrangement years ago: Where sex was concerned, her husband was off the hook. He wasn't into it, and she wouldn't demand it. How she satisfied herself was her own business. He didn't want to know. She wanted to discuss it, this theory of hers. But she stopped herself. Her infidelities weren't merely the dalliances of a frustrated wife and at last she knew it.

Sitting in my office, uncharacteristically unkempt and ashen, Claire finally admitted that she had a problem. (Progress!) "My husband's right. I'm sick. I've been sick for a long time." She pulled a tissue out of her purse and dabbed at her eyes, then delicately blew her nose. "The town whore. Can you believe it?"

Well, yes, of course I can believe it, I thought. I looked at the clock. It was time to end the session. "Now you're ready to make real progress," I told her. "I know it feels like your world is caving in, but believe it or not, you're going to get through this."

I picked up Petey from school and listened to his amiable chatter and thought, this is my life, and my life isn't so bad after all. By the time I pulled into the driveway, I literally craved my husband. I decided to put my petty complaints about peanut butter aside and just love him. I imagined walking into the house and kissing him long and hard.

What I hadn't imagined, though, is that he had company. As I opened the door from the garage, I heard him say, "She's home." And then I heard a woman say, "Do we tell her now or later?" And then Roger: "I'm not sure. Why don't we play it by ear?"

'Til next time,

V

April 16

I thought I was hallucinating when I saw Diana sitting in my rocker (*my* rocker) in the living room, a club soda in one hand and an unlit cigarette in the other. She was wearing khaki slacks and a periwinkle knit top with a plunging neckline and cap sleeves that revealed toned, strong biceps. Her hair, now shoulder-length and glossy black, was swept into a loose ponytail at the nape of her neck. Her face had a few more crow's feet, but her olive skin was clear, her lips plump (collagen injections? hmmmm . . .) and her teeth brilliant white (bleached?). Jeez, I thought to myself. Maybe I should get myself arrested too. She looked incredible for a woman fresh out of prison.

She stood as I entered, set her glass down on the side table, called out, "Darling! Darling!" and extended her arms to hug me. I let her. She pressed her lips to the side of my face, then whispered, "Don't fret, darling. Everything's kosher."

"They let you out?" I couldn't help myself.

Diana let the comment bounce off her like a Nerf ball. "Oh, darling, don't put it that way," she said, laughing. "I'm out. Free and clear." She lifted her pants cuffs to show me her unencumbered ankles. Tan legs, white Hilfiger crew socks. "See?"

I looked at Roger and waited for an explanation. I could see the sweat on his upper lip. "Sit, sweetheart. Can I get you a drink? You look like you need it!" He giggled nervously. I hated that giggle. And all these terms of endearment—sweetheart, darling—were making me sick.

"I'm fine," I heard myself say tightly. I wanted to appear casual but couldn't. I was hurtling headlong into major PMS and knew I'd sound as pissed off as I felt. Here was my nemesis sitting in my living room, apparently cooking up some scheme with my husband while I'm at work. I know she thinks prison and that twelve-step program of hers transformed her life, but she'll always be a bitch as far as I'm concerned. I looked at Diana, then back at Roger. "So, what's going on?"

Roger rubbed his hands together and took a deep breath. "I've decided . . ." Uh-oh. Anytime he starts a sentence with "I've decided," I know there's trouble ahead. It's a kind of preemptive strike, as if to say, "I know you're going to hate this idea, but this is my business, not yours, so shut up and listen because you have no say in the matter."

". . . to hire Diana as my new research assistant." He raised his glass of wine. "I think this calls for a toast." I couldn't believe my ears. As if the week hadn't been bad enough, now this. Welcome to my world. "Really," I managed weakly as they clinked their glasses together. "So, how did this all, uh, happen?" I glanced over at Diana. She was literally beaming. I took deep cleansing breaths. I counted to ten in my head. I tried to remind myself that Roger and I were on firmer footing, that there was nothing to fear.

"It was serendipitous, really," Diana started. "I was picking up some clothes at the dry cleaners, thinking that I really needed a fresh start, a new career, no more number crunching." She fiddled with the unlit cigarette, stared at it, ran it across her lower lip. "Then I'm thinking, but who would hire me? How would I explain the, uh, gap in my employment? So do you know what I did next?"

"No, Diana, I can't say that I do."

"I prayed, of course. Right there in the dry cleaners. I said, God, grant me the serenity to accept the things I cannot change, the courage to change the things I can, and the wisdom to know the difference." She smiled brightly. "It's the Serenity Prayer."

I wanted to choke her scrawny neck, but immediately I felt guilty. Many of my patients have literally been saved by twelve-step programs. I just couldn't believe she was serious. "Then my higher power answered my prayers," Diana continued. "Precisely—I mean, precisely—at the moment I finished praying—"

"—in I walk," Roger interjected. "And I have my own

worries. As I'm driving to the dry cleaners, I'm thinking, I'm getting deeper into the new play, and it's time to start adding the sort of detail that will make my characters come alive. Even though I invented them, I know so little about what they do. What I really needed—"

"—was a researcher." Now, wasn't this special, the two of them finishing off each other's sentences like an old married couple. I wanted to scream. "Roger needs someone to investigate his characters' careers, and present a kind of executive summary, you might say," Diana continued. "I'd do the legwork while he concentrates on his . . . craft." Diana shot a dazzling smile at my husband. He grinned back appreciatively. I continued my deep cleansing breaths.

"Isn't that . . . I don't know . . . kind of cheating?" I asked. The two looked at each other.

"What do you mean, exactly?" Roger finally replied.

"Well, I mean, isn't research part of the creative process? Is that something you can just farm out to someone else?"

"Sure, of course, it's done all the time," he said, a bit of defensiveness registering in his tone. Then, "Diana, can I freshen your club soda?" I noticed he didn't bother to ask if I wanted anything.

"That would be lovely." She offered him her empty glass. I watched my husband saunter out of the room and imagined how satisfying it would feel to kick his ass.

Diana jumped up from the rocker to the sofa and now sat inches away, her tight thigh almost touching my not-so-tight thigh. I started to move away but she restrained me with a hand on my arm. "Don't. Please. Sit."

I don't know why, but I flopped back into the couch. Breathe, I told myself. Breathe.

"I know how you must feel. I really do."

"Really? And how's that?"

"Let's see . . . you thought you'd gotten rid of me, and now I'm back to haunt you. You ruined my life by turning me in, and now you're terrified that I'll take revenge, that all this twelve-step talk is just an act, that I'm really the same crazy bitch that made your life a living hell. Oh, and you're convinced I'm going to get Roger into bed . . . Am I getting warm?"

She was flaming. But I refused to give her the satisfaction of a response. "Oh, you poor darling. Of course you'd feel that way," she went on. "And why shouldn't you? And I suppose there's nothing I could say or do today to prove that your fears are all unfounded. You'll just have to wait. And see." She reached over and gave my hand a little squeeze. "You'll see."

Now the question is, do I just let Roger go through with this? Do I have the right to ask him not to hire Diana? Has she really changed? Am I right to be afraid? Or is this some kind of opportunity for spiritual and emotional growth? I honestly don't know what to do next.

'Til next time,

𝒱

April 23

I'm depressed. It's almost the end of April, and where's our spring? It's rainy, icky, windy, and cold. I had an entirely unfulfilling day at work: two cancellations and a double session with Rita, my biggest failure, a thirty-eight-year-old speech pathologist who's been stuck in a dead-end relationship for nearly seven years. I wanted to throttle her, to tell her to shut up and quit whining. I have no patience for people who won't even do the minimal legwork necessary to change. Maybe I need a new career. On the drive home I had to listen to this radio talk show host vilify mothers who put their kids in day care. (Of course, I could have switched stations, but instead I masochistically forced myself to listen to every word.)

Also, I'm pissed at Roger. And not just because of the Diana thing, which I'll get to later. When he was at the writer's retreat, I hired Red Ripley to build an entertainment center for the family room. Real cherry cabinets, glass doors, storage space for Pete's games and puzzles, plenty of room for the TV, stereo, etc. Red came highly recommended, and it's almost impossible to get on his schedule. I signed a contract and gave him 25 percent down. Yes, it was pricey, but Roger and I had talked about doing this ever since we moved into the house, and I felt we could afford it. I also felt flush: I've picked up twelve new clients since January and an outpatient consulting gig with the hospital.

When I mentioned it to Roger yesterday, he hit the roof. How dare I sign the contract without consulting him? Where did I come off hiring a fancy carpenter to build an entertainment center when we could buy one for half the price at IKEA? Or better yet, he screamed, he'd build it himself! (Sure. He couldn't even assemble Pete's swing set, let along construct an entertainment center.)

He would not let up. At 2 A.M. he was still at it! I finally tore up the contract and yelled: *"Fine! You build the friggin' entertainment center!"* The next thing I know, we're having the hottest sex we've had in months—maybe years—but I was angry the whole time. I even left teeth marks in his shoulder. And I'm still angry. Does every single decision have to be a *committee* decision?

I continued to be disturbed by Diana's reappearance, thanks to my darling husband's decision to hire her as a research assistant. I called my parents and told them what Roger had done. Dad said Roger was "up to his old tricks."

Mom agreed. "You'd better watch that man," she told me. She urged me to get one of those video monitoring systems that people use to spy on their nannies. "Forget the camera," Dad chimed in. "Tell him he can't do it. He's got a history. It's just not appropriate. He's just setting himself up for another . . . situation." Then I heard him mutter, "The rotten bastard."

I didn't want to hear that. Three months ago I did, but not now. Not when we're trying to work things out. I had naively wanted to turn this Diana thing into some sort of healing experience, a chance to fully trust Roger and forgive her. But my father's words emboldened me.

When I got home tonight I found a vase of creamy pink tulips on the kitchen table. A note: Meet me upstairs. I could hear the water running in the Jacuzzi. I saw two empty wineglasses and a bottle of Merlot. Roger emerged wearing the red silk boxers I'd bought him for our second anniversary.

He slipped off the shorts and silently proceeded to nuzzle my neck from behind. "Where's Petey?" I said into his chest. "Next door at Hunter's," he said, reaching around to unhook my bra. "Lynette said she'd take him for at least an hour, maybe more."

He bent down and put his lips on my left breast while

I watched the top of his blond head move up and down with every lap of his tongue. But I couldn't relax. "Where is she going to work, exactly?"

Roger continued at my nipple. "Who?"

"You know who. Diana."

"Shhhhh. Not now. Please."

I had a choice. I could focus on sex, enjoy myself for an hour, get closer to my husband, and demonstrate to both of us that I had transcended all the Diana crap. Or I could pull my breast out of my husband's mouth and decide that standing my ground was more important than sex, intimacy, transcendence, or chocolate chip cookies. I chose sex, and I'm glad I did, but I'm still mad. Diana starts on Monday and I find myself wondering where I should hide a nanny-cam.

'Til next time,

V

April 30

There seems to be some movement on the lawsuit. Alyssa's lawyer told Roger's lawyer that he's planning to gather some damning depositions for the stupid sexual harassment case. I say, enough with the friggin' depositions! This is torture! At this point I just want to get it over with. Even if it turns out he's guilty, I just wish it would end.

Right now I have to focus on repairing my marriage. After all the crap we've been through, pulling together is my number one priority. I know how strange that must sound coming from me—so Tammy Wynette, so Laura Schlesinger. Even though I've always wanted to keep it together for Petey, I wasn't fully committed to Roger in my heart. Word of his transgressions would have been enough to get me fantasizing (or more) about other men, whether it was Eddie or Ben. Now I realize I have to *grow up*. I've got to rise above Roger's mistakes and my own destructive impulses. I have to believe that Roger can change. I've tried to talk to Betsy about this, but I've got to say, she's not giving me a lot of support right now. It's almost as if she wants my marriage to fail. This may be the biggest spiritual and emotional challenge of my life.

Diana hasn't made it easy. I can't stand having her in the house. I go into the kitchen, she's sitting at the counter (my counter), drinking coffee from the belly-shaped mug Roger bought me when I was pregnant with Petey. (She had nine million mugs to choose from. Why that one?!) I pass by Roger's study, and the door's closed, and I can hear them giggling or talking in hushed tones. I pull out of the driveway, and she's pulling in, waving and smiling brightly. One day I came home and found them in the family room watching *Xena* together. (What is it with guys and that show, anyway? Roger claims he likes it for the martial arts, but Dale says its the lesbian subtext.) When I walked in, Roger obviously anticipated my concern, because the first thing he said was, "We're just taking a break. It's been a grueling day."

How grueling is it to sit at a computer?!? It's not like he's digging ditches or working on an assembly line. Give me a break! Oh no. There I go again. I've got to get a handle on this negative thinking. God, give me strength!

'Til next time,

𝒱

May 7

When I came home from work today, I found Diana and Roger at his computer looking at pornography. Roger fumbled for the mouse, presumably to put the computer to sleep, but he was too late. I'd already seen the picture, a brunette stimulating herself with a sex toy. I wanted to scream, "What the hell do you think you're doing?!" but knew that would only make matters worse. So I tried the bemused approach: "Researching the play, Roger?"

He swiveled around. His mouth worked crazily, but no sound came out. His face was flushed and sweaty. "Actually, we're taking a little break."

Diana giggled. "Roger insisted there was a woman on this site that looked exactly like me." She pointed to the brunette. "But I don't agree. I think my breasts are a lot nicer." She looked at me.

"Don't you?" She arched her back like a '40s pinup and laughed. I didn't find it amusing. "Come on, baby. It's all in fun."

I walked out, grabbed Petey, and left the house. I wound up at my parents, and called Roger from there. I told him that Diana had better be gone by the time I got home. She was. And Roger was sound asleep. I got Petey to bed, then woke Roger up and insisted he fire her. "You're overreacting," he mumbled. "We were taking a break. It's just a picture. Come on. Get into bed. I missed you."

If there are two words in the English language that make me absolutely homicidal, it's "You're overreacting." It's almost as bad as "You're too sensitive." Growing up, that's all I ever heard from my mother.

Whenever I expressed any strong emotion, the reaction was, "You're too sensitive. You're overreacting." That's probably one of the reasons why I became a therapist. In therapy, no emotion is dismissed as an overreaction.

"You've got to trust me," Roger said. "We were just looking. We weren't aroused. She didn't touch me. I didn't touch her. It was just amusing, that's all."

I didn't sleep in my bed that night. And I'm still mad at Roger.

'Til next time,

V

May 14

I've got a new problem at work. Her name is Cadence Bradley (what kind of a name is Cadence, anyway?!). She's a clinical psychologist, and the Westfield Center wooed her as soon as her husband was hired by the medical school. She (grudgingly) agreed to give up her job in D.C. to follow him here. Cadence isn't just a big fish in a small pond, she's orca in a goldfish bowl. The partners are falling all over themselves trying to please her. It's sickening. They made her a senior partner in wellness, so she'll be voting on administrative decisions and getting a share of the center's profits when she reels in new clients. They also gave her Penny Lyon's old office—the one with the private bathroom and fireplace.

Already I hate her. It took me three years to become a senior partner in wellness. She got the title merely by accepting the job offer. Cadence is tall and big-boned, with coarse, cropped black hair and a small scar over her lip that gives her face a perpetual sneer. No makeup, trimmed, buffed fingernails.

The day I met her she was wearing a suit the color of a Mary Kay Cadillac. Sounds tacky, but it was truly gorgeous on her—and expensive-looking. While I'm rifling through the racks at T.J. Maxx, she's shopping at Bergdorf's. Next to Cadence, I felt like a fat, frizzy dwarf. Suddenly all my fashion mistakes came clearly into focus. I noticed the ink marks on my fingertips where my (brand-new) fountain pen had leaked. I regarded my toenails with alarm (what had possessed me to paint them with blue glitter?). I ran a hand through my hair and found that patch I can't straighten no matter how much styling gel I glob on.

When I reached out my hand to greet her, she gave me a limp-fish handshake and barely listened while I talked about the eating disorders program I'm developing with Dale. Her expression fluctuated between bored detachment and bewilderment, and after I'd blathered on and on, her only response was, "I'm sensitive to perfume." She flared her cavernous nostrils imperiously. "Go a little more lightly tomorrow."

Now I've got this incessant monologue in my skull that goes something like, Who the hell does she think she is? I'll show her! Maybe I've never chaired a congressional subcommittee, and maybe I've never been interviewed by the *Today Show,* and maybe I make a tenth of what Cadence Bradley pulls down every year, but I'm no slouch. I developed the center's early childhood program. I've been published in the most respected journals. I have the most referrals in the office. I want to grab her by those quarterback shoulders of hers and say, "Look, Miss Fancy-Washington-D.C.-Senate-Subcommittee-Big-Shot, I'm just as smart as you are.

Maybe you're taller and younger than me, but I bet I could kick your ass. And has anyone ever told you that you look a little like Henry Kissinger? Because you do!"

The thing is, I must admit that if I were the boss, I'd put her, not me, in charge of the center's eating disorders clinic. It doesn't take a genius to see she's better qualified than I am to head up the project; I happen to know that she was instrumental in devising professional guidelines for the diagnosis and treatment of anorexia and bulimia.

I'm scheduled to unveil the preliminary plans for the center's new eating disorders clinic at next Thursday's management meeting. I'm curious (no, scared) to see how Cadence responds. If my instincts are right, she'll either gun down the project or commandeer it.

Then there's my other headache, Diana. I'm drawing on all my spiritual resources to remain sane and serene, but she's practically living here now. I leave for work in the morning, she's pulling into my driveway. I come home in the afternoon, she's sitting in my kitchen or upstairs with my husband. Yesterday I left Petey alone for three minutes and came back to find him in her lap while she played "little piggy" with his feet! I wanted to yank her hair.

I also realize that unless I have evidence that she and Roger are fooling around, I really have no case. Their friendship pre-dates me. They were college drinking buddies. They backpacked through Europe together. Anything I do now will only drive a wedge between me and my husband, and I don't want to do that. As it is, Pete heard me yelling at Roger last week. At breakfast the other day, he asked me, "Does Daddy have to leave again?"

The question made me sick. I feel like I've put this

poor kid through the wringer. Why should I do it again? Because Roger hired his best friend as a researcher? Yeah, I hate her, but that's my problem and I've got to deal with it.

I may also have to deal with something else, something I'd never anticipated. As I was dressing for work this morning, Roger stared at me from the bed, then suggested we let Petey sleep for an extra twenty minutes.

I watched his reflection in the mirror. He was on his belly, head perched on his hands, naked except for the white towel draped over his butt. I'd already showered, dried my hair, and put on my makeup. Normally I would have asked for a rain check—I didn't want to get all sticky and sweaty—but didn't feel comfortable leaving a sexually frustrated husband alone in the house with Diana. I knelt by the side of the bed. "How 'bout I just take care of you?" I checked to make sure the door was locked. "You can do me later. Tonight, I said."

He rolled over onto his back. "Have your way with me."

After he came, I admitted to him that I hadn't wanted to leave him and his blue balls in Diana's clutches. "Funny you should mention that," he said, calling out to me from the bathroom. He flushed. "If there's anyone she's interested in, it's probably you."

My heart smacked against my ribs. I must have heard wrong. I waited for the toilet to stop roaring. "Say that again?"

Roger walked back into the bedroom and pulled his underwear drawer open. "You heard me. I think she's got the hots for you."

Now this was news. And it made me queasy. "What makes you think that?"

"The way she stares at your ass when you're stomping out of the room." Roger laughed and yanked on his jeans. "Don't tell me you haven't suspected something." Then he leaned over and kissed me on the mouth. "I've got to get Petey up. Thanks. I'll make it up to you tonight."

The thing is, he never did. And I can't stop thinking about Diana.

I've got to go get some lunch.

'Til next time,

𝒱

May 21

In search of guidance, I went to church. I know how bizarre that must sound: a therapist seeking guidance from a pastor? But something compelled me—literally took me by the hand and pulled me to St. Mark's. Reverend Lee was in his office, and when I appeared at the door feeling shy and awkward, he bounded out of his seat and greeted me like an old, dear friend (in truth, I've seen him perhaps twice in the last six months, both times at the supermarket).

I spilled the whole sordid story of my marriage, Roger's philandering, my own affair with Eddie, Diana's unwelcome reappearance in my life. "You are a brave woman," he told me, reaching for my hand across the table. "And you have come to the right place to find the power of forgiveness." He suggested we pray together, and I agreed. He held my hands and asked God to bring peace and loving kindness to Roger and me, and by the time he was done, I felt as if a brick had been lifted off my collarbone. I could breathe again.

As for work: You think you're emotionally evolved, successful, confident . . . then someone like Cadence Bradley appears, and all the old insecurities and unresolved issues are flushed out and exposed. Now I'm convinced everyone in the office hates me. Here's my evidence:

Monday: Walked into a staff meeting. No one but the secretary greeted me. I'd brought brownies for everyone, but no one thanked me. Cadence didn't look at me once during the whole meeting. In fact, when I offered some ideas on boosting our referrals from physicians at Burrows Memorial, she actually started talking *over* my voice on an entirely different subject, as if I wasn't even there. I felt like a ghost. It was eerie and disturbing. I stared at the side of her head as she talked, at that single flared nostril and pearl earring, and imagined a malevolent insect burrowing its way into her ear and chewing her brain tissue.

Tuesday: Michael Davis, the marketing guy we hired in January, stopped making eye contact with me. I walked in, and he looked down. Whenever I talked to him he looked away, or responded with something curt and cold. Example: He recommended we put Pam Reister on the board of directors. Now, I happen to know for a fact that Pam is a flake, a contentious and confused woman who manages to alienate everyone on every committee and board she's ever been on. She's also loaded, which is why (the *only* reason why) she is asked to serve on all these boards and committees. At a board nominating committee, I said that Pam Reister would be a liability, based on my own experience serving on the United Way board with her. Mike looked straight at Leo Chambers, the chairman of the board, and said something like, "I put no stock in secondhand information. Pam Reister would be perfect." *What* secondhand information? I served with her on the United Way board! Why wasn't anyone listening to me? I wanted to scream! (Now I want to kick myself for spending so much money on gifts for Mike's new baby!)

Wednesday: I discovered that Cadence Bradley has been named director of the eating disorders clinic. She's *supervising* it! Dale and I will report to her, and our first meeting is set for this week. I decided to pull a power play; I had Rita, her secretary, pencil me in for Thursday afternoon, then sent Cadence this e-mail: "I'll see you in my office on Thursday at 3 P.M. to discuss the clinic. Look forward to hearing your ideas. I'll contact Dale and let him know about the meeting."

Thursday: 3 P.M. came and went. No Cadence. I could have called or simply walked over to her office, but decided to work at my desk instead. At 4:30, the phone rang. It was Cadence. She said, "I've had meetings all day so I couldn't possibly meet. Would you buzz Rita to reschedule for next week? In my office." Damn her!

'Til next time,

V

May 28

Bad chemistry. That's what I've got with Cadence. It's primitive, this immediate revulsion she seems to have for me. I don't know what set her against me so quickly. She's organized, linear, elegant, no-nonsense; I'm free-flowing, spunky, emotional—maybe she sensed this difference between us and reacted viscerally. I dread going to work. God, it's only been two weeks since she's arrived. How could my life change so rapidly in such a short period of time?

The latest episode in the Cadence saga: The Kirby Institute has agreed to partner with the Center on a project to identify and treat depression in high school students, a program I helped initiate two years ago. How do I know about Kirby's decision? Because I read about it in the local paper! And who was quoted in that article? Cadence Bradley! I stared at that article a long time, feeling my insides twist and clench.

Instead, I called Cadence. I said, "I'd appreciate it if you would keep me informed of significant news. The Kirby partnership, for instance." Silence. I continued, "I don't know if you're aware of this, but I was the original contact on that project. I cultivated their CEO, and I wrote the proposal. I think someone should have told me when the deal was signed." More silence. Finally, Cadence said, "We don't have the time to call you whenever someone signs a deal with the center."

I was steaming! I pulled myself together and said, "Cadence, it's entirely appropriate for the person who made the proposal to be kept informed and—"

She cut me off. "Look, I've got another call on hold. This conversation will have to wait." And then she hung up on me. *She hung up on me!* I wanted to strangle her! I spent the rest of the afternoon fuming. I could barely concentrate on my clients. As they spoke, I doodled pictures of Cadence with horns, Cadence with spears poking through her chest, Cadence with a knife in her neck. I couldn't wait to get home, couldn't wait to tell Roger everything.

I picked up Petey from day care after work and tried to listen while he talked about his day. The worst part about interpersonal conflicts at work is that they make it impossible for me to enjoy my family. No matter how cute Petey may be, no matter how charming his tale, I just can't do it. All I can think about is Cadence, our conversation (if you can call it that) running through my brain like a tape loop.

I told Roger everything. He was even angrier than I was (which pleased me). He urged me to confront Cadence. "Threaten her. Tell her she's a liability. How will it look to the board of directors—not to mention the public—that the person most responsible for developing the Kirby partnership was kept totally in the dark? You must face her down on this. Don't let her get away with it! Focus on protocol, not on your feelings. Don't whine. Don't tell her she's a meanie. Tell her she behaved unprofessionally in a manner that will hurt the center."

"I'm so upset!" was all I could think to say in response.

"This isn't about feelings!" Roger exhorted, slapping the kitchen counter with his palm. "Cadence doesn't care about your feelings! Stick to the facts. She understands facts!"

"She should understand feelings, too. It's her business!"

"But you're not her patient! You're her underling. And for one reason or another, she has placed you on her shit list. Now pick up the phone and set up an appointment to talk to her. Be brave!" Roger put his hand on my shoulder and gently pushed me toward the phone. He whispered in my ear, "Call her. Now."

Reluctantly, I punched in her number. "Dr. Bradley here," she said.

"It's Dr. Ryan." (An affectation, I realized, but why not? Though I thought I heard her snicker.) Silence.

"Are you there?" I asked.

"Yes." Man, she was cold.

"I'd like to arrange an appointment to chat with you. Monday at eight A.M., perhaps?"

"My office."

"How about the coffee shop on the corner?"

"No. That won't do. My office, please." What could I say?

"Fine." I said. She hung up without saying good-bye.

So now I've got all weekend to prepare my script. There's so much I want to tell her: Work with me. Be nice to me. Don't undermine me. Don't wreck the one place in which I feel secure and accomplished. But how do I say it? How deep and honest can I be?

Whenever my clients are experiencing tremendous stress in one area of life, I always advise them to keep things stable in all other areas. For example, if you're under fire at work, now is not the time to stir up trouble in your marriage. So I'm letting myself coast at home, not dwelling on problems with Roger. We're having sex, he's being nice, I haven't found any diaphragms in his car lately . . . all is right with the world.

There are problems, of course. One big one: Diana. Now I'm certain Roger's right about her. I'll find her staring at me (or, rather, my chest) from across the room. Or when she brushes past me, I'll feel her hand fleetingly on my ass, though if this had been any other woman, I'm not sure I would even notice. She saw me rolling my head and suddenly began massaging my neck and shoulders. (I quickly sprang to my feet and told her something like, "I'm fine. That's okay. You don't have to do that." I reluctantly had to admit the massage felt incredible.) So what can I say? These little moments are adding up, and I'm feeling increasingly uncomfortable in my own home. I don't want to be Diana's object of affection. This is insane! She's like a tick. I can't seem to pull her out of my life!

'Til next time,

V

June 4

Sunday

I'm dreading tomorrow's meeting with Cadence. The only thing that's made me feel better is a voodoo doll that Roger, my biggest fan and ally in all of this, bought me. He bought it at Borders. It came with instructions. I stuck a pin in the doll's head, another in her ass, and one right in her heart. It gave me a guilty pleasure. I also typed up a script for the meeting, reduced it to a 6-point type, and glue-sticked it onto an index card that I can hold discreetly on my lap. I know how infantile this all sounds, and how ironic—a therapist who dreads communicating.

Monday morning

The meeting with Cadence was anticlimactic, to say the least. I bounded into her office, pumped up and prepared for battle. (Remembering her sensitivity to perfume, I had even made a point of giving myself a good spritz of Obsession on my way out of my bedroom.) I eased into her guest chair and searched her desk for some knickknack or photo to inspire small talk, but it was bare except for a small black clock, hardly a conversation piece. So I just started. "I need to talk about that Kirby article." She deflected me swiftly, gracefully. "Yes, I understand your concerns," she said, launching into the kind of sanitized neutral-speak you get from hotel concierges when you complain about the dead lightbulbs in your room. "From now on, any time there's big news at the center, it will be communicated to all personnel. Immediately. Through interoffice e-mail. So now everyone can be kept in the loop." The insincerity in her broad smile was deafening.

I ran my fingers over the edges of the index card in my lap. I could almost hear Roger whispering in my ear, "Say it! Her conduct was unprofessional and potentially damaging to the center. Don't let her push you around! You're better than that!" Cadence sat there in her lime green suit and Gucci scarf. She drummed her fingertips on the table. She glanced at her watch. Clearly she had a busy day ahead. "Will there be anything else?" Again, Roger's voice in my ear: Say it! *Now!* But instead of following his advice, I fell back on the touchy-feelies. "Cadence, I came here prepared to talk about professional protocol but . . ." My heart hammered in my chest. ". . . what I really want to say is, I am sorry we seem to have gotten off on the wrong foot. And if there's anything I can do to change your feelings about me, I hope you'll let me know." I gulped, took a deep breath, and waited.

Cadence leaned forward. For a minute I stupidly thought she was going to smile and apologize. Instead she said, "Let's get something straight. I'm not your little playmate. I was hired to do a job. Pussyfooting around you and your feelings is not in my job description. If you've got a problem with me, take it up with personnel."

I could feel the stinging of mascara and saltwater in my eyes. I told myself, Don't cry. Don't cry. Whatever you do, *do not cry*. I stood up, nodded, gesticulated psychotically, and left the room. I knew if I tried to utter even a single word I would have started bawling. Roger called, as planned. "Well?" he asked.

"I blew it," I told him.

"Oh, no. Honey. What did you say?"

"Don't ask. I said it all wrong. Everything you told me not to say, I said."

Surprisingly, Roger did not respond with "I told you so," or any variation on that theme. Instead he encouraged me to come home early, promised to make me feel better. I plan to take him up on his offer.

Monday night

Roger is sound asleep—snoring like a St. Bernard—and I am wide awake. We just got through a marathon screwing session. Now why didn't I say an hour of tender lovemaking? Frankly, because it was *not* an hour of tender lovemaking. I felt like I was drilled by a jackhammer for forty-five minutes. What was he trying to prove? Now that he's hurtling toward the big four-oh, does he think he has to demonstrate his stamina and endurance? Does he think I actually *like* that?

It just went on and on and on. I tried to position myself in a way that might actually bring pleasure to my lower region, to no avail. I begged silently, "Will you just *come* already?" Each time I thought he was nearing climax, I felt such joy and relief . . . but then he slowed his rhythm and I knew he wouldn't let go. Occasionally he would whisper into my ear, "Am I hurting you?" Or, "Shall I stop?" I could have told him the truth, but then he would have wanted me to go down on him (I know his pattern all too well). I was too exhausted and not feeling particularly generous. So I let him hammer away until he mercifully exploded, rolled over, and fell asleep.

I once read a book by a radical feminist who believes that most women, if forced to answer truthfully, would admit that they don't enjoy intercourse. I wouldn't go that far. I like it for the first forty seconds. Then I stop liking it.

'Til next time,

V

June 8

What should have been the proudest day of my life has turned out to be the most embarrassing. I was awarded a "CAPPY" for one of my journal articles on childhood depression and family systems—not a huge deal, but a nice honor. Most of the center's upper management, therapists, and secretaries came to see me receive the award—including Cadence. The luncheon, hosted by the local chapter of the American Association of Clinical Psychologists, was quite an elegant affair at the Hilton.

I ate my lunch at the dais, onstage, with other award recipients. Emilio Arpetta, president of the local chapter, introduced me. I searched the audience for Cadence's face as Emilio read the highlights from my CV. It would have given me tremendous pleasure to watch her as my achievements were publicly announced and celebrated. She may think I'm dryer lint, but to the

AACP I'm a star. I finally found her at a table in the back, whispering behind her hand to another managing partner. She shut up when my name was announced, and even clapped along with everyone else. I stood up and smiled, aiming for a humble yet happy expression.

Then I heard a loud crash.

Apparently, thinking the edge of the tablecloth was my napkin, I'd inadvertently tucked it firmly into the waistband of my skirt. When I stood up to receive my award, I dragged the entire tablecloth with me, toppling the water goblets. Half the plates fell on the floor. It actually took me a few moments to realize that I was responsible for that horrible, clattering noise. There was an awful collective gasp from the audience and then a smattering of laughter.

I looked helplessly at the wreckage I'd caused, watched as one of the other honorees frantically dabbed at the salad dressing on her cream-colored suit. I pulled the tablecloth out from under my belt. I could see Cadence shaking her head, rolling her eyes.

I gripped the sides of the podium to stop myself from shaking. "I was told it's always nice to start a speech with a joke, but I thought I'd try something entirely different this time." Amazingly, everyone laughed. I felt a lot of empathy and appreciation from the group. And soon into my comments, I knew they were listening to my talk, not thinking about the tablecloth fiasco. All's well that ends well, I suppose. But I don't think I'll ever get Cadence's expression out of my mind.

Friday
What a pleasant surprise! Reverend Lee just called. He wanted to know how I was doing, whether I'm finding time for daily prayer. He also wondered whether I

might like to come in for more pastoral counseling. I agreed to meet with him again next Tuesday at noon. I'm looking forward to it!

'Til next time,

ᢦ

June 12

Tuesday

Today I had my session with Reverend Lee. I actually found myself staring into my closet this morning wondering what I was going to wear for it, as if I were going on a date instead of getting spiritual counseling from a man of the cloth.

I told Reverend Lee about my conversation with Cadence last week, how I tried to connect with her and she snapped back, "I'm not your plaything. Take it up with personnel." I even told him about the voodoo doll Roger bought me. I expected the Reverend to frown or remind me that the church abhors witchcraft, but he only laughed and asked me where he could get one for himself. "There are a few people I wouldn't mind vexing with a pin or two," he said. That comment alone ratcheted up my opinion of him. Did I mention that his whole face crinkles when he smiles? Or that his eyes, which can only be described as merry, are the most amazing hazel? Or that he has a ponytail? It suits him.

We started with a quote. Not from the Bible, but from Hermann Hesse. "If you hate a person, you hate something in him that is part of yourself. What isn't part of ourselves doesn't disturb us." Reverend Lee asked me what part of Cadence I hate in myself. It was a wonderful question. It was, in fact, the sort of question I pose to clients who, like me, are marinating in resentment. I tried to piece together a coherent response. What I hated most about Cadence was her self-confidence, her arrogance, her superciliousness. I am not consciously aware that I embody any of those traits—if anything, I'm too self-deprecating.

"Oh well. Perhaps something will come to you later. Or maybe it doesn't apply at all. Don't force it." He smiled that giant, face-crinkling smile of his and I felt instantly at ease. We ended the session by joining hands and praying for Cadence. The Reverend is a big believer in praying for one's enemies. His hand was big like a bear's paw, and warm. I didn't want to let go.

We made an appointment to meet again next week.

Wednesday
I wish the serenity I felt in Reverend Lee's study would sustain me at work. But the minute I walk into the center, my stomach starts churning again. I used to love my job. Now I can't stand this office. I know this sounds paranoid, but I just feel so . . . alienated. I want to work in a place where people greet me when I walk in, where coworkers and supervisors are genuinely glad to have me on board. That's definitely not the vibe I'm getting these days.

Friday
Oh God, I can't believe what I've done. I came into work early today—6 A.M. Even The Bitch doesn't get here until 7:45 A.M. But instead of catching up on paperwork (the explanation I'd given Roger), I went straight into Cadence's office. Fueled by equal measures of paranoia and self-righteousness, I decided to

read her e-mail. That's right, I have finally hit rock bottom. I still can't believe I did it.

I switched her computer on and double-clicked on the Eudora icon. It asked for a password. I took a wild-ass guess. Though I know almost nothing about Cadence's personal life, I remembered someone mentioning that she and her husband, Barry, had two beloved Rottweiler show dogs. I held my breath as I typed in R-O-T-T-W-E-I-L-E-R. In an instant I saw the "Checking Mail" box in the upper-left-hand corner of the screen. Oh God. I did it. I broke into her account! (I must admit that even in my crazed state, a small part of me was proud of this accomplishment.)

I was dismayed to find that her in-box was totally empty, until I realized she transferred all her messages into separate folders (how characteristically anal of her). I scrolled through the folders. Barry. Conference. Eating Disorders. Grants. Then I found one with my name on it. *My name!* I was about to click it open when I thought I heard the elevator. I panicked and quickly shut down the computer.

Obviously I feel guilty. And so hypocritical—what would Reverend Lee say if he knew? But I am completely fixated on that folder with my name on it. What was inside? And do I dare break in again?

'Til next time,

V

June 18

Monday
It's official: I have a crush on Reverend Lee. And I guess that's okay, as long as I can somehow limit those feel-

ings. That's always been my problem, keeping it contained. Over the years I've sought to understand that impulse: Why am I not satisfied with a simple crush? Why, always, is there the drive to expand it to something larger, more consequential, more damaging, more real?

I don't think it's about lust. In fact, I suspect it's not even related to romance, necessarily, but ownership. I can't simply enjoy gazing from afar. I must possess. It's why I've never been inclined to lease a car or rent an apartment or use the public library.

Now I find myself fantasizing about Reverend Lee's wife, Michelle, running off to the Bahamas with Roger. Then Reverend Lee invites me for a prayer session which turns to—oh, this is gross. What am I *thinking?* This is a man of the cloth! I've got to stop this.

Tuesday
Well, temptation strikes in more ways than one. This morning, I got to work at 6 A.M. and, finding myself all alone in the office, couldn't resist trying to get back into Cadence's computer. But when I typed in "Rottweiler," I got a "Bad Log-In" message! She changed her password! I immediately became flushed and felt as if my heart had wedged itself in my throat. Could she have known someone broke into her account? Does she suspect it's me? She hasn't behaved any differently toward me—she has been her usual dismissive, remote self.

I feel myself spiraling downward. What once gave me joy at work—brainstorming at staff meetings, working with Dale on the new clinic—are closed off to me now. My ideas are no longer welcome. The staff seems to have sided with Cadence, and now I'm on the outs, the unpopular girl rejected by the clique. Cadence has chipped away at my responsibilities so that my involvement in the eating disorders clinic is all but symbolic; Dale reports directly to Cadence. I am miserable.

Wednesday
Oh, the joys of living in a small town. A few well-placed questions and I've uncovered all sorts of interesting tidbits about the good Reverend: He went to college on a wrestling scholarship. He minored in bass clarinet. He plays in an amateur jazz trio and performs every Thursday night at Chico's. His parents are still alive, still married. He has a brother in high school, the product of his mother's surprise pregnancy at age forty-four. He plays basketball at the Y. He doesn't drink or smoke but is addicted to a computerized basketball game called Slam Dunk. He's a Big Brother to a boy named Jason who lives in the Altamont housing projects. He and Michelle have been married for thirteen years but, most intriguingly, were separated for nine months during a period of marital strife. Couldn't get further details on that one.

Thursday
Roger and I are starting to disagree about how to raise Petey. That's never been a problem before; we've been a united front on all the major issues, from spanking (we're both against it) to TV (weekends only) to toy guns (no). Now, suddenly, we disagree. For instance: Last week Pete said a boy in class (Louis, the troublemaker) had slammed him with his lunch box. The next thing I know, Roger is in the basement with Petey, teaching him how to fight! I hear him say something like, "One quick hit to the stomach, with all your might, and Louis won't ever bother you again."

I ran downstairs and said, "Excuse me, but do you really think this is the message you want to give Petey? That it's okay to hit other kids?" Roger said it's his "duty" to teach our son to fight. Then Petey gets into the act and chimes in, "Yeah Mom. I *want* to learn." I looked at him, his tank top hanging off his bony little shoulders, and imagined some bully crushing him against the wall. Wouldn't fighting back just provoke creeps like Louis? Wouldn't it be better just to involve the teacher?

Roger dismissed me with, "Let me handle this. It's between me and Pete." I looked at the two of them staring back at me and felt like I was intruding in some kind of male ritual. Part of me believes it's my responsibility to stand firm; I am the boy's mother, after all. And yet, I know all those drum-beating Robert Bly fanatics would tell me to back off and let men be men.

Friday
Alyssa's lawsuit against Roger seems to be moving toward a firm court date. I've been dreading this. I don't want to relive all the tawdry details of their affair, and frankly I fear that stirring this up again will put our marriage to the test once more. I'm not in the mood for another test. I have the power to stop Alyssa and her attorney in their tracks. I know she was a hooker, a fact that could cost her her teaching job.

That's been my trump card all along, but I've clutched it in my fist as a kind of collateral. I've always known I could save Roger, but what if he doesn't deserve to be saved? What if there were other women? What if he was making it with Diana? Taking Reverend Lee's advice, I "prayed on it." And the answer that came to me was this: Let it go. So tonight I will tell Roger about Alyssa, and together we will confront her and her attorney. I'm nervous.

'Til next time,

V

June 25

I finally told Roger that Alyssa was a hooker. I'd expected a positive, even celebratory conversation. But Roger accused me of inventing stories, picking at old scabs, even losing my mind. I tried to assure him I wasn't fabricating anything. I told him everything Dale had shared with me last winter, about Alyssa showing up at the CD release party with some gross guy who couldn't get a girl unless he paid for one; about her being his "escort." I watched as Roger's look of incredulity faded. Then I thought I heard him mumble something like, "That explains the phone calls." I asked him to repeat himself, but he wouldn't answer me.

For a long time he just sat there, slowly shaking his head. He had a knuckle wedged between his teeth, as if to plug the impulse to scream. Maybe I should never have told him. Maybe I should have gone to Alyssa on my own. She'd have withdrawn the charges, Roger would have been surprised and happy, and it would have been over. Instead, I was sitting on the deck in the glow of a yellow bug light with a husband who seemed filled with antipathy toward me. What was he thinking? That he was a big sucker, dumb enough to imagine he was the only man to share Alyssa's bed? Was he worried that she'd given him an STD?

Eventually he'd have to say something. I crossed my arms and waited. As I sat in the rocker I realized how nice it felt to be out on the deck on this balmy night, smelling steaks on other people's grills and watching the pink-streaked western sky. The geraniums were thriving. The new mulch on the flower beds was deep brown and fragrant. The deck, warmed by a day of strong sunlight, now radiated a soft, woodsy, sauna smell. Pete was at his grandparents' house.

Roger's voice interrupted my thoughts. "I can't believe you. I can't believe you. How could you wait so long to tell me?" He was almost yelling now. I could see my neighbors out on their deck. They had company. Suddenly nobody on their deck was talking. Clearly, our conversation was more intriguing than their own. I didn't want to give them the satisfaction of seeing Roger and me argue. Dave and Genevieve Wright are model citizens. Two children, perfectly behaved and regularly pressed into service scrubbing down patio furniture, planting impatiens, hosing down the van, raking up leaves. While my garage looks like the aftermath of Hurricane Mitch, theirs is spare and clean, with color-coded cardboard boxes on wire racks and a smooth cement floor that's cleaner than the floor in my kitchen. Even their garbage is neat: recyclable cans and plastics washed and sorted, papers stacked and bundled, trash cans sparkling on the curb. Though I'm experienced enough to know you can't judge a marriage by its surface, I'm amazed at the congeniality and open affection between them. The only noise I've ever heard coming from their house is the ethereal plucking of Genevieve's harp.

"Shhh. Roger. The neighbors will hear you."

"Screw the neighbors." He grabbed a pebble from the flowerpot on the table and tossed it in my direction. It hit the sliding door with a loud "ping!" He wasn't trying

to hit me—at least I don't think that was his intention—but it still got me mad.

"Are you insane? If you want to sit out here and announce our business to the rest of the neighborhood,
fine. But I'm going inside."

The thing is, I knew he was right. It was senseless,
almost sadistic, to have kept this secret to myself for so
long. I had no good excuse. But then again, there was
no point in flogging myself. The only thing I could do
was apologize. It's what Reverend Lee would call "taking the high ground."

"Look," I told Roger, as I rose from my chair. "I don't
know why I kept this from you. But not everything happens when we want it to happen. Things happen in
God's time." As soon as I said it, I realized how bizarre
it must have sounded. Roger knew about my meetings
with Reverend Lee and didn't seem particularly threatened; I guess he figured it was yet another of my self-
improvement projects, like my brief fling with Bud-
dhism or the tai chi class I took three years ago. But
working God into everyday conversation—actually
using Him to justify human behavior—was something
else altogether. It surprised me, too.

"What the hell are you talking about?" Roger narrowed his eyes, as if perhaps I wasn't his wife, but an
evil holographic impostor.

"I just mean, we don't always have control over
things."

"Of course we do. What are you talking about?"

I didn't know what to say. Reverend Lee had put it
so much more eloquently.

"Look, I'm not in the mood for this religion crap.
And if you're thinking about becoming one of those

born agains, you can forget it. For once in your life, stay in reality. Be accountable. Grow up, dammit!"

So I tried again. I apologized. I admitted that I held on to the information because I didn't completely trust him; I needed to know that we were solid, and he was trustworthy, before revealing the one thing that would get him off the hook for good. I told him I planned to confront Alyssa and was confident she'd drop the lawsuit once she realized I had no qualms about taking the matter to the principal of her school, even the school board.

Suddenly, almost tangibly, the balance of power shifted. Roger fell back onto the couch and blew out a long breath. I don't know what finally clicked into place for him, but I suppose he realized the woman he'd betrayed was presenting him with a precious opportunity. In other words, he knew he owed me bigtime. "God, I'm sorry," he sighed. "I'm so sorry. You are being very, very good to me."

"As a matter of fact, I am." It was a rare moment: Roger, contrite and, if my hunches were correct, willing to grant any request I desired. I could have asked for a vacation in Tuscany. But I chose something closer to home. I asked him to fire Diana.

He reflexively pulled his hand away, then quickly realized how that must have come across, and attempted to take my hand again. It was too late. I didn't want him to touch me. I'd wanted him to agree without hesitation.

"So, what's it going to be?" I asked. I could almost see his brain grinding. How would he tell his old college buddy she was out of a job? Wouldn't he look pussy-whipped to capitulate to his wife's demands? "Okay. Fine. I'll do it."

"When?" I wanted specifics. I could see this dragging out for weeks.

"I don't know."

"Well, I need to know."

"Okay. She'll be gone by Friday. I promise."

I don't know if I was right to extract this reluctant concession when I probably should be working on acceptance and trust. But I can't stand Diana, and her sudden sexual interest in me gives me the willies. Whether Roger fulfills his promise remains to be seen. In the meantime, I called Alyssa; her father told me she's on vacation until Monday. I didn't leave a message but plan to call her first thing next week. I can't wait!

'Til next time,

$\mathcal{V}$

July 2

Petey started day camp at the Y today. I spent last night loading up his backpack: sunblock, cap, insect repellent, swimsuit, towel, clean underwear, peanut butter on whole wheat, two drinks. When I picked him up at the end of the day, he told me I'd forgotten to pack a snack. "Everybody had something except me," he said. Luckily, the counselors keep a stash of cookies for just these sorts of emergencies. I know it's minor in the scheme of things, but I still felt awful and wanted to make it up to Petey somehow.

So Roger and I took him for ice cream after dinner. We sat on the bench outside the Dairy Queen and watched the lightning bugs hover over the grass. It was a small but perfect moment.

Tuesday, 6:30 P.M.

I overslept and missed my eleven o'clock! This is unfor-
givable. It would have been my second session with
Molly, who is, quite possibly, the unluckiest person I
have ever met; in a span of thirty-six months Molly lost
her job, discovered that her husband was having an affair, underwent a double mastectomy, and lost her
grown son to AIDS. She hadn't known he was sick,
hadn't known he was gay. She's on four different medi-
cations for depression and stress. She told me I was her
only hope.

And now I've had to put off seeing Alyssa again.

When I got to the center around 2 P.M., I found a
yellow Post-it from Cadence on my door. It said, simply, "See me." I peeled off the note and examined it
more closely. All the letters were capitalized and the
words were underscored. Twice. It reminded me of a
teacher's note, the kind you'd find at the bottom of an
essay test you fudged your way through. I wanted to
ignore it. Screw Cadence and her notes, I thought. If
she wants to *see me* so badly, let her drag her fancy ass
down the hall to my office.

But that's just not my style, I'm afraid. Knowing Cadence needed to see me made it impossible to focus on
anything else. I had to know what she wanted with me.

Was it the appointment I'd missed? Was there a
problem with the grant I'd written for the eating disorders clinic? Or—and it gave me palpitations just con-
templating it—had she found out that I'd broken into
her e-mail account?

I had to know. I stopped at the bathroom to make
sure I looked more self-assured than I felt, then walked
briskly to her office and rapped on the open door.
I tried to make it a sharp, professional, almost-

militaristic knock instead of a soft, tentative, scared-shitless one.

Cadence was on the phone. Though I stood in plain view, she continued talking as if she hadn't seen me. I debated whether to walk in and sit myself down, or simply leave. I decided to stand there. She looked up, then waved me away with her free hand. I didn't move. "Hold on a sec," she said into the phone. Her smile, clearly reserved for the person on the other end, instantly vanished as she addressed me.

"Later. Okay?"

I wanted to *kill* her. Who did she think she was talking to, one of the summer interns?! "Actually, that's not okay."

She looked up. "Excuse me?"

From some hidden spring, I found it. Courage. "I said, 'Actually, that's not okay.'" I pulled myself up straighter. I watched her nostrils flare. She ended her phone conversation, wheeled her seat back, and folded her arms, appraising me with a subtle look of amusement. I said, "You wanted to see me. I'm here now. Later isn't good for me. I've got a client."

As soon as I uttered the word "client" I knew intuitively what would come next. I had just set myself up. I could feel it.

"I'm so glad you plan to be there. For your client." She didn't say anything else. She just stared at me. We both knew what she was talking about.

"So, what did you need to see me about?" I asked, suddenly not so brazen.

She picked up the phone and swiveled her chair so that I was now facing the back of her head. "That will be all," she said. "Please close the door behind you."

Typical Cadence: with minimal effort she had produced maximum results. I hate that woman. God, how I totally despise her.

Thursday
Yesterday turned out to be the day I finally confronted Alyssa. All day long I imagined how things would turn out. Would she recognize me? Would she try to throw me out of the house? Deny everything? Get violent?

My last session ended at 1:50. I punched in Alyssa's number and waited. I had a plan; I would pretend to be some kind of delivery service, maybe a florist, just to make sure she was going to be home later that afternoon. The phone rang twice. An airy, "Hello?"

"Alyssa Elkins, please."

"That's me!"

"I have a delivery. Will you be there in fifteen minutes?"

"Uh-huh."

"Thank you."

"Wait! What kind of—"

I hung up, grabbed my briefcase, and ran out the door. As I pulled into her driveway I saw the screen door fly open. I slowly walked up the drive, feeling like I was finally at the denouement of some cheesy made-for-TV movie.

Alyssa was wearing white linen drawstring pants and a white tank top, no bra. I tried not to look at her nipples. Clearly she was anticipating flowers, something lovely from a satisfied customer, perhaps. She looked at me expectantly, searched my empty arms. The little nitwit was obviously confused.

"Delivery?" she asked.

"No." I stepped onto her porch. "Do you know who I am?"

She stared blankly. "Uh, census?"

"Roger's wife."

She gasped. "What do you want?"

I had rehearsed this moment in my head four thousand times. I looked at my watch. "Sometime before five o'clock today, your lawyer will call me to tell me you are dropping your lawsuit."

Her eyes bugged out. "What?"

"And then he will fax me a letter confirming your decision."

"What are you talking about? I'm not dropping the lawsuit." She turned and put her hand on the screen door handle. She wasn't wearing underwear either. I thought of those lean, young legs wrapped around my husband's waist and suddenly wished I had a stronger weapon than words. (And yes, I do realize that this is the second time in a week I've contemplated killing someone.)

"In that case, I guess I've got my work cut out for me this afternoon. Because as soon as I pull out of your driveway, I'm heading straight to Jan Dawson's house to tell her how you whored your way through college."

Alyssa released the handle and turned to face me. I continued, "You do know who Jan Dawson is, don't you? The head of the school board?" Alyssa nodded weakly. Things were going even better than I'd imagined. She looked like she was going to throw up.

"And I guess after I talk to Jan, I'll have a talk with the news editor at the *Morning Herald* and let her know that the new kindergarten teacher happens to be a hooker."

Just then Alyssa's father called from somewhere in the house. "Everything okay out there, dear?"

She yelled back, "It's fine, Daddy." She reached behind the screen and pulled the door shut.

I stuck to my script. "You know what I really love about e-mail?"

She didn't say anything but kept her eyes on me.

"I love how you can reach hundreds, even thousands of people in an instant. Like, I can make up a recipient list of all the teachers in your school, and all the parents whose kids go to that school, and all the news editors at all the TV and radio stations in town. And then I can send a message about anything—you being a whore, for instance—to all those people, just . . . like . . . that." I snapped my fingers for effect. She jerked back as if I'd pulled a trigger.

I looked at my watch again. "I've got to pick up my kid from camp." I started down the porch steps, then turned again to face her. She was literally trembling. I loved it.

"So, shall we be expecting a call from your lawyer this afternoon, then?"

She nodded her head.

"Very good!" I flashed a smile. "You have a nice day."

I was home by 3:30. At 4:03 the phone rang. I checked the Caller ID. It was Bill Kalman—Alyssa's lawyer. I told Roger to pick up the phone. "You're about to get some very good news," I said, almost delirious with pleasure. I watched a smile spread slowly across his face as he held the phone to his ear. When he hung up, I asked him, "Is it over?"

"It's over." He hugged me. "It's over."

Friday

True to his word, Roger ended Diana's stint as his research assistant today. When I pulled into the garage she was loading a cardboard box into her trunk. She straightened up and stuck out a hand.

"No hard feelings, babe," she said. I didn't know how to respond. What, exactly, had Roger told her about the circumstances surrounding her dismissal? I shook her hand. She held on a little too long. "Let's stay in touch, okay?"

No, not okay, I thought. "Yeah," I said.

"Maybe lunch sometime soon?"

"Maybe."

Diana hopped into her car and backed out of the driveway. She grinned and winked as she drove away. I'm relieved to see her go but have a nagging feeling that I'm not done with her. Or perhaps I should say, she's not done with me.

'Til next time,

V

July 9

I have just endured the most unpleasant dinner party of my life. It was at Evan and Lucy Child's magnificent house in the hills. (Evan was one of the producers of Roger's play, Lucy is a landscape architect). I wore the black fake-silk outfit I bought at Ann Taylor Loft, the silver jewelry Roger gave me on Mother's Day, and a pair of sexy strappy black sandals. Thanks to low humidity and jumbo Velcro rollers, my hair behaved. I looked really good, if I may say so myself. Among the guests was a famous actor who I will refer to as T. (I can't bring myself to use his full name; I'm convinced the guy's unstable, and if this story ever got out, I'd fully expect him to come after me with either a lawyer or a semiautomatic weapon. So I'm not taking any chances.) I'd seen most of T's movies and, frankly, was thrilled to find myself seated across from him. Since he tends to play good guys in his movies, I naively assumed he was one.

For the first half hour, T simply watched me. I pretended to listen to Lucy talk but really I was focused on T, feeling his eyes on me, wondering what he was thinking. I found it flattering at first, here's this famous actor staring at little me, a non-celebrity who (well-behaved hair notwithstanding) pales in comparison to his magnificent wife, a dancer and choreographer.

All of a sudden he says, loudly, "Are those your real tits, or what?" Everyone stops talking. T's wife looks embarrassed, but says nothing. I pretend I haven't heard him but inside I am dying. When I don't respond, T says it again, but more loudly this time: "ARE THOSE YOUR REAL TITS??" I should have ignored him but couldn't.

"Yes, they're all mine," I tell him. "Why do you ask?"

"And how 'bout your hair. You dye it?"

I feel my throat tighten. "Yeah, to cover the gray." Why did I feel compelled to respond to this jackass? If he'd been an ordinary guy, I would have rolled my eyes and told him to mind his own business. And everyone at the table would have told him to shut up. But because he was a movie star, we indulged him. My husband laughed nervously, our hostess looked the other way, and nobody tried to change the subject. "So," he persisted. "how old are you, anyway?"

Was this a trick question? I cleared my throat. "I'm thirty-five."

"Damn, you look good." There was nothing about his

tone or expression that indicated he meant to praise my looks. If anything, he sounded jealous. And, actually, it made sense. He was at least forty, and I imagine he's lost more than a few good roles to younger actors. His face had the grooved, baggy look that comes with years of cigarettes and hard liquor.

I thanked him for the compliment, but he wasn't done with me. "Of course, your hands give you away. You've got old lady hands." He peeked under the table. "And old lady feet. All hard and veiny." I felt as if someone had dumped a bucket of ice water on my head. I was shocked, stunned. I suppressed a gasp. I wanted to curse him, but how could I? He was a celebrity, and I was a guest. I didn't want to make a scene. I looked at Roger at the other end of the table. He watched me helplessly. I wanted him to jump in, to defend me. But he was as dumbstruck as I was. I looked down at my hands. My "old lady" hands. Why hadn't I used moisturizer before I left the house? Why did I even care what this jerk thought about my hands? Why was I still sitting there like a boob instead of walking away, or responding with something witty? The rest of the evening proceeded uneventfully, if awkwardly. I picked at my food. T did not say another word to me. We left early.

Roger tried to console me on the ride home. "What an asshole," he said. "I wouldn't see one of his movies now if you paid me."

"Yeah."

Roger looked over at me. "What is it?"

"What do you think it is, Roger? I was just publicly humiliated by a movie star while my husband sat there!" I snapped at him.

"Hey, you're a big girl. You're perfectly capable of handling yourself. Don't lay this on me."

He was right, of course. My anger had nothing to do with Roger, and everything to do with the fact that T had, wittingly or not, zeroed in on all my vulnerabilities. I haven't fully accepted the damage done to my body by age, pregnancy, and breast-feeding. I don't like the fact that every four weeks I cover encroaching gray with semi-permanent hair color.

"Don't let it get to you, hon." Roger pulled into the driveway and turned off the engine. He put his hand on mine. "That man thinks his fame allows him to behave boorishly and with impunity. He needed a target. You were handy. Forget it ever happened."

If only it were that easy.

Saturday
With the Alyssa episode behind us, Roger and I decided we deserved a little vacation. We dropped Pete off at my parents and drove to Chicago for the weekend. We spent most of the morning at the Art Institute, which was wonderful until I noticed Roger eyeing a drop-dead gorgeous girl in a red micromini. My heart sank. I still hadn't recovered from the incident with T. I felt old and fat and ugly. I drifted over to a Renoir. Roger was close behind. "God, I love it here," he whispered, gazing at the painting. "Art appreciation was one of my favorite courses in college, you know."

I felt the jealousy well up in my stomach like acid. "Really, Roger?" I stared straight ahead. "Are you sure you don't mean, 'hot young women appreciation'?"

He kneaded my neck. "Oh, no," he answered, instantly catching my meaning. "I'm quite sure I mean art appreciation." He leaned in closer and whispered, "As for young women . . . you're my only major." He said it with affection. I responded with anger: "Get your hands off me." I wanted to cry. I wanted to slap him. Our little vacation was quickly curdling.

Roger reached out for my hand. "Come on, sweets," he said in a singsong voice. "Hey. We're here. In Chicago. Just the two of us." He launched into a dopey rendition of "Just the Two of Us," and raised a pinky to his lips a la Dr. Evil. I tried not to laugh. "Come on, honey. Snap out of it." He pulled me toward him and kissed my neck. He was right. I was being a baby. I managed a smile and kissed him back.

But as we navigated the rest of the museum, I watched for Miss Miniskirt, and worked hard to ensure our paths would not collide with hers again. That night, when Roger and I made love in our hotel room, I never fully surrendered myself to the pleasure and intimacy. I was still in the museum, still on the lookout for the young woman in the red miniskirt. And I was in Lucy and Evan's dining room, staring down at my old lady hands.

Wednesday

I'm convinced that everyone is purer than me. At a church picnic last weekend I became fixated on the idea that I might be the only one who (a) used a vibrator, (b) had an extramarital affair, (c) enjoys the occasional porn flick with her husband, (d) thinks about the Reverend's sex life. All the other women looked so pure, so sanitized, so Junior League. There they are in their pastels and nautical motifs, creaseless and clean. And here I am in black capri stretch pants, giant platform sandals, deep spandex T-shirt, and Wonderbra. I thought I caught the good Reverend gazing at my ass but I probably imagined it.

Thursday
When I picked Petey up from camp he announced that he has a girlfriend. "Do you mean a friend who's a girl?" I asked him.

"No, I mean a girlfriend. We're going to get married." I watched him through the rearview mirror. He was picking his nose.

"Well, you probably ought to quit that before you march down the aisle, huh?"

He looked confused. "What aisle?"

"You know, the aisle in church you march down when you're going to get married."

"We get to march? Aw right!"

"So who is this girlfriend, anyway?" I asked him. He was still picking. I couldn't watch. "Hey. You need a tissue?"

"Nope. I'm doing okay just with my finger."

"Let me put it this way. Use a tissue or quit doing it. Picking your nose is gross!"

"Kelly picks her nose."

"Who's Kelly?" I asked, sensing I already knew the answer.

"My girlfriend! Except she eats it."

Yuck.

Friday
I'm so angry I could spit blood. Guess who took over as the center's liaison to Wilton Clinic? Yes, Cadence. Now the clinic I started—the clinic I got the grant money for six years ago, the clinic I served on the board of until the Alyssa lawsuit took up too much of my time and energy—is in *her* hands!! And just like that, she's totally squeezed me out of the loop. This morning I ran into one of Wilton's original benefactors at the

health club. She asked me how the clinic's new child care center was going. I was thinking, What child care center?!? No one had told me. I was furious! I sped to the center and marched into Cadence's office, slamming the door behind me. She looked stunned.

"Why didn't anyone tell me about the child care center at the Wilton?" I demanded.

"You would have found out at the next board meeting, along with all the other board members."

"But I'm not just another board member! I started that clinic!"

She smiled. "But you left the staff. That was your choice. Sorry, but I guess that puts you out of the loop." She flipped her mouse over and began scraping the lint out with a fingernail. If that wasn't a blatant act of hostility, I don't know what is.

"Cadence, I've got to stay informed. People still ask me about the clinic. They assume I'm on top of things. I need to know what's going on."

"Go to board meetings."

"The board meets three times a year. That's not good enough. I'm going to start sitting in on staff meetings."

She glared at me. "No, you're not."

"Why not?"

"You chose to leave the staff. You can't now suddenly decide to pop in on staff meetings. People will resent you. They'll think you're checking up on them."

"Bullshit."

"Excuse me?" she said, as if she'd never heard the word before.

"You heard me. Bullshit. The only one at that table who will resent me is you. And that's your problem, not mine."

"You're not welcome there." She dared me to defy her.

"You can expect to see me at the next meeting." As I walked out of Cadence's office I heard her say, "Not if I have anything to do with it." I couldn't let her get away with this. I turned back around to face her. "Look, I don't know what your problem is, or why you've decided to make me your enemy, but I started that clinic and I'll be damned if I'm going to let you stop me from staying involved. And until you get a restraining order against me, I'm going to be at those staff meetings!"

She looked at me with a cold stare and said, "I'll do better than that."

'Til next time,

V

July 23

Monday
It feels like Roger and I are heading into another cold war. I have never understood this cycle of ours, affectionate and companionable one week, distant and edgy the next. It has been days since he smiled, made eye contact, greeted me with enthusiasm, extended the crook of his arm for cuddling in bed. I've tried to understand what role I've played in this withdrawal of his. Was it something I said or didn't say? Something I did or didn't do? After dinner, I finally decided to ask him, but realize now that I'd approached him the wrong way. I asked, "Is something wrong?"

"No. Why?" He was wiping the kitchen counter and watching *Xena* on the small TV near the sink.

"I don't know. You're acting sort of weird."

He groaned. "Please don't start with me. There's nothing wrong." He threw the sponge in the sink and went upstairs. When he came downstairs for dinner I apologized. "I'm sorry, Roger. I went about that the wrong way. What I should have said was, 'I've been feeling some distance from you and wonder whether there's something wrong.'"

He looked at me blankly. "I *said*, there is nothing wrong."

I already knew how this conversation would play out, should I choose to pursue it. I'd insist that he was being disingenuous. He'd say I was too sensitive. He'd say I was inventing problems. He'd complain that I could never leave well enough alone. His face would darken and he'd leave the room, muttering, "Satisfied now? You got what you'd wanted. I'm withdrawing."

Before Alyssa, I could attribute his emotional leave-taking to his depression, or his frustration with work, or his concern that I'd spent too much on new bath towels. Now I worry that he's cheating again. Maybe there's someone else he is smiling at, making eye contact with, greeting with enthusiasm, tucking into the crook of his arm.

Tuesday
The next Wilton Clinic staff meeting is tomorrow at noon. I'm going to get there at 11:45 to get a strategic seat, to the right of the director, Marlena Swede. I helped recruit Marlena when she was an administrator with an outpatient program at Northwestern. She nominated me for a Women in Well-Being leadership award last year; I didn't win, but I've always been grateful for her support.

I can't stop ruminating about the meeting. The whiny victim in me wants to hole myself up in my office, collapsed under the weight of Cadence's decision to push me out of staff meetings. But my inner bitch made an appearance in Cadence's office last week, and I sense that she's here to stay. Throughout my life I've operated from a position of approval-seeking and submission. This new persona is scary. And exhilarating. I don't know where it will take me, but it's got to be a hell of an improvement over the pathetic little cave I've inhabited with my chastised inner child. I shared this revelation at lunch with Dale. He said he wants to throw a party for my inner bitch. What a guy.

Wednesday
I showed up at the meeting at 11:45—early as planned. Everyone was already there. I didn't understand at first—how could everyone be early? Cadence, sitting at Marlena's right, glanced at her watch and announced, "I guess that covers everything on the agenda, unless there's new business." Suddenly it dawned on me: Cadence had changed the time and notified everyone—but me. I whispered to Wey, "What did I miss?" She patted my arm.

"Everything, I'm afraid. We started an hour ago. You're late, girl." I looked at Cadence. She was shuffling her papers, ignoring me. I demanded, loudly enough for everyone to hear, "Why didn't you tell me you rescheduled the meeting?" Everyone froze. These were, after all, mental health professionals; they know a good interpersonal dysfunction when they see it. They waited for Cadence's reaction. She wouldn't answer me. Instead, she asked Louis, "So you'll get back to me on that proposal?"

Louis looked at me apologetically. "Yeah. Some time next week, okay?" "That would be fine." Cadence strode out before I could say anything. Where was my inner bitch when I needed her?

'Til next time,

𝒱

July 30

Saturday

Today at Barnes & Noble, I told Petey I'd buy him a book—a little paperback based on the new Tarzan movie. When Roger came over to us, I handed him the book and asked him to go pay for it. He looked at it and frowned. "Do we really want our son reading this kind of tripe?" he asked. Petey, who was sitting on the chair next to mine, was already bracing himself for an argument. "But Mom said she'd buy it for me," he protested, voice wavering. Roger sighed one of his big theatrical sighs. "I think we need to discuss this."

"Now?"

"Now is as good a time as any," he said. "I'm sorry, but I just can't abide this kind of reading material." He folded his arms like a schoolmarm, a disapproving old biddy. "Now that Pete's taken a real interest in reading, he needs quality. Not stupid books based on stupid movies."

Pete looked at me hopefully. I reached for the book and tucked it under my arm. "Sorry, Roger, but I already told him he could have it."

"Fine. Then you pay for it. I'll be waiting in the car." Exit stage left. I offered to read the book to Petey at bedtime but he said he didn't want to hear it. "Maybe some other time," he said, looking sad. Roger didn't talk to me for the rest of the night. Welcome to my marriage.

Sunday

The Tarzan episode continues. This morning I woke early to buy Roger breakfast—a scrambled egg and cheese on an onion bagel, his favorite—and he barely thanked me. "What is it with you?" I asked him. "Would you please talk to me?"

He put down the newspaper and stared at me. "I'm tired of you dismissing me in front of our son."

"What do you mean, dismissing you?" I said.

"I mean, I told you I didn't want him reading that crap and you went ahead and bought it anyway. What kind of message does that send?"

I wanted to choke him! "Excuse me? And what kind of message does it send to have Mommy capitulate every time Daddy snaps his fingers? Huh?"

"You know what? You know what? It makes me absolutely sick to my stomach that you let him read that crap. What the hell is wrong with you, anyway?" That ugly, bulging vein on Roger's forehead was throbbing now.

"What's wrong with me?" I demanded. "How about you? You encourage him to watch *Xena!* You've rented *A Very Brady Sequel,* like, four times! You let him stay up until ten P.M. watching Nick at Nite. Don't talk to me about crap!"

Then Roger did something that made me absolutely maniacal. "Look at you. Just look at you," he said, gesturing toward me. "What is this, some kind of performance?" He looked around the room in search of imaginary spectators.

"Bravo! Bravissimo! Such drama. Such projection."
He cupped his hands around his mouth to form a
megaphone. "Are you auditioning or something? Is that
what's going on? An audition?" Then he dropped his
voice to a whisper. "There's no need to emote, you
know. I'm only two feet away."

I grabbed a hairbrush and threw it. It hit the wall, six
inches from his ear. I was filled with unspeakable rage.
I screamed, "I hate you!" My throat burned and I
sobbed into my hands, feeling my nose and eyes swell.
Roger sat there, serene and fully in control. He had
won. "Maybe we can revisit this issue after you've
pulled yourself together," he said coolly. He put a hand
on the doorknob and turned toward me once more.
"That time of the month?"

As a matter of fact, it is. God, how I hate my husband
right now.

Monday
Big improvement. Roger actually apologized. While he
still insists I was wrong to buy the Tarzan book, he
realizes it's something we should have discussed privately and understands it was wrong to expect me to
back down in front of Petey. Wow. *Big* progress. I'm
still mad at him but things are so lousy at work I can't
afford to be in a fight with him right now. I've got this
theory that if something's wrong in one important area
of your life, you'd better work like hell to keep things
stable everywhere else, or you're headed for a breakdown. When Roger apologized, he gave me a smile that
literally melted the anger. It's hard to stay mad at him.
Does that make me a wimp, or a wife? Is my ability to
recover so quickly a sign that I'm incredibly strong, or
incredibly screwed up?!?

Tuesday
I've decided to take a chance and show up at the next
Wilton staff meeting. I called Marlena this morning to
confirm the day and time: Wednesday, 11 A.M. "We've
missed having your shining face at the table," she said,
her voice genuinely warm, as usual.

"Yeah, thanks," I said. "I've missed you all too."

"What happened last week?"

"What do you mean?"

"Oh, you know, coming in at the end of the meeting.
That's not like you."

"It's not me. It's, well, there was a miscommunica-
tion, I guess." It took all my self-restraint to keep from
mentioning Cadence. I didn't want to drag Marlena
into this ugly mess, especially now that she'll have to
work with that Amazon.

"So we'll see you tomorrow, then?" Marlena chirped.

"I'll be there!" I said, trying to sound bright.

Wednesday
The meeting went without a hitch. The Amazon
blanched when she arrived to find me sitting at the
table, already engaged in light banter with Marlena and
Wey, the young, funny therapist who works as an art
therapist, mostly with kids. I took the role of elder
stateswoman, offering my wise counsel when consulted, and (thankfully) I was consulted frequently.
(Jack, the fortyish social worker who came on to me
at the center retreat two years ago, seemed especially
interested in what I had to say. Maybe because things
have been so rotten at home, I found myself staring at
his sexy mouth.) In fact, once I stopped focusing on
the Amazon, I actually enjoyed myself. Wilton is like
the center's feisty, scrappy alter ego. It's always invigor-

ating to be around the staff, makes me feel like a graduate student again. It was hard to go back to my quiet office, harder still to find the following message from Cadence in my e-mail box: "See me." I decided to ignore it. See yourself, you big moron.

Thursday
Get this: Tonight we interviewed a potential baby-sitter for Petey. When I opened the door, my first thought was, Not a chance, kiddo. This girl was a *knockout*.

She was wearing a gauzy little top, tiny shorts, gorgeous smile, long blond hair. "Hi, I'm Amber." I must have been staring, because then she said, "You know, I called about the baby-sitting job?"

Roger, who should have been deeply immersed in *Xena* and has never shown any interest in interviewing baby-sitters, suddenly materialized. "Well, aren't you going to introduce me?" he asked.

I glared at him. "Amber, this is my husband, Roger Tisdale." She practically jumped off the sofa.

"Roger Tisdale? You wrote *Basic Black*? Are you that Roger Tisdale?"

Roger pulled himself up to his full five feet eleven inches. "That's me." He extended a hand. I hated that eager look on his face. "Wipe the drool off your face," I mumbled. They both looked at me. God, I think I'm developing Tourette's. I couldn't restrain myself.

"I auditioned for Jasmine." She pouted. "But I didn't get it. They said I was too, uh, sexy."

"Indeed," my husband said, smiling. Leering.

I want to finish this story but I see I've got a client coming in a minute and I've got to review her file.

'Til next time,

CV

August 6

Friday
So there we were yesterday, in the living room: Amber, the baby-sitter candidate, radiating erotic youth, my darling husband practically ejaculating into his Dockers, me feeling fat and jealous. Had I known that this girl would turn out to be so perfect, I wouldn't have answered the door in a stained oversized T-shirt and baggy jeans. The truth is, she sounded ugly on the phone. She had one of those mucus-clotted voices that suggests a deviated septum or harelip. I expected slow and fat and jolly. I never expected long and lean and stacked. Nor did I expect a theater aficionado who just happened to audition for a role in my husband's play but got rejected because she was "too sexy."

When I left the room to answer the phone, Amber was sitting on the piano bench while Roger stood at the archway, chatting amiably. When I returned, they were both on the sofa, Roger's arm draped over the back, his fingers just barely touching her bare, tanned shoulder. I knew that would happen.

They were discussing Roger's work. He looked elated, charmed, smitten. "And it's precisely that yearning I explore in my new play," he said to her.

"Your new play?!" Amber widened her eyes and opened her mouth to reveal two rows of perfect teeth. She was really turning it on—and so shamelessly, given the fact that Roger's wife, the woman who would ultimately determine her employment, was standing right there.

Neither one seemed to notice or care that I had returned to the room, or that we'd lost sight of the original purpose of the meeting. I sat on the piano bench and waited, trying to appear respectful as Roger summarized his plot. At some point Amber must have remembered that she'd come to interview for a babysitting position. "So. Where's the little guy?" she asked.

"He's in the family room," I answered. "His name is Peter."

"That should be easy to remember. That's my little brother's name."

"Oh, really?" I said as Petey walked into the room with his bucket of Legos. Amber immediately squatted beside him and said playfully, "Oooh! Legos! My favorite. Can I play?" I could see the outline of a thong through her shorts.

Petey regarded her cautiously. "I guess so." He pushed a handful of blocks in her direction.

Roger shot a look at me that said, "Isn't she just wonderful? Aren't we the luckiest family in the world to have found such a delightful young woman to watch our child? Won't she make a fabulous baby-sitter?" I shot back a look that said, "Not on your friggin' life, kiddo." I watched the smile fade from Roger's face. I glanced at my watch. "Roger, it's almost nine. Would you get Pete in the tub, please?"

"Oh, hon, I think we can be a little flexible with bedtime, don't you?"

"Actually, no. He's going on a field trip tomorrow. He needs his sleep. I'll be up in a few minutes."

My husband didn't budge. It was like wrenching a kid out of a candy store. Finally he said, "Well, okay, then." He extended a hand to Amber. "It was a pleasure. I imagine we'll be seeing more of you." Amber put out a smooth, tanned arm. She didn't shake his hand, exactly. She sort of rocked it sideways, as if she planned to take off with him. I waited until Roger was safely upstairs before I turned to Amber and said, "Well, thanks for stopping by."

She looked surprised. "We're done?" She moved toward her bag and reached in. "I brought my resume. I've got references. I was a nanny for the Friedmans. They live around here, somewhere. Do you know them?"

"I don't believe I do." I took the resume and unfolded it. Lots of experience. She even knew CPR. She'd probably make a terrific sitter. But then I remembered that look on her face when she met Roger. And then I thought of Alyssa, the first time I spotted her with Roger outside the school, how they looked like they were in their own little lovers' bubble, impervious and oblivious. Suddenly I felt my inner bitch rocket to the surface. What I said next was so uncharacteristic, so incredibly Jerry Springer-ish, I almost scared myself: "I know what you're thinking, and you can forget it."

"Excuse me?"

"Number one, you're not getting this job." My heart lodged itself in my clavicle. "Number two, you're not going to contact my husband. You will not audition for his next play. You will not ask to be his intern or assistant or gofer or anything. You will not call here under the pretext of doing an article for your school newspaper. You will not," I stopped myself. This girl didn't know what had hit her. She looked like she was going to cry. I'd scared her. She was just a kid. I felt horrible. "Look. I'm sorry. It's just that, I've been through this before. I don't want to go through it again."

Amber had recovered. Now she was insolent. She rolled her eyes. "Fine. Whatever."

I watched her hop into her Miata. She floored the

pedal and roared away. Roger trotted down the stairs. "Where is she?" he asked.

"Who?" As if I didn't know.

"You know. The girl. The baby-sitter. Amber."

"Oh, she's gone."

"So, what did you think? She's something else, isn't she?"

"What do you mean, Roger?"

"What do you mean, what do I mean? You know what I mean. She's great. Don't you think? I mean, the way she bonded with Pete so quickly, just got down on the floor with him and really clicked with him, don't you think?"

"No, Roger, I don't think." I started up the stairs. "Do you have any idea what just happened in that room?" I asked, pointing toward the sofa.

"What do you mean?"

"Forget it, Roger. She's not getting the job."

"Oh, dear. Is the green-eyed monster rearing its ugly head again?"

"Shut up, Roger." I was drained and shaken by the fact that I'd unleashed all my paranoid fury at a young girl. I didn't want to talk. I put Petey down for the night and collapsed into bed.

'Til next time,

V

August 13

Saturday

The new neighbors up the street, Hanna and Craig, invited us to have coffee and dessert tomorrow night. Naturally, I cannot find a sitter. I've called everyone on my list. Called Pete's counselor. Asked Rachel Becker's mom if she'd take him for a couple of hours. No luck.

I was wildly flipping through my phone book when Roger walked in and waved a sheet of paper in my face. It was Amber's resume. "Won't you please stop this foolishness already and call her?" he asked wearily.

"No, Roger." I knew she'd make a great sitter. She knew CPR. Even I don't know CPR. I felt like a big, stubborn baby.

"Come on," he said, almost whining now. "I've got a hunch she's one of those sitters who comes with a backpack full of coloring books and Play-Doh."

"Right. And you'll pull out your Erector set and the two of you will have a grand old time." I can't believe I said that.

He started to walk out of the room, then turned around and said, "Look. We've been through a lot. I was an awful shit to you. So I don't blame you if you don't trust me. But if we're going to move forward, I mean, if we're aiming for some semblance of a happy marriage, then at some point you're going to have to give up this routine of yours. And for both our sakes, I certainly hope that happens sooner rather than later."

I thought of Reverend Lee. He's on vacation in New Hampshire somewhere. I missed his big, warm hands. What would the good Reverend want me to do now? Roger and I haven't had a grown-up's night out in a while. And I do want to get to know the new neighbors. Should I get beyond the jealousy and call the girl?

I thought of that thong, the pert breasts, and silver toe ring. I remembered my husband's flushed, animated face. Screw it. I'd rather stay home.

Monday
Roger was cold and remote all evening. He's treated me like an acquaintance, one he's not particularly fond of but willing to tolerate. He communicates with minimal output. It's almost like he's playing some kind of board game, where you get more points for using fewer words. I'd say, "How did your meeting go with your agent?" and he'd say, "Okay." I'd say, "Where's the permission slip for Pete's field trip?" and he'd say, "Fridge." Not "On the refrigerator." Just "Fridge." When he does make small talk, he looks at a spot just to the left of my head, and speaks all formally, with the slightest hint of an English accent. I find this infuriating.

Tuesday
I was going over my records and realized that I have not had a single referral from the hospital or the county mental health center in more than two months. I still see new people, but most of them lately have come to me through other therapists. This makes no sense at all. Normally I do two intake interviews a week. Most of the referrals go through Filomena. I'm going to talk to her tomorrow to find out what's going on. I'm hoping there's a reasonable explanation.

Wednesday
Filomena looked pained when I asked her about the referrals. "What can I say?" She shrugged helplessly. She rubbed the tattoo on her wrist, Chinese characters drawn in a deep green.

"Say anything. You've got to know what's going on. Tell me."

She looked around then leaned toward me. "It's her. Quasimodo."

Even in my rage I wanted to laugh. "You mean Cadence?"

"Whatever." Filomena rolled her eyes in disgust.

"What? Did she just tell you to stop sending me intakes?"

"Nope. That bitch took over referrals, you know what I'm saying?" She rubbed her tattoo again. "Look. I know it's none of my business but . . ."

"What? Say it."

She looked around again. "Word is, you're out."

I felt sick. I wanted to throw up. "What do you mean, I'm out?" And what did she know, anyway? She was one of the clericals.

"Look. I'm sorry. Forget I said anything."

I had to grab my hands to keep them from shaking.

When I got home I tried to talk to Roger but he was deeply engrossed in a *Xena* rerun. As I talked he reached for the remote, not to lower the volume so he could hear me (as I originally assumed) but to actually intensify the volume so I wouldn't drown out the show's profound dialogue. He pulled Petey onto his lap.

"You've got to see this," he whispered to my son. "It's the best part."

I stared at my husband, really took him in. So tidy, almost fey, in his creased khakis, Eddie Bauer madras plaid shirt, and moccasins. His glasses were pushed down to the tip of his nose and his lips were pursed like a fussy old lady's. How did I wind up with this man? I wondered. And how would I possibly endure the next thirteen years, until Petey was out of the house and in college?

It's 2 A.M. I can't sleep.

Thursday

Didn't see Amazon all day. Filomena said that one of Cadence's Rottweilers was having surgery. It would not surprise me to find out she's interviewing for my replacement.

This afternoon I had a session with Pauline Willis. Pauline started seeing me two years ago to deal with anorgasmia. I directed her toward a few self-help books, the kind designed for women who use phrases like "down there" or "female plumbing" to describe their genitals and reproductive system. When I hadn't heard from her, I assumed that the books must have scared her away.

Now Pauline is back, and she's convinced that someone is watching her through a crack in the ceiling of her office. "What makes you think there's anyone spying on you?" I asked her.

"It was weird. All of a sudden it felt like I wasn't alone. I looked up and noticed this gap between the ceiling tiles."

"And you're sure this gap wasn't there before?"

"That's the thing. I'm not sure. I don't remember ever looking up there before."

"What exactly are you worried about?"

She stopped, pulled her thick brown hair to the side of her neck and twisted it with both hands. A crimson flush spread from her neck to the tips of her ears. "I don't know." She did know. She just wasn't ready to say. And then we were out of time.

'Til next time,

V

August 20

Monday

Pauline was so panicky last week that I had to make time for her today. She finally admitted that she has a habit of masturbating in her office after hours (apparently those books *did* help), and now she has convinced herself that someone was monitoring her. I guess there was a time when a notion like that would have been ridiculous, but now it seems entirely plausible. I've seen this on TV: people discovering hidden cameras in office bathrooms, locker rooms, even their own homes. Still, it's hard to believe someone would go to the trouble of spying on someone like Pauline, a quiet albeit nerdy claims adjuster at Carmichael Insurance. Since she noticed the gap in the ceiling above her desk nine days ago, she hasn't slept and can't keep food down. She's terrified that everyone at work knows about the masturbation.

Normally I'd focus on the guilt and shame associated with her sexual behavior. But what if there *is* a hidden camera above her desk? Why dredge up her entire childhood when we can, at least, solve her short-term issue by peeking behind the damn tile? I suggested she climb on her desk and take a look, but she wouldn't even consider it. "Can't you just see it?" she said. "My big face staring right into that camera. Bad enough they've got me doing—you know. Do I have to humiliate myself even more?"

She looked so anguished and desperate, and since Carmichael Insurance is just across the street, I offered to help her. I realize I was mucking up the boundaries, but this woman doesn't have a friend in the world. I felt I had to help her. We made plans to meet on Friday at 5 P.M.

Tuesday

I'm sad today. I'm thinking about my marriage—all the small, significant things that have fallen away. The casual, almost absentminded caresses. The unexpected flowers for the dinner table. The words of praise: "You have a beautiful voice." "You look pretty tonight." There was a time when Roger automatically said "Bless you" after I sneezed. He still says it when Petey sneezes, but has stopped sending blessings my way. There was a time when Roger was actually interested in me, a time when he put down the paper or switched off the TV so he could hear what I had to say. There was a time when he would ask, "What are you thinking right now?" because he noticed a certain expression play across my face, or "What did you dream about last night?" because I cried in my sleep and he heard me.

And there was a time when Roger didn't seem to notice other women, let alone screw them. Now he is almost shameless in the way he stares, twisting his chair or contorting his posture so he can get an eyeful. At Dairy Queen last night he was talking with his back turned toward me, in that unnatural way soap opera characters converse so that both are facing the camera. I followed his eyes to a young woman straddling a nearby bench. She wore a white tank top, no bra, and shorts so tiny I could see her labia. "Will you please turn around so I can see you?" I hissed. He reluctantly twisted his body around and asked impatiently, "This better?" By then I was so angry at him I no longer wanted to see his face. We sat in silence until Petey finished his cone.

I know that marriage changes, and that romance is for the discovery stage of courtship. But something else has happened. Not just the fading of romance, but a kind of rotting, a decomposition like an old stump. Most of the time I just don't think about it. I can't.

Friday
When I met Pauline, she admitted that she'd spent the previous half hour in the women's room, retching into the toilet. She had the distinct odor of vomit and perspiration. Her uncombed hair hung limply around her ashen face.

She looked like she's lost ten or twelve pounds in the last two weeks (here I have to force myself not to envy this about her; I've gained five pounds and feel grotesquely corpulent). We ascended to the eleventh floor in silence. I held my breath.

The elevator doors slid open and Pauline led me to her office. The room was small and spare, tidy as a nun's. My eyes immediately found the suspicious tile above her desk. If there was, in fact, a camera hidden there, it had surely caught Pauline's every action.

"Well, shall we?" I asked, trying to sound casual. Pauline made the slightest movement with her head. A nod.

I hoisted myself up on the desk, took a deep breath, and pushed the tile up. It flopped back down, sending mats of lint and dust into my face. This time I managed to pull it out. I peered into the darkness, saw nothing. "Have you got a flashlight or something?" Pauline said no at first, but then poked around in her top drawer and found a penlight.

I took it from her and looked around in the space above the ceiling tiles. There was nothing there. Absolutely nothing. Pauline started to cry. But then, as I slid the tile back into place, something dropped onto her desk with a sharp ping. It was a case. An empty video-cassette case.

'Til next time,

$\mathcal{V}$

August 27

Pauline is a mess. After we found the cassette case, she refused to go back to her apartment and has moved in with her sister. I hooked her up with Marion Kleibaum, a rabid civil liberties attorney I met on a ski trip in Colorado three years ago. Marion was still feeling victorious after a lawsuit she'd won against some big chain store that videotaped employees while they went to pee. Pauline wanted to quit her job but Marion told her she should tough it out until they firmed up her case.

In the meantime, Pauline's not eating or sleeping. She's seeing one of the center's psychiatrists, Jeff Goodman, a sweet guy who put her on Zoloft and Xanax. If the drugs don't kick in soon, she'll be in the hospital before she ever makes it to court.

Tuesday
It doesn't seem possible, but things have actually gotten worse with Roger. Earlier today I was unpacking the groceries when he walked into the kitchen and pulled a box of chocolate Pop-Tarts out of a bag. "Oh, God. Don't tell me you're planning on feeding this to our son?" He pushed his glasses up his long nose and began reading the ingredients in that smarmy, pseudo-English accent of his. By the time he got to sodium acid pyrophosphate I was ready to throw the carton of eggs in his face.

But then he moved on to the Quaker oatmeal. "Don't you realize we already have, like, three of these?" he asked icily. He swung open the pantry and giddily called out, "Here's one . . . and a second . . . and, by God, here's the third." He smiled triumphantly and grabbed the new canister. "What, are you starting some kind of oatmeal collection?"

Why didn't I walk away, or tell him to shut the hell up? Why did I stand there like a beaten dog, waiting for the rest? I don't know. I should know. I'm trained to know. But I might as well be figuring out hieroglyphics. I'm mystified. And I hate myself for being so passive.

He ended his routine by pointing out that I should have used a coupon for the Tombstone pizza. "What coupon? I don't have a coupon," I told him. He spun around and clawed at the refrigerator, sending the magnets flying to the floor.

"Oh no? What do you call this?!" He waved the coupon in front of my face.

"You're right again, Roger. It must be such a burden to be the standard bearer of truth in this household. I pity you."

He smiled derisively. "Know what? You're a piece of work. A real piece of work."

"And you, darling husband, are a piece of shit."

"Spoken like a true lady." Roger reached for the newspaper. "I'm going out."

I put my hand on the paper. "Please. Don't. Can't we talk about this?"

He looked at me. "What is there to discuss? You just spent two hours and $84 on four bags of crap that we either don't need or shouldn't eat. Any responsible husband would behave exactly as I did."

"You've got to be kidding, Roger. This isn't about Pop-Tarts or oatmeal or coupons for frozen pizza. Don't you see that? Surely a man of your intellectual depth understands that there's something deeper going on." I watched his face. It seemed to soften. He was listening. "What is it, Roger? What are you so angry about? Why are you so contemptuous of me?"

He lowered himself to the stool and stared at the wall. Then: "I don't know." He looked up at me as if in pain. He shook his head. "I just don't know."

I told him he'd better find out because I couldn't live like this anymore. I hated him and I hated our marriage and would rather be alone for the rest of my life than live out my years with a man who made me feel defensive, self-conscious, and hyper-vigilant. I could deal with the affair. What I couldn't handle were the snide comments and reproaches, the mood swings and oppressive monitoring of my behavior, my choices, my mothering. I always said I'd never divorce, but suddenly I'm warming to the prospect of living without that ever-present layer of static and anxiety this husband brings to my life and our household. Then when I think about the details—just the prospect of going through our papers, sitting with lawyers, hammering out a custody arrangement, dividing all our worldly belongings—it's all so overwhelming!

Wednesday

Dale and I drove five hours down to Indiana to see the Dalai Lama speak, then five hours back home. It's now 2 A.M. I'm completely wiped out but glad we made the trip. I never imagined that His Holiness would be so funny and self deprecating and, frankly, adorable.

The topic was vague, ethics for a new millennium, I

think. He told the crowd that the new millennium would be pretty much like the old one. I'm not surprised, but I'm disappointed. My marriage and job are so crappy, I was beginning to hope there might be something to this Armageddon business. Dale tells me I should quit my job, go back to marital counseling with Roger, and stop whining already.

I'm not ready to quit my job, but I do believe I'm ready to try therapy one more time. If I'm going to file for divorce, I need to feel as if I've exhausted all my options. Now I just need to find the right therapist.

Thursday
I'm sitting here, listening to Al Green and torturing myself. In this particular masochistic mind game, I imagine what Roger's second wife will look like. She is in her late twenties and has a body like Nicole Kidman's. She is highly fertile and can't wait to have many children. She keeps house like June Cleaver, cooks like Wolfgang Puck, and insists on stripping for him (to music) every night, which leads to passionate and extended lovemaking. Her favorite position is on top (Roger's fantasy and my nightmare, given what my belly looks like from that angle). She massages his feet without being asked, has hot cocoa waiting after he's shoveled the driveway, and gets along swimmingly with his parents (who tolerate but hardly adore me). She builds instant rapport with Pete, who insists on calling her Mommy and suddenly decides he likes her better because she's prettier and knows every single Pokemon character (I'm still not sure which one, if any, is Pokemon himself).

For this woman, Roger does all the things he wouldn't do for me: learns to line dance, shaves his goatee, takes a cooking class, wears silk boxers. I think I'm getting some kind of cardiac arrhythmia. Every time I think about this I notice my heart's not beating right.

I must stop.

Friday
Oh God. I think I just managed to get myself fired. I confronted Cadence. Actually, it wasn't a confrontation. I cursed her out. At a staff meeting. In front of everyone. I want to write more but I've got a client outside and I've got to pull myself together. More later.

'Til next time,

V

September 3

Monday
I could tell I was headed for trouble today as soon as I woke up this morning. Everything felt wrong: Roger had left a wet towel on my only clean bra (the damp cups against my skin made me want to scream); my hair looked like straw, and when I slicked on too much mousse it looked like greasy straw; my face looked gray, no matter how much blush I smeared on my cheeks; I wore that stupid coral-colored linen dress that makes me look like death; all my clothes felt constrictive (I'm up another two pounds); my bra straps dug into my shoulder and back; and my pantyhose stopped three inches short of my crotch. I fantasized about slicing off my thighs and belly with a carving knife. I clutched my blubber in both hands and stared hatefully

at my reflection. All I wanted to do was peel everything off and climb back under the covers, preferably with the leftover cookie bars Pete and I made the night before. But I had to go to work. I doused myself with coffee, rammed a cereal bar down my throat, dropped Pete off, and picked up another cup of coffee at Starbucks.

I was consumed by road rage. A woman in a feeble Geo was puttering in front of me at a slug's pace. As the light changed, she miraculously found the gas pedal and scooted through, leaving me stuck at the red light! I swear, I was homicidal. I pulled up alongside her and put down my window, motioning her to roll down hers.

She looked about ninety. "Time to surrender those car keys!" I screamed.

She smiled and cupped a gnarled hand to her ear. "Sorry?" She hadn't heard me.

"Oh, forget it!" I tore ahead of her. Hello, I'm a therapist. I'm a healer. I know how to handle rage.

I switched on the radio and heard the radio shrink tell someone that doing well at work was the best revenge against crazy bosses. Or something like that. That's it, I decided. I'd transcend Cadence by focusing on my job. I'd get myself on a panel at the next conference of the American Association of Marriage & Family Therapists. I'd publish an incredible journal article. Maybe I'd start an obsessive-compulsive disorder group; I bet I could get Jeff Goodman to team with me.

As I arrived at the office—now ten minutes late for the staff meeting—I decided I had to be poised and commanding. I would reverse whatever the Amazon had already set in motion against me. And one day I would root out some awful secret, some hideous and destructive flaw that would turn the staff and center's administrators against her.

With this infantile monologue looping through my skull, I grabbed yet another cup of black coffee from the cart in the lobby and jumped into the elevator. By the time I walked into the conference room the blood was pounding in my ears. I pulled up a chair and thought I heard Cadence say something about canceling the Open Mind fair, a kind of public convention I'd started five years ago as a way of demystifying mental illness.

"Excuse me, Cadence," I started. "Did I hear you say you wanted to cancel Open Mind?"

"It's canceled," she said, never lifting her eyes from the paper in front of her. "And we're moving on to the next item on the agenda." I could feel my throat tighten. I looked around the room for a sign of support. Dale rolled his eyes. No one else would look at me. "With all due respect, Cadence, could we please discuss this first?"

"We just did. If you'd arrived on time, you could have participated in that discussion. Now, if you don't mind?"

"Please. Cadence. I started that conference."

"So?" Cadence flashed her hideously huge teeth. Today she looked more like Kissinger than Kissinger himself.

"So, I feel a responsibility to keep it going."

"Responsibility. Now there's a word."

Jesus. What was she doing? What was going on? My skin prickled as if lightning were about to strike. I knew something awful was coming. I just didn't know how awful it would be. Poised and commanding? What a joke. I was a pathetic seventh-grade loser, striking back blindly at a snide bully. My ears rang with the white noise of animus and caffeine.

I opened my mouth and heard myself say: "Cadence, you are one butt-ugly woman."

I wished I could reel the words back but they just hung there. The room was stone silent. Cadence actually smiled at me. I'd just hammered the last nail into my own coffin and she didn't have to do a thing. Bert Wiley, the center's director and a generally amiable guy, stood up. "Step outside, please," he said to me. He wasn't smiling. His face and neck were deep red.

"No. That's okay. I'm okay. It's over. Everything's cool."

"Step outside, Valerie."

I was afraid to stand up, certain my legs would buckle beneath me. I grabbed my clipboard and walked out. My ears burned.

"What just happened in there?" Bert stared at me.

I felt like a child. "I don't know, Bert. I guess I lost it. I'm . . . I'm sorry. It won't happen again."

"I think it best if you skip the rest of the meeting. You know. Take a breather."

"Look. Bert. Things haven't been great between Cadence and me. I don't know what it is. Bad chemistry, I guess. I don't know."

Bert didn't say anything. He turned and slipped back into the conference room. At the end of the day I got the message from human resources. They wanted to talk to me first thing on Monday.

Dale stopped by to see if I was okay. Also to suggest I start packing my files. "You know," he said. "Before they lock you out."

"They're going to can me, aren't they?"

"I guess you'll find that out next week, won't you?"

"I guess I will."

Dale put a hand on my shoulder. "Just remember. One door closes, another door opens. Or something like that."

Yeah. Something like that.

'Til next time,

V

September 10

Sunday

I've spent my weekend consumed by fear. Thank God for Tylenol PM. Now I sit and wait. Twelve hours until I meet with human resources. They're going to fire me, I know it. I called Reverend Lee but he was at some kind of religious retreat in Lake Geneva, Wisconsin. His wife sounded almost angry.

Here's how screwed up my marriage is: I haven't told Roger that I've been forced to resign. I guess it's possible he would have been supportive and compassionate, but more than likely—given how awful things have been between us—he would have been incredulous and snide.

With everything that's going on at work, I forgot to mention that we had our first therapy session last week. The therapist I chose, Charles Moseman, has a sort of absentminded professor reputation, and when we arrived, he wasn't even there! When he finally showed up, exclaiming, "So sorry, so sorry! I've been running late all day," Roger shot me a look that said: "This guy had better be as good as you say he is because right now I'm completely unimpressed."

Our first session went too quickly. I wished I'd
booked a double appointment. We touched on Roger's
affair but not mine since Roger doesn't know all the
details, and I wasn't ready to open that Pandora's box.
I felt like I blathered too much and Roger didn't say
enough, but Charles scribbled furiously in a battered
loose-leaf notebook. He asked only a few questions, but
each one was unexpected, surprising, almost profound.
He asked Roger why he was afraid to be nurtured by
me. He asked me whether I felt I could handle being in
a relationship with a faithful, loving husband (suggesting that I've got exactly the type of marriage I set out
to get). The rest of that session is a blur. I left feeling
completely drained and desperate for a nap, but Pete
would have his first Tiger Cub meeting in an hour so I
had a large cup of coffee instead. Roger isn't sure
Charles is any good, but he's willing to give it a few
more sessions.

Monday
It's over. I'm out. Under the pretext of an annual evalua-
tion (which normally doesn't happen until November),
Sharon Harris-Jackson, director of human resources,
has informed me that I had violated item number three
in the center's code of ethics.

She pulled out a document from a manila file—my
file—and showed me my signature. "Do you remember
reading this when you were promoted to senior partner
in wellness?"

I nodded dully.

Sharon was an inoffensive woman, colorless but benign. She had returned to the workforce at fifty after
her husband died. She'd started as Bert Wiley's secretary. I knew this wasn't easy for her.

Sharon cleared her throat and proceeded to read aloud. " 'I understand that as senior partner at the Center for Mental Wellness I am responsible for conducting myself in a professional manner at all times, and behaving in a way that demonstrates respect toward supervisors and support for coworkers.' "

She flipped to the last page. "A violation of any of these terms may lead to suspension or immediate dismissal." She returned the document to the folder. "Valerie," she said, her cheeks flushing, "I think you can understand how calling Cadence Bradley 'one butt-ugly woman' qualifies as a violation."

I guess she was waiting for me to resign, but I wasn't biting. She waited. I waited. Finally, Sharon cleared her throat and said, "It's Bert Wiley's recommendation that you consider filing your resignation." She said it was in my best interest to do so, because my record would remain "unblemished" by termination. What she didn't mention, however, is that if I resigned the center wouldn't have to pay me unemployment benefits.

I told her I had no plans to resign. So she mentioned Alice, the young client who walked in front of a bus the day I canceled out on her to be with Eddie. She said, "We have reason to believe you were out with a friend that afternoon." Sharon arched her eyebrows ever so slightly, a signal that she could go on and provide more details if need be.

I stopped breathing. I wanted to get out of there. "Fine, then. You'll have my resignation this afternoon."

"Very good." She stood up but didn't extend a hand. "I know how difficult this must be for you," she said.

"Right." With stinging eyes and a constricted throat, I staggered out. By the time I got to my office, the files were gone, as Dale had predicted they would be. The only thing left was a manila folder of Christmas crafts I had begun collecting last year. I picked up my phone, half expecting it to be disconnected. I got a dial tone. I watched my fingers punch in numbers, as if they were commanded by an outside force. For reasons I still can't explain, I dialed Eddie at work. He picked up on the second ring. I asked him to meet me tomorrow at noon. He agreed without hesitation. I went home. I still haven't told Roger. I have no idea what I'm going to do next.

'Til next time,

$\mathcal{V}$

September 17

Wednesday

Tonight I told Roger about Cadence's obviously vindictive decision to cancel the Open Mind conference. Then I told him I resigned from the center. "I just couldn't stand it anymore," I said. "I really felt I had no choice but to leave. It became a matter of pride."

"What's that?" Roger retorted. "A matter of pride?" The vein on his forehead was starting to throb. It was going to be a long night. Roger didn't just mute *Nash Bridges*. He turned the television off completely. For once, I had his undivided attention. Except now I didn't want it.

"Is that so weird?" I asked him. "That I'd want a job where I'm actually respected? Where my ideas are valued? Roger, you have no idea how miserable I was there!"

"Apparently I don't." He was frowning; I searched his

face for some signs of empathy but found none. "So, what, she cancels your conference and you just walk out? Just like that?"

Roger couldn't understand why I'd give up my job just because Cadence canceled Open Mind. And he'd be right—if that was the real reason I resigned. But I couldn't tell him that I was forced to resign. I didn't mention that I'd called Cadence "butt-ugly," or that the center had linked Alice's suicide attempt to my rendez-vous with Eddie.

There was a time when I could be completely honest with my husband, a time when I knew he'd offer solace and support and compassion. All I can expect now is shaming denigration and incredulity, and I wasn't in the mood.

"So now what?" he asked, his voice brittle with exasperation.

"I don't know." And, truth is, I really don't. I feel so unmoored right now. I'm literally dragging my body through the day. I can't even contemplate finding another job.

Every time I think about my upcoming meeting with Eddie, I get nauseated. I should take this as a sign, and yet I feel compelled to go through with it. He's a friend.

Monday

Eddie called me to say he'd rather meet at his office. When I got there he was talking to one of his employees. He poked his head out of the door, told me he needed a few more minutes, and winked. He looked tanned and relaxed and a bit older, but also sexier. His mouth—that overbite!—was just as delicious as I remembered it.

I felt disappointed and a little insulted that he left

me waiting in the reception area, like I was one of his customers. I expected an entirely different reunion. I wondered whether I should get up and leave.

But something kept me rooted to my seat. I wanted to see him. Eddie's office was nicer than I'd imagined. Of course the place was full of robust, glossy plants and trees, including a ficus that looked a lot like the one that first brought us together. The furniture was surprisingly sleek. There were stark black-and-white photographs on the walls, and a small stone fountain in the corner.

I decided to use the bathroom to freshen up. I stared at myself in the mirror, angled my face so I couldn't see the second chin. I scrutinized my hair: Did long hair make me look sexy or like a hag? Should I keep it loose or put it up in a ponytail? I had every hair accessory known to womankind stuffed in my bag and I tried them all, frantically. I finally settled on leaving it loose. Eddie always liked long hair. He had this amusing theory about men who insisted their girlfriends cut their hair off. "Repressed gays," he called them, so sure of himself. "Same for guys who like flat-chested girls." Eddie could be such a dope, but I laughed anyway. I suspected the same thing, but would never have the guts to say something so un-PC out loud.

By the time I came out of the bathroom, Eddie was waiting for me on the leather couch. "Nice place," I said, trying to keep my voice steady. "I'm impressed."

"Hi," he said in return. He was staring at me. "You look fantastic."

"Hi, yourself," I said, suddenly shy. He stood up and led me to his office. I spotted a pin-up calendar taped to the filing cabinet. He is such a *guy*. I was dying to kiss him.

I told him everything and when I was through, he had two words: "That bitch." I suddenly had a flashback to grade school. Reggie was an enormous, strong, sweet boy who had a crush on me. I didn't want to date him, but Reggie wasn't easily deterred; he asked if he could be my bodyguard. One day I got a death threat from Lydia, a bully who had decided I had to die because I wouldn't share my Fritos with her. I told Reggie. The next day Lydia didn't just leave me alone, she left a bag of potato chips on my desk in homeroom. The rest of that school year, I was untouchable because Reggie was my bodyguard and everyone in school knew it. I *loved* it. I realized now that I wanted to see Eddie in the same way. He'd already helped me with Diana. Now I wanted him to help me with Cadence. But how could he?

There's lots more to say about Eddie (suffice it to say, my lips are still swollen) but if I don't leave right now I'm going to be late picking up Petey.

'Til next time,

$\mathcal{V}$

September 24

Tuesday

Back to Eddie. The abridged version of the story is this: He told me he has thought about me every single day since he moved back in with his wife, and, yes, even when he's having sex with her. (He says, "Otherwise it's just not bearable.") He said he'd thought of me while his wife was literally pushing out the new baby. I found this last comment too gross to be flattering, but didn't say anything.

He pulled me onto his lap. We made out. His mouth tasted exactly the way I remembered it, like lollipops and beer. He tried to unhook my bra. I wriggled out of his grip. I couldn't go on. Roger and I had started with Moseman. I wasn't about to break the cardinal rule of marriage counseling: no screwing around.

But I realized I'd gotten what I'd really come for. Proof that I was important to at least one human being in this great big rotting world. Maybe Roger didn't want me, and Cadence didn't want me, but this man with massive arms and a delectable mouth did. And right at that moment, that's all I needed to know.

There wasn't a thing Eddie could do about Cadence, of course. What was I thinking? That this blue-collar tough guy would have some underworld connections? That he'd offer to whack the Amazon for me? This wasn't *The Sopranos*. This was my real, relatively boring Midwestern life, and there would be no adventure, no intrigue, no great acts of revenge.

"Look. Cadence is a bitch and you got screwed. That's life, sweetheart." He pulled me close and said the five words I expected and dreaded.

"Can I see you again?"

I shook my head, told him that would be a mistake. We were both stuck in crappy marriages and neither of us had any intention of bailing. He held me tighter. I felt his little finger slipping beneath the waistband of my panties as he buried his face in my hair. "Change your mind," he whispered.

I pulled away. "No."

When I got back to the house there was a message on my machine from someone I hadn't seen since high school: Sunny Rose (her real name, believe it or not). I'd worked for Sunny the summer of my junior year. She'd accused me of flirting with her husband, Barry. (I knew he was hot for me but he was so old he didn't even register a little blip on my radar. He was probably thirty-five.) She fired me during one of her bizarre jealous rages, and I cried all the way home. I never heard from her again until tonight. She'd gotten my number through my mother. She said she was calling to apologize, to set things right before Rosh Hashanah. "I've felt just awful all these years," she told me. "Can you ever forgive me?"

"Of course. Please. It's ancient history." I was dying to know what had brought her around. I mean, there have been lots of new years since high school, lots of opportunities to make amends. Why apologize now?

"You came to me in a dream," she said. "And I put tremendous stock in my dreams. I've got ESP, you know."

"No, I didn't know."

"I do. I dreamed the whole Kennedy thing. Not the assassination, I mean Junior's plane going down."

"I hope you didn't dream about me dying or anything," I said, trying to sound jokey. This was getting creepy.

"No, no, nothing like that! I dreamed you were me. I mean, you were all grown up and you had hired a mother's helper just like I'd hired you. She was gorgeous, just like you were. And you were yelling at her because you were so jealous. You thought she was flirting with your husband. And even though she was a great sitter, you had to have her out of your house. Your face was all twisted with anger and jealousy. Just like mine must have been. So I figure it was a sign. I'm not sure what it means, but I knew I had to call. To say I'm sorry. And even though you're not Jewish, I wanted to wish you a sweet New Year . . . Hello?"

"I'm still here." I gulped. "Listen, all is forgiven, Sunny. Ancient history. By the way"—I had to ask this—"how's Barry?"

"Barry is Barry, what can I say? We split in '89. He screwed anything that moved. I remarried in '95, and I've never been happier. It's true what they say—it really is better the second time around." She giggled girlishly. "So, how about you? Your mother tells me you're happily married? To a big-shot writer? And you've got an adorable little one of your own?"

"All true."

"And, you're happy?"

"Very."

"Oh, I'm so glad to hear that. That's just wonderful!"

I'm still stunned. I thought of that sitter—Heather? Amber? What was her name? I remember how overcome I was with the purest jealousy. I hated everything about her: the high tits, the tight little ass, the way she fawned over my husband. I blasted her like a cruise missile. What did Sunny's dream mean for me? Am I now supposed to call Amber and apologize?

As long as I'm home, I figured I might as well clean. I decided to make it a research project. I went on-line and searched "housecleaning tips." It turned up 3,080 sites. After two and a half hours I was ready to clean. I did seven loads of laundry and ironed a basket of Roger's shirts, picked up Pete's room and packed away his out-of-season clothes, reorganized the front hall closet, cleaned the bathroom grout with a toothbrush, wiped the windows and mirrors with newspaper and Windex, cleaned the kitchen floor on my hands and knees, tile by tile. I put potpourri sachets in the sock drawers, refilled all the liquid soap dispensers, replaced all the dead lightbulbs, wiped all the baseboards, and vacuumed the dust from all the air conditioning registers. I wiped the grime off the phones, cleaned the bread machine, and reorganized the medicine cabinets.

Now I sit in my clean and shiny reorganized home and wonder, what's next? Part of me wants to rededicate myself to my career. Another part wants to chuck it all, stay home, and be the wife and mother Roger and Peter need me to be. But the part with the loudest voice right now simply wants to climb into bed and pull the quilt over my head.

Saturday

This morning when I went out to get the paper, I found a trail of tampons leading from the front door to the sidewalk, wrapped but soggy from last night's rain. I ran inside, grabbed a rubber glove from the cabinet under the kitchen sink, pulled it over my hand, and went back to gather the tampons. There were nine. I picked up the first and examined it closely. At first I thought it was smeared with blood, but quickly realized it was lipstick. The imprint of a kiss. In fact, every single tampon had been marked with a kiss.

I felt like a crime victim, shaky and scared. Who could have done this? And why? I knew that some of the neighborhood houses and trees are occasionally festooned with toilet paper, but this was different. The only clue I had was that the tampons were slim, the kind worn by younger women and girls. I ran upstairs and woke up Roger. He rolled over and looked at me with half-closed eyes.

"Do you know anything about this?" I asked him,

holding up one tampon in my gloved hand. Roger fumbled for his glasses and slipped them on.

He squinted. "A tampon?"

"A tampon. Size slim. Someone went to the trouble of kissing nine tampons and throwing them in front of our house."

Roger shook his head as if to clear it. He probably thought he was dreaming this conversation. "What the hell are you talking about?"

Until that point I had assumed it was one of his past or present lovers, but it suddenly occurred to me that perhaps this was the work of a disgruntled client of mine. It was possible. "What should we do?" I asked, not so cocky anymore.

Roger flopped back into bed, pulled the quilt up to his chin, and rolled onto his side. "Forget it. Crazy kids. Halloween. They probably got the wrong house anyway."

I suppose Roger might be right. But I can't shake this feeling that whoever left the tampon is someone who knows Roger, or me. And I'm certain we're going to be hearing from her again.

'Til next time,

V

November 5

Monday

We just got back from the therapist. *I am so mad at Roger!* Moseman asked me to describe the experience of feeling rejected (familiar terrain), but just as I was about to answer, he changed his instructions. "Wait. Do

this instead. I want you to face your husband and tell
him how he might benefit if he were faithful to you.
What's in it for him?"

The thing is, I was still caught up with his first question. Suddenly I was sobbing convulsively. I couldn't
stop. I cried to the point of nausea. Aware that Roger
and Moseman were staring at me, I shook my head and
tried to apologize through the sobs, but the therapist
encouraged me to keep crying.

"Don't shake your head! That blocks the feelings.
Nod your head. Let it come. Let it out. Please."

I'd never heard that before—that shaking the head
blocks feeling—but it made sense. As soon as I stopped
shaking and started nodding, the sobs grew louder and
stronger.

I described the experience of trying to climb on my
mother's lap while she and my dad were locked in an
embrace. I remembered her casually elbowing me off,
and I remembered trying again to climb on her lap. I
could see my father scowling and telling me, "Not now.
Mommy and Daddy need time alone. Go watch TV upstairs." And I remember stumbling to the archway between the family room and kitchen, and watching them
kiss. My father gave me one last menacing look over
my mother's shoulder and I slouched out of the room.

Moseman passed me a full box of Kleenex and slowly
I regained my composure. When I finally looked up
again, spent and congested, I found Roger glaring at
me.

"It's always about you, isn't it?"

"What do you mean?"

"You know *exactly* what I mean." He smirked derisively. "Typical. So typical. Dr. Moseman's question, as
you would have known had you been paying attention,

was to face me and tell me how you think I'd benefit if I were faithful to you. So what do you do instead? You go on and on about you." Roger raised his arms and mimed playing a violin. "Poor little you. It's always about you." My husband slumped back into Moseman's overstuffed couch and rubbed his eyes wearily. "Typical."

I wanted to kill him! I still do! Moseman squinted at Roger, then pulled out his notebook and jotted down a few words. I hope one of them was "ASSHOLE." My only consolation is that I've lost another two pounds. And still managed to eat sweets—I figured out that if I skip a few fruits and breads, I can double my dessert portions. This makes me very happy.

Tuesday
Without work to distract me, I find myself fixated on the stupidest things. Like the size of Julia Roberts's mouth. It seems extraordinarily large and somewhat scary. I'm thinking about Jennifer Love Hewitt. She's on every magazine cover, and yet I don't believe I have ever seen her in anything, which is disorienting. Then there's Clinton. I just saw him on CNN and all I could think about was fellatio. This man could announce that he has singlehandedly negotiated world peace, and I'd still be thinking: fellatio. And am I the only one who thinks Lauryn Hill looks exactly like a younger, thinner version of Oprah? Or that Leelee Sobieski is a young Helen Hunt? Or am I just going crazy from all the Soft Scrub fumes?

Thursday
I'm beginning to think that what I really need isn't a marriage counselor but a private therapist, someone

who can help me deal with the true issue: *How can I ever trust Roger again?* (Of course, he might ask the same question. Why should he trust me?)

My distrust of Roger runs like a contaminated brook under the foundation of our lives. I see betrayal, or the threat of betrayal, everywhere, in every interaction. He's auditioning actors now, and I'm grateful that his new play has only two female parts, and they're both very small, but every time he comes home from auditions I smell his clothes, searching for the telltale scent.

A few nights ago, I saw Roger chatting a little too long with the pizza delivery girl. I watched from the top of the stairs as she moved closer toward him and my heart froze. I couldn't hear what they were saying, but I knew she was no stranger; she stood too close, they talked in quiet and familiar tones. I hurried down the steps and glared at them both through the screen door. She couldn't have been older than nineteen. She had a stud in her nose and a thin ring through her lower lip. Her long dyed red hair was parted in the middle and hung to her waist. She looked at me with huge green eyes. She wore no makeup. Her skimpy green nylon top clung to her small, braless breasts.

Roger greeted me brightly. "Isn't this a coincidence? Look who came to deliver our pizza. This is Julia Gottleib, Ken's daughter. Isn't that something?" I watch my husband eye the girl's nipples.

"Yeah, Roger. That's really something." Ken Gottleib was one of Roger's racquetball partners. The girl hadn't taken her eyes off my husband. I pulled the pizza box out of her arms.

"How much do we owe you?" I turned to Roger. "Do you have the checkbook?"

"It's inside, hon."

"Would you please get it?"

"Yeah. Okay."

He reluctantly left me alone on the porch with Julia. I stared at her, aware of the jealousy that curdled all rational thought. She wouldn't look at me. She said nothing. Roger quickly returned with a check.

"There's a little something in there for you," he said.

As I watched my husband come alive in the presence of this young girl, I had to ask myself, How much longer can I live with this? Even if he never fondles or kisses or penetrates another woman, how can I live with myself? How can I live with the suspicion and rage that seems to stain every single day of my life with him?

Then I remembered the soggy tampons. I'd saved one just in case I might need it later for evidence. I asked Julia to wait for a moment, then ran inside and grabbed the Ziploc bag from under the sink. I was breathless by the time I got back to the porch.

"Just one more thing before you go," I said, holding out the bag.

"Do you know anything about this?"

The girl peered at the bag. "What *is* that?"

"Just what it looks like. A tampon. With lipstick kisses," I said, bringing the bag a bit closer to her face.

She started backing off the porch and shook her head. "Yuck." Then she looked at me as if I might be deranged.

"Why would I know anything about *that*?"

"I don't know."

Roger pulled the bag out of my hands. His face was purple.

"What the hell are you doing?"

I suddenly felt hot with shame. "I don't know. I just

thought maybe Julia might know something about this."

Roger grabbed the bag out of my hand. "Julia. Please. Go. My wife obviously isn't feeling very well this evening. Please go." He pulled some stray bills from his pocket and pressed them into her hand. She didn't resist. "Here," he insisted. "Take it. Please."

As Julia backed her Blazer out of the driveway, Roger grabbed the sleeve of my sweatshirt.

"Would you tell me what's going on with you?"

I tried to pull away but he held on and the fabric ripped along the shoulder seam. "Get your friggin' hands off me," I yelled. "Look what you did! God! Leave me alone!"

Naturally, our neighbor Roz Eberley just happened to be putting her trash out at precisely that moment. She stared scornfully at us. I ignored her.

Friday

The Tampon Queen has visited again. This morning when I went out for the newspaper, I found a small padded envelope, the kind you might use to mail a book. It had no return address. I don't know if it was meant for me or for Roger, because there was no name, either. I decided to open it outside. Roger and Pete were eating breakfast. Whatever was inside, I was pretty sure I didn't want my son to see it.

The envelope was as light as air; I considered the possibility that it might be empty. I could feel my heart pulsing in my throat as I slipped a fingernail beneath the flap and loosened the adhesive.

The first thing I glimpsed was a bit of fabric, deep magenta, satin, elasticized. Something told me this wasn't an early Christmas gift from Roger. I held my breath, tugged gingerly. I pulled it out. It was a pair of panties. A thong, to be precise, Victoria's Secret, size small. I let out an involuntary shriek; in retrospect, a bizarre reaction—it's not as if I'd pulled out a severed finger. On closer inspection (and breathing through my mouth), I discovered that these panties weren't new and in fact were definitely not laundered. *Ugh!* I shook the mailer out, hoping for a note. Nothing. This time I decided not to tell Roger.

At least not yet.

'Til next time,

V

November 12

Saturday

Well, I guess I won't be talking to Shannon Herringshaw again, all because of a stupid Pokemon pencil box. We were at the annual silent auction at the church today. I didn't see anything worth bidding on and was getting ready to leave, when Petey drags me over to the kids' table. He wants this little plastic pencil box in the shape of one of those bland little Pokemon characters. I put down a bid of $2.

Next thing I know, Shannon's there with her nine–year–old daughter Talisha. She doubled my bid! So I doubled her bid while Shannon and her daughter looked on in horror. This went on until the frigging box was up to sixteen bucks and Chrissy Miller announced that all bidding on the kids' table had officially ended; my bid had been the last one, so I won. I felt triumphant, but also totally crappy. As I walked into the parking lot, Shannon pulled up beside me and lowered the window of her sparkling silver Lexus. "Was that really necessary?" she asked me. Her eyes were rimmed in red. Her daughter was sitting in the back seat scowling. I wanted to say, "Get used to it, kid." I didn't know how to respond to Shannon's question, so I just shrugged and said, "What can I say? Your daughter wanted it, so did my son. At least we made money for the church, huh?"

She shook her head sadly and drove on. Petey tugged my hand. "You could have let Talisha have it, Mom," he said. "I didn't want it that much anyway."

Monday

Got a phone call from Reverend Lee. He said he was hoping to continue our prayer sessions, but I told him I wasn't in the mood to make contact with my higher power these days.

"That's exactly the time to do it," he urged.

"Why don't you stop by this week?" I said I'd think about it. I wonder if everything's right between the Reverend and his wife. He seemed awfully insistent. I really don't feel like praying with him, especially not this week. I think I must be getting ready to ovulate, because even my fat old dentist looked good to me this afternoon when I went for a cleaning. Who knows what I might do to a really attractive man like the good pastor.

I took the bag with the tampon and the panties from the Halloween attack on our house to the police station. I asked to speak with one of the detectives, female, preferably, but she was out sick so I got stuck with Mike Lundgren, who happens to be my father's best friend from high school. I'd totally forgotten he was a detective. As I watched Mike saunter toward me, I panicked. I hadn't told my parents any of this. I didn't want to worry my father, who hasn't been feeling especially well lately.

"What have you got there?" Mike asked me, tugging the bag from my hands. He grimaced when he saw the tampon. I knew I'd made a huge mistake. This was the kind of guy who calls female anatomy "plumbing." I wasn't about to show him the panties. "Oh, I think it's probably just a Halloween prank," I told him, quickly shifting gears. "I just wanted to show it to you, you know, in case you had other complaints and needed, I don't know, some sort of evidence."

Mike rubbed his bald head furiously, as if enough rubbing might produce some information. "Beats me," he said finally. "Tell your pop I said hey, okay?"

Tuesday
I volunteered in Pete's class today. It was fun but draining. The big news is that Alyssa no longer teaches there. All I could get out of Nancy, the normally talkative office administrator, was that there was an "incident" involving Alyssa and the janitor, the vaguely sinister Mr. Reilly. I tried to get Pete's teacher to fill me in on the details, but didn't push it. She's nice enough, but I didn't want to do or say anything that could affect the way she treats Pete.

On my way out, the principal asked if I'd be interested in subbing. I was surprised that he knew I was available. "Word has it you may have some extra time on your hands," he said, smiling solicitously. Damn these small towns! God only knows what else people know about my untimely departure from the center.

But I was intrigued by the offer. I wouldn't mind

working at the school while trying to figure out what to do with the rest of my life. I told him I'd think about it.

Later . . .

I guess I never really noticed how awful this neighborhood was until I stopped working. All these big fancy facades and no signs of life! People drive straight into their garages, close the automatic doors behind them, and that's it for neighborly conversation. One block over, all the neighbors arrange activities. One year when the creek flooded, they had a bullfrog race. They have a little parade on the Fourth of July, block parties on Labor Day, and caroling on Christmas. But they're all so damn precious that I can't stand them either.

Wednesday
It's 1:00 A.M. and Roger still hasn't come back from auditions. Naturally, tonight was the final audition for the two female parts. Knowing Roger, he's probably doing just that: auditioning female parts.

I've got to stop thinking like this. I have no reason to believe Roger is still cheating on me, other than the fact that he has a history of cheating, which certainly traumatized the marriage but in itself does not support any suspicions I might have. There haven't been any of the telltale signs (I don't think leering at the pizza girl's chest counts), and the tampon/panty incident proves nothing—so far.

Thursday
Roger ended up stumbling in at 2:00 A.M., reeking of gin. I woke up but kept my eyes closed. I didn't want to talk to him. I could hear him stripping off his clothes,

throwing them on the rocker, peeing, gargling. He banged his foot on the NordicTrack, suppressed a profanity, then flopped into bed. Two minutes later his arms were wrapped around my waist and he was pulling me against him. He was completely hard.

"Where were you?" I mumbled, trying to sound more asleep than I really was.

"Mmmmm," he said back. "Quiet. Just let me do this." He started working himself into me from behind. I wanted to be angry, but the truth was, I was wildly aroused. So I pressed back toward him, and it felt incredible. But when I woke up in the morning and saw him lying there naked and hung over (in more ways than one), I wanted to kill him. I threw my towel on his face and demanded to know why he was so late. He insisted that the auditions ran late.

Afterwards, one of the *male* actors insisted on buying him a drink. He wanted to discuss his role. That was at 10. Before they knew it, three hours had gone by. He would have been home a bit earlier, but he ran into traffic on the road. "A big accident," he said. "Tied up the highway in both directions for miles." Roger raised a hand to his heart. "I swear."

Friday
Oh my God, oh my God, oh my God. I just got into my Jeep. Right there on the driver's seat was a small tin. I've got it in my hand right now. It says Kama Sutra Edible Body Powder. It's tied with a black velvet ribbon, and slipped between the ribbon and the tin is a black feather. At first I thought it was a gift from Roger—a sexy follow-up to last night—but when I thanked him he honestly had no idea what I was thanking him for! Oh my God, oh my God, oh my God. What is going on?

As I reached for the tin, my car phone rang. When I picked it up, I heard a long silence, faint breathing, then a quiet click. Whoever left that in my Jeep must have known I'd find it at precisely that moment. Or maybe they were actually watching me. I ran in the house and quickly pulled all the drapes closed. Roger was gone. It's just me now, and I'm scared shitless.

'Til next time,

V

November 19

No more gifts from Tampon Queen. At first I thought they were meant for Roger, but after I found the Kama Sutra powder in *my* Jeep, and after the call came in on *my* cell phone, I'm not so sure. But who could possibly want to torment me like this? Alyssa is absolutely twisted enough to pull a stunt like this, just to make me crazy. Among my former patients, the only possibility is Maria, the volleyball player, who once confessed to having vivid erotic dreams about me and gave me a box of chocolates on Valentine's Day. Unless it's Eddie, and those panties were mine, from my pre-blubber days. They did look familiar—could I have left them somewhere?

The truth is, I find it more than a little arousing that these gifts might be meant for me. I'm the object of someone's horny fantasy! If I thought it was a stranger, I'd be terrified. But I'm certain it's someone I already know. *But who?*

'Til next time,

V

November 21

Still trying to adjust to being home. I'm lonely. I thought it would be hard being home with Roger here all day, but it turns out he's rarely home. They're starting rehearsals now. I've hinted that I might like to stop by the theater to watch, but he's distinctly unenthusiastic. That hurts. I know he thinks I cramp his style. It would be like having his mother there. I might just stop by anyway.

I wish I could stop thinking about Cadence. She had spurned me since the day she started at the Center, and I had to know why. I finally decided to deploy my only true ally, Dale Miller. I called him this morning and suggested he engage the Amazon in casual conversation about my sudden departure. He agreed without hesitation.

He called me during his lunch hour from the pay phone in the lobby.

"Well, I got her to talk," he whispered into the phone, "and it wasn't pretty."

"What's that supposed to mean?" I asked.

Dale sighed. "Are you sure you're up for this?"

"Just tell me," I told him, bracing myself. "I can handle it."

"Fine." He took a deep breath. "She said you had some good ideas, but your image was all wrong. She thought you dressed inappropriately. In other words, too sexy. She hated those black spandex pants, by the way, as if she could fit her amazonian ass into a pair of spandex pants. And she said she knew you were out with Eddie the day your client tried to kill herself."

"Wonderful," I said.

"I'm not done. Should I go on?"

"Yes."

"She saw you dancing in a Greek restaurant. Like a wild woman, she said. With Eddie. That's before she took the job here, before she even knew your name. Then when she started at the Center, she recognized you. And hated you right away." Dale paused, then added: "Jealous bitch."

So now I knew. It didn't make me feel any better, though.

The most frustrating thing about being fired is knowing I can't reach my old clients. I don't have any of their files, and even if I did, I'm contractually prohibited from contacting any of them. There's no way they can reach me because my home number is unlisted.

I did run into Claire—at Oooh La La, the lingerie shop in the mall. She approached me as I pawed through a stack of gray cotton briefs, probably the least attractive undergarments in the entire store. She seemed happy to see me. "What do you think?" she said, holding up a hot pink, fur-trimmed teddy.

"It's you," I told her, wondering whose husband she planned to seduce this week. As it turns out, it would be her own. Claire told me that after the picture window scene on her anniversary, her husband unleashed his inner satyr. "He's an animal," she whispered. "I can't keep up with him."

"I've meant to send you a note," she continued. "I know I sort of dropped off the edge of the earth. It wasn't you. I just needed some time to process everything, to get centered. I just wanted to thank you for helping me turn my life around."

I didn't know how to respond. I didn't think our sessions had made a difference. I found it hard to believe she credited me with saving her marriage, let alone her life. "You're welcome," I said, and then moved toward the cash register.

"Hey," she said, tugging my sleeve. "Give your husband my regards."

Huh?

'Til next time,

V

November 23

The stalker is back and wants Roger. A package was left in the big pot of dying geraniums on the porch. Inside was one of those little books they sell by the counter at Barnes & Noble. *The Tiny Book of Big Sex.* On every page a full-color photograph of a couple in a different position. There was a yellow Post-it note tucked inside the first page. My heart pumped wildly as I read the message, written in a distinctly feminine hand. Saturday. 2 P.M. Room 219. Econolodge. At the bottom of the note, another of those tacky lipstick kisses.

The only thing I've told Roger is that I'll need him to watch Petey Saturday afternoon. I said I needed to visit a former client at Meadowfield. I'm going to the Econolodge myself to find out, once and for all, who is pursuing my husband.

'Til next time,

V

November 26

Friday night
Mom just called. Dad's blood tests came back from the lab. It doesn't look good. Dr. Bendel suspects the cancer

has spread, possibly to the liver. He scheduled a biopsy for next Thursday. Ever the stoic, Dad's telling Mom he's going to be fine. "You're stuck with me, kiddo," he keeps saying. "I'm not going anywhere for a long, long time." His optimism, feigned or not, is something I find heartbreaking. He is the consummate Good Provider. He knows Mom would be helpless without him.

In the meantime, Mom is convinced that she caused Dad's cancer. Apparently she read somewhere that men who have lots of sex and eat lots of tomatoes have a lower incidence of prostate cancer. "I should have cooked more Italian food . . . and . . . we haven't been, you know, as active since I went through, you know," she whispered on the phone. It must have taken all her courage to share that. I know that impotence and in-continence are common after prostate surgery. It was hard to imagine my father wearing Depends, harder still to imagine how my parents got along without the sex. But now I knew that perhaps it wasn't so difficult for my mother, given what she'd just told me.

I'm having a harder time dealing with the really im-portant issue: the possibility that Dad might not make it, and what that means not merely for Mom, but for me. I've secretly believed that among his three daugh-ters, I was his favorite. Why else would he take me alone to skip stones and watch the sunset by Lake Je-rome? Why did he teach me and not the others to throw a football, to play his old bass clarinet, to make a campfire? He'd joke that Mom and my sisters were too prissy, that I was the real trooper in the family. From a man who didn't readily dole out praise to any of his daughters, these words were like gold nuggets. I gathered them and preserve them to this day. I think of how Roger and I lavish praise on Petey, often when it's not especially deserved, and I realize how meaningless that praise has surely become to a boy who hears it almost as often as he hears his own name.

So it's hard for me now to imagine my father dying. Instead I'll distract myself by thinking about my husband, and the slattern who will be waiting for him in room 219 tomorrow afternoon. And I'll set up an appointment with Reverend Lee. I suspect I'll want some spiritual guidance after tomorrow.

Saturday morning

I'm too nervous to relax, to eat, to breathe. Have to remind myself: inhale. When I manage to sleep a few hours, my dreams are filled with images of tampons strewn on the front path. Dirty panties in the mail. I keep thinking of that phrase: Be careful of what you wish for. I've been bored out of my skull since I lost my job at the center. I wanted a little drama. I never expected this.

Despite Moseman's most heroic attempts to steer us toward healing, it's clear that my husband is a chronic cheat. I feel nothing for him but anger, but this worries me: rage and lust are twin emotions—both are passionate, both can be barometers of attachment. I won't be ready to walk away until I feel detached disgust, disdain, more like a spectator than a participant in this car wreck of a marriage. Thank God Roger's taken Pete to visit his parents. I think I'd rip his eyeballs out if he were here now. Which reminds me: I called the sheriff's department last week, after Roger had claimed he was delayed that night because of a terrible accident on the 246 bypass. It was Betsy's idea to call. They put me through to a female deputy, the one who keeps track of highway "incidents." "Nope, it was a quiet night," she

said in a flat, nasal voice. After a pause, she said something so unbelievably unprofessional, I'd have reported
her if she hadn't been so eerily accurate: "Husband's
been cattin' around, huh?"

"Excuse me?" I don't know why I felt it necessary to
sound so indignant, when she happened to be right.

"We get this all the time," she said, sounding sincerely sympathetic. "Let me guess. Your old man was
real late getting home. And he told you he was held up
because of an accident, right?"

"Right." I felt completely defeated. This stranger
knew more about my marriage than I did. I had to ask
again. "Are you sure there wasn't anything? Could you
just check one more time?"

I heard a loud sigh, and a shuffling of papers I'm
certain was for my benefit alone. "I'm sure," she finally
said. "You open to a little unsolicited advice?"

"Sure," I told her, correctly sensing what would come
next.

"Dump the jerk," she told me. Then, "If I could do it,
believe me, anyone can."

I was filled with awe and admiration for this tough
woman. I pictured her sitting at her desk in her navy
blue sheriff's uniform, single but strong. I imagined her
gun and wondered whether she'd brandished it as she
kicked her own jerk's ass out of the house. I'm going to
hold that image in my head as I drive to the Econolodge.

I've spent an hour dressing, putting on makeup. I
figure, if I'm about to confront Roger's lover, I'd better
look good. I ran back in the house, found my camera,
and popped in a fresh roll of film. I impulsively grabbed
a steak knife on the way out and slipped it in my bag.
Just my luck, I'll probably stab myself while rooting

around for my car keys. Before I go, I feel impelled to send a quick prayer: God, please give me the courage to handle whatever I happen to find in that room. Amen.

Saturday night
I am feeling what can only be described as shock, the kind of stunned numbness that you see in people with post-traumatic stress syndrome. My impulse is to get drunk and pass out in bed, but if I don't write about this now I'm only going to feel worse tomorrow.

I drove to the motel with the female deputy's words ringing in my ears. I had decided that I would tell this new whore, whoever she was, that she could have Roger. I'd make a joke of it, like someone giving up an unwanted mutt, because that's what Roger was to me now, a mangy dog I'd sooner dump on the highway than allow back into my house. I found a spot around the back and scoped out the room. The curtains were drawn. I couldn't see a thing.

I grabbed my bag and walked up the steps to the second floor. I stared at the dingy door, then knocked hard, like a man might (but quickly realized that a philandering man wouldn't pound, he'd tap quietly, discreetly). I heard a woman's voice. There was no answer. I tried the doorknob. It was unlocked. The door creaked open. The room was dark. I felt something at my feet. At first I assumed it was one of those moist towelettes I always carry in my bag in case Pete needs a quick cleanup. But when I bent down to pick it up, I realized it was a condom. Tied around it, the same ribbon that held the feather to the can of Kama Sutra powder I found in my Jeep. This woman obviously knew my husband wasn't keen on rubbers; she'd brought her own.

I gripped the ribbon as it snaked into the room. I flipped on the light. Both beds were empty. The room was empty! But the ribbon didn't stop there. It led me to the doors that adjoined room 219 to 221. I knew there was someone on the other end of that ribbon, because as I approached the adjoining doors, I felt a distinct tug. With one hand on the doorknob and the other grasping the steak knife in my bag, I pushed open the door. And there in bed, lolling like a sultan amidst a pile of pillows and wearing nothing but her Cheshire cat grin, lay Diana.

"Right on time." Her eyes glittered and she tossed her head back.

"Right on time."

'Til next time,
𝒱

December 3

"What do you mean, right on time?" I asked Diana, my blood pounding in my ears. The brain is an incredible organ, it really is. How's this for multitasking: as one part was registering total mortification, the other was taking in every inch of Diana's naked body.

I saw firm, round breasts that hadn't been flattened and sagged by nursing, and a flat belly that never had to expand to accommodate a growing baby. Her hips were narrow, boyish. (Of coure, those panties had belonged to her, I suddenly realized.) And Diana's skin was smooth and unblemished, like a young girl's. No stretch marks, no shrivels, no varicose veins. Her shiny black hair was longer now, and curled around one rosy nipple. A bull's-eye.

Diana snuggled back into the pillows. She giggled. "Oh, baby. Do you have to analyze every single thing I say?" She twirled her hair around a finger. The nails were short, squared, buffed to a soft shine. "Right on time means right on time."

"You mean, you were expecting me?" I noticed she'd lit some incense. Something musky. I recognized it. They sold it at that funky gift shop in the Castle Creek mall. It was Roger's favorite. He said it made him horny.

"Expecting you?" Diana's eyes widened. "Of course I was expecting you. I've never known you to pass up adventure."

I noticed the bottle of Merlot on the chipped laminate side table. There were two glasses. So much for AA, I thought.

"Did you enjoy my little—gifts?"

"Those tampons. That was you?"

"You betcha!" Diana beamed like a flashlight. "The kisses were a nice touch, don't you think?" She puckered her lips and blew a salacious kiss. I could almost see it sliming its way toward me.

"No, I thought the whole thing was disgusting."

"Disgusting? Ouch!" Diana pouted, feigning insult. "Don't tell me you forgot!"

I stared at her. I had no idea what she was talking about.

"You remember. Prince Charles? Camilla?"

Oh yes. It was all coming back to me. It had been one of those exceedingly rare moments of harmony between Diana and me. A staff luncheon at Bellamy's. Hot topic of the week: Prince Charles's secret desire to be a Kotex in Camilla Parker Bowles's love canal. Most everyone agreed that Charles was a royal pig, but I argued that it was a private comment between lovers and wasn't meant to be publicly aired or judged. Diana vociferously agreed, then winked at me in a way I suppose I should have noticed. She caught up with me later, said she believed that anything is permissible between consenting adults.

I looked down at the condom in my hands. I figured it was only a matter of time before my husband would arrive. And when he did, I planned to tell him our marriage was officially and finally over. It seemed totally appropriate that I'd end my misery in some motel room with its stain-flecked walls, chipped laminate furniture, and forlorn drapes. I was actually looking forward to it.

I reached into my bag and felt for the camera. It was still there. "I can't wait to see the look on Roger's face when he walks in and finds me standing here with his whore."

"Roger?" Diana grinned impishly and shook her head. "Oh, baby, you've got it all wrong. I'm not that kind of girl. I mean, that's not my or-i-en-ta-tion."

With every syllable of the word she tugged sharply on the ribbon, reeling me in toward the bed. I lost my balance and flopped beside her. I could smell the incense in her hair.

"I've never been interested in Roger. Don't you know that?"

I pried her fingers off me and turned to face her. I was sure she was bullshitting me. "Cut the crap, Diana. How many times have you told me you should have grabbed him when you had the chance? You were married once. And how about all your boyfriends? Roger told me you had a new guy up to your dorm every week."

Diana snorted, "Boyfriends, shmoyfriends. Listen. You're a therapist. You're supposed to know this stuff."

She grabbed a pillow and playfully bopped me over the head. What did she think this was, a slumber party? "Sexuality is a continuum, babe. I used to be on this end of the continuum"—she lightly traced a line from one end of my lips to the other—"and now I'm on this side."

"Give me a break," I told her. "How stupid do you think I am? What about *this?*" I waved the condom at her. Diana licked her lips.

"Oh, sweetcakes, that's not for Roger." She leaned forward to brush the hair away from my face. It was a gentle, affectionate gesture. It made me shudder.

"But let's not rush it, okay?"

"But the book, the body powder—that wasn't for Roger?"

Diana was radiant now. "Oh, this is too perfect. Just perfect!" she said.

At this point I didn't know what to think. I was sitting in a cheesy motel room, with my nemesis, who just happened to be naked. To complicate matters, I was aware of an intensifying heat spreading like a rash over my body.

"So, were *you* planning on wearing that thing?" I pointed toward the condom.

Diana giggled. "No, I'm afraid I don't have the right equipment." She shifted her legs provocatively, watching me watching her.

"You are delectable, you know that? Delicious. And Roger doesn't deserve you, that rat."

She reached for me again but I stood up and glanced perfunctorily at my watch, as if the time even mattered at that point. The truth is, I felt suspended in time, as if I'd stepped outside myself and now watched this entire sordid scene unfold from a corner of the room.

"Look," I heard myself say, "it's been real. But I've got to go."

"Oh, no! You can't!" Diana grabbed my hand and held fast. "Please. Not yet. You'll miss the best part!"

Just then I heard the door in the next room open.

"Yes!" Diana whispered. "Finally."

I held my breath and waited.

'Til next time,

V

December 10

It's 1 A.M. The locksmith has finally left and Roger's clothes are now sitting on the curb in Hefty bags that also happen to be filled with broken eggs, coffee grounds, old tuna fish, yogurt, and everything else in the kitchen trash can. I took special care to dump the slop on his favorite Armani suit, then emptied Pete's acrylic paints into the bag with the Tommy Bahama trousers and silk ties. I poured bleach over everything else. I would have puked into his $160 shoes if I thought I had anything left in my stomach, but I'd already heaved up dinner into the toilet. With any luck the raccoons will tear into the bags and drag his crap all over the street.

But I'm getting ahead of myself.

As soon as the door creaked open in the next room, Diana slinked out of bed and started moving toward the bathroom.

"Just where the hell are you going?" I whispered, instinctively reaching for the steak knife.

"Don't say I never did anything for you," she muttered.

I watched her scuttle into the bathroom and close the door behind her. And then I knew.

"Hello?" I heard him call from the adjoining room.

"Hel-lo?" The voice was playful, but a little tentative.

A faint rustling of tissue paper. He came bearing flowers. Red gerbera daisies and tiny yellow roses. Eddie's smile was as big as the bulge in his pants. He offered the flowers. Reflexively, I brought them to my face and inhaled deeply. He grinned at me. "You naughty, naughty girl."

"What?"

"What? What?" he mimicked. "Don't give me that innocent routine." He unzipped his leather jacket and tossed it on the wobbly Formica table. He wore a crisp shirt, azure blue. I wondered if he'd asked his wife to iron it this morning. He looked beautiful.

"You're something else, you know that?" He pulled me toward him with authority and entitlement. "First, the panties. Then that little sex book. And the Kama Sutra powder?" He suddenly looked stricken. "Damn! I left it in the car! I could run out and get it. Wouldn't take more than a minute." He pulled me closer and put his mouth against my ear.

"On second thought, let's forget the powder. We really don't need props, do we?"

"Wait, Eddie, you don't understand."

"Oh, I understand just fine." He put his hands beneath my blouse and fiddled with my bra. "What I *don't* get is why you picked this place? We could have met at the Roundtree. For old time's sake." He gently lifted my chin with his hands and ran his tongue lightly across my lips. "God. I've missed you." He tried to lower me to the bed.

It took all my willpower to stop him. It was all happening so quickly. Knowing that Diana was sitting in the bathroom, stark naked, possibly watching us—I should have been freaked out, but I felt intoxicated. For a fleeting moment I wondered what it would be like to have Diana in bed with us. I thought, I could do this. What guy wouldn't want to have two women in bed? And I could give Diana what she wanted: a piece of me.

I was still having that weird out-of-body feeling. Even while I tasted Eddie's tongue in my mouth, part of me seemed to float around the room observing—the dead horsefly squashed against the mirror, the stray puzzle piece under the bed. And then I thought of Petey. He loved puzzles. I thought about the bad dream he'd had the night before, something about this boy in his class cutting up all his Pokemon cards with scissors. I'd chuckled as I smoothed his forehead. "That's the worst that should ever happen to you," I whispered as he drifted back to sleep. I kissed his face.

Now Eddie was kissing mine. I couldn't go through with it. "Eddie. Stop." I mumbled the words into his neck. I finally pushed him off me.

"Please." I whispered. "We're not alone." I cocked my eyes toward the bathroom.

"Huh?" Eddie looked bewildered.

"Remember Diana?" I mouthed.

Eddie nodded, wide-eyed. He pulled himself onto his elbows. His face was flushed. You're kidding, right?"

"Diana!" I yelled "Get out here! *Now!*"

No response at first. I knew there was no window from which to escape. Either she'd slit her wrists (unlikely, given her Montana-sized ego) or she'd fallen asleep (also unlikely, given her avid interest in my sex life). After what felt like ten minutes but was probably more like four seconds, Diana appeared, fully clothed.

"Hey, don't let me stop you. I was just leaving." She reached for the faux fur coat hanging on the bar near the door. "You kids just go about your business. I'll be out of your way in a minute."

"What the hell is this all about?" Eddie looked angry. I realized that the prospect of a three-way probably would have been more repellent than appealing to him. He detested Diana. "What is this, some kind of sick joke?" Eddie shot me a dark glare. He thought I'd set him up!

"Don't look at me that way," I told him. "I had nothing to do with this." I implored Diana to explain herself. She hoisted herself up onto the dresser.

"Okay. It's like this." She took a deep breath. "You know I'm in AA, right?" Oh no, I thought, here we go with this again. What could her twelve-step program possibly have to do with this?

"I'm still sober, believe it or not." She gestured toward the Merlot. "That was for you two. Not me."

Eddie reached for the bottle and took a swig. "Not bad," he said, grinning. Good old Eddie. He wasn't angry. He was amused.

"Anyway, part of my recovery involves making amends. And I thought one way to make amends would be to get you together, you know, give you the opportunity to have a little fun, rekindle the old flame, whatever."

"You made amends to me already, Diana." This twelve-step stuff was getting tiresome. "You don't owe me anything."

"Oh, baby, I do." Her smile faded. She was truly earnest. "See, I still feel terribly guilty for trying to break you and Eddie up. Your little dalliance drove me crazy. I made you think I was looking out for Roger, but that wasn't it at all. It was more complicated than that. And . . ." Her voice softened. ". . . more pathetic. I had a crush on you. And I thought maybe you might like me too."

I glanced at Eddie. His eyes crinkled. "Oh, this is sweet!"

Diana tossed a small stack of wrapped plastic drinking cups at him. "Oh, shut up! It's not funny! I'm pouring my heart out here!"

My head was spinning. Nothing made sense. "If all you wanted to do was make amends, why were you naked when I got here?"

Eddie perked up. "She was naked?"

Okay. Maybe I was wrong about his interest in a three-way.

"Well? Why were you naked?" I demanded.

Diana shrugged sheepishly. "A girl can dream, can't she?" I thought I could get you warmed up for Eddie.

I pulled on my coat. This was too bizarre. I was standing in a motel room with two people who wanted to get me in bed. At the very least, it was an ego boost. But it was still friggin' weird. "Okay. Fine. But I'm married."

Diana sighed. "Barely."

"What do you mean, 'barely'?" I asked.

"I mean, your husband is a dog." Another big sigh. "Roger's a dirty dog."

"Look, I know all about Alyssa, okay?"

"Alyssa?" Diana snorted. "Old news!" Her face filled with pity. "Baby"—she shook her head slowly—"you don't know the *half* of it."

Eddie reached out for my hand and squeezed. I knew he meant to offer support, but he must have felt at least a little jubilation. Here was the opening he was waiting for.

"Okay," I told Diana. "You've got my attention. Start talking."

Diana pulled a pack of cigarettes out of her bag, shook one out, and lit up. She waved toward the bed. "Maybe you'd better sit down for this," she suggested. "And take off your coat. We're going to be here a while." I chose one of the chairs near the window. Eddie stretched out on the bed, hands behind his head. I took a deep breath and tried to look neutral. Even though Diana thought she was doing me a favor now, I had yet to eliminate the possibility that she might take some pleasure in my anguish. She took a deep drag and began.

"Remember Lola Jacobson?" Of course I remembered her. When Roger and I were engaged, I rented the upstairs of Lola's house on a quiet street in West Liberty. Lola was a sculptor, fortyish, married, no kids. She had jet black hair and straight bangs, long legs, and strong arms. Her husband was a swami, of all things, the charismatic leader of an ashram on the fringes of the state park, about six miles outside of town. His name was Swami Muktananda but we always called him Mike. She told me they had tantric sex. I had to look it up in the library.

I knew Lola enjoyed talking to Roger. Lots of women seemed to. Unlike most guys, Roger was at ease on the emotional plane. Women found it refreshing. He had a way of drawing them out, getting them to talk about the kinds of intimate topics they'd normally reserve for female friends. Just last month, for instance, when I was about to run next door to ask my neighbor for olive oil, Roger advised against it. "She's just had a D & C, you know." Actually, I didn't know that. But how did he? Apparently this woman had confided to Roger that she'd been having irregular periods. I couldn't believe she had told him that.

Now I can believe it.

After we'd been engaged for about six months, Roger moved his things into my apartment. He'd write while I was in class. He spent a lot of time alone there. At least I used to think he was alone.

"Did you know he used to pose for her?" Diana asked. No, I said, I hadn't known. I was beginning to feel sick. Then I remembered the Sunday morning that Roger and I joined her and Mike on the sun porch for herbal tea and scones. Lola had put one of her nude figures—an extremely well endowed figure—right in the middle of the rattan table.

I joked that the man looked a little like Roger, the same high brow and clefted chin. "But there's a *big* difference between you and this guy, isn't there?" I said, giggling. No one else laughed. Still, I suspected nothing. I knew I'd embarrassed him. I assumed that Lola, a fellow sensitive artist type, was feeling his pain.

It turns out Lola was feeling a lot more than Roger's pain. "He told me all about that time on the porch, how you embarrassed him with some comment about his dick." Eddie put his hand up to his mouth, suppressing a laugh. "He also told me Lola was playing with him under the table. And I don't mean footsy."

"What else?" I asked Diana masochistically. I had to know. Diana took another drag on the cigarette and stared at me. "Everything else. With and without the swami."

"What, you're telling me Roger went both ways?"

"No, God no. I mean, sometimes the swami watched, and sometimes Roger watched."

I felt a hard lump rise in my throat. I used to like Lola and Mike. I thought they were nice people. A little weird, maybe, but nice. "So, how long did it last?" I asked Diana.

"It started a couple of weeks after he moved in with you. As far as I know, it lasted until you guys moved into your place on Heath Street."

"In other words," I said, "it lasted until we got married."

"Not exactly." Diana walked to the bathroom and tossed the cigarette butt into the toilet. I heard a quiet sizzle as it hit the water. Eddie looked at me. "Are you okay?" he asked. "I'm fine," I lied. I wanted to grab the bottle of Merlot and bash myself in the head. I'd been such an imbecile. I thought bitterly of our little apartment on Heath, how I'd decorated it with frilly curtains and cheap prints from the Art Institute. Roger helped me stain a hope chest. It held our grandmothers' table linens and silver. We kept it at the foot of the bed. Everything was so new and full of promise. And I was the world's biggest sucker.

"Lola and Roger kept it up for a while," Diana continued. "Three, four months after you guys were married." Diana watched me for a reaction. I refused to cry in front of her. "They only stopped when Lola and the swami moved to Sedona, except for that time, uh . . ."

"Except for the time he went out to Sedona, right?" Roger insisted he had to go out there to "get the feel of the place" for a new play. He never wrote anything even remotely related to Sedona. I'd heard enough. I was anxious to leave. I knew I'd have to change the locks. I knew I'd have to call a lawyer. I'd have to find a job.

And I'd have to tell Petey. I stood up. "Thank you, Diana. My husband was a dog. You've made your point."

"No, sweet love, not *was* a dog. Roger still *is* a dog. We're not talking past tense, baby." Diana hopped off the dresser and put her hands on my shoulders. "You're not getting it, are you? I haven't even scraped the surface here."

"Really, Diana. I don't need to hear this."

Now it was Eddie's turn to talk. "Yeah, honey, you do. It'll help you later, you know, when you start duking it out with the lawyers. You'll need all the ammunition you can get." He was right, of course.

"Fine." I reached into my bag and hunted for scrap paper. I pulled out a long cash register receipt and flipped it over. It would have to do. "Okay. Keep talking."

I grabbed the wine and filled my glass halfway. I battled a visceral impulse to soothe (or maybe destroy?) myself with alcohol. I'd wanted to remain clearheaded, but I also wanted to numb out. I didn't want to feel the excruciating feelings, not just the anger but also the embarrassment. I remembered, bitterly, the time I'd driven Lola to the hospital when she had diverticulitis and thought her intestines were going to rupture. I baked her cookies. I walked Berkeley, her Pekingese. She was my landlady, but I'd also come to care about her. I'd been such a fool!

After Lola Jackson, Diana (now the archivist of my husband's infidelities) explained that Roger took a hiatus from infidelity—two years, give or take a few months. I remember those times as the best years of our marriage. Roger was fully present, physically and emotionally. That was before we had a TV in our bedroom. When I talked, he actually listened. There was a sense of our building a life together, not just in the material sense of buying and furnishing a home, but also in the way we'd shared the same values and goals. We talked about starting a family. We grew a small but productive vegetable garden. We took a cooking class together. And we joined the governor's reelection campaign, stuffing envelopes, knocking on doors . . . and then Roger grew remote, distracted.

"Then there was Jacqueline Leland. Or was it Lehman?" Diana asked rhetorically.

"Leland," I said, staring at my hands. "Jacqueline Leland." Jacqueline had been a local strategist on the governor's campaign. She was smart, wiry, blond, single. I once found them in the hallway giggling quietly, Jackie with her back against the wall and Roger leaning inches from her face. I'd accused Roger of flirting with her, and he'd protested vehemently.

"She's not even my type," he'd insisted. "She's too bony. And she has no chin!"

I looked up at Diana. "So—what about Jacqueline Leland?"

Diana reached for another cigarette, but Eddie stopped her. The smoke aggravates his allergies. She sighed, put the pack away, and continued.

"He took Jacqueline to his parents' cabin on the lake. The fire was her fault. Her curling iron, something like that."

Oh God. That was the year his parents' cabin, a sweet little place on a magnificent lake in Door County, burned to the ground. Roger had said the furnace had exploded. His parents decided not to rebuild and wound up selling the lot. I was so disappointed. I'd hoped it would stay in the family. I used to imagine bringing our kids, and eventually our grandkids, there. One weekend during the campaign he drove up to get the cabin ready for winter. At least that's what he told me. He encouraged me to stay behind and help with a telephone fund-raiser. Now that I think of it, Jacqueline had called me to ask if I'd direct the effort, and I'd been too flattered to turn her down. She said I was a "gifted communicator."

"They'd been together maybe a half dozen times," Diana continued. "Mostly at night, mostly on the conference table." I winced. "Roger finally took her to his parents' cabin after she started complaining about back problems. It ended after the cabin burned down. Jacqueline knew it would scandalize the governor if it came out, so she dropped ol' Rog like a hot potato. But he recovered just fine, with the help of a cute little thing named Dara."

Dara Rosario was Roger's first intern. He'd advertised at the university for a writing major. He offered an unpaid internship—essentially a gofer's job—in exchange for writing advice. He said he picked her because he pitied her. She came from poverty, the only one of nine children with any scholarly ambition. Dara was studious and quiet. But I remember noticing how her wardrobe seemed to change as the months wore on. The dumpy flannel shirts and baggy jeans gave way to short skirts and skimpy tops. And suddenly there was lipstick. She'd come to the house once a week, presumably to help him with filing and to clean his office. I once found her perched on his desk while he typed. Her legs were open wide enough for him to glimpse her underwear, if he'd been so inclined.

"Roger bragged about changing Dara's mind about virginity," Diana said.

"What do you mean?" I asked.

"What I mean is, little Dara had strong views about preserving her virginity for marriage. Your husband convinced her that sex was a good thing, a healthy thing. He gave her a good dose of feminist conscious-ness-raising. Told her the idea of virginity was just an-other way of oppressing women." Diana grabbed her cigarettes and lit up, shooting a defiant glare at Eddie.

"Baby, you have no idea how he relished the idea of popping that girl's cherry. I never heard the end of it!"

My resolve to stay stoic had vanished. I lurched toward the bathroom and threw up in the toilet. I rinsed my mouth with water and staggered back to the chair. Eddie was standing now. He held me for a long time while Diana smoked and watched us.

"I'm almost done," she said, softly. "Sit down and keep writing." I'd already filled up the back of the gro-cery receipt. Eddie found an old invoice in his jacket pocket. Wearily, I uncapped the pen and poised it above the paper. "Go ahead," I said.

For the next hour Diana recounted tales of stolen kisses and fondling, cyber sex, phone sex, and oral sex. And intercourse. There were two actresses in *Basic Black,* the computer repairwoman, a camp counselor, a three-night fling at a writers' retreat, and, of course, Alyssa. "I think that covers everybody," Diana said. "Wait. One more. There was this really crazy chick, a total sex freak. Met her at a gas station. She was pump-ing gas and flashing her booty. I think they did it in the men's room." Diana stubbed out her cigarette and chuckled. "She actually gave him her business card. Claire Something. CPA."

I felt the blood crash behind my eyeballs, my stom-ach clench like a fist. I started to laugh, and then I was sobbing. "I'm sorry, love," Diana murmured. "I'm really sorry."

It was a miracle I hadn't contracted herpes or chlamydia. Or HIV. I closed my eyes and tried to feel gratitude. I desperately needed to find one thing to be happy about. I couldn't be happy about the imminent dissolution of my marriage. I was terrified. But the prospect of living with Roger was even scarier. He had led a double life for years. He was a stranger to me.

It was 5 P.M. when Diana finished recounting the list of Roger's sexual conquests, and it was starting to snow. I looked through the stiff curtains, out at the dreary sky and parking lot, and wondered whether I had the stamina to drive home. I thought about my father. If he knew what I'd just discovered today, he'd probably dust off his old hunting rifle and blow Roger's brains out. Then I remembered that my father barely has the energy now to dress himself. My father was dying. My marriage was over. Where would I possibly find the strength to pull myself out of bed tomorrow morning?

I stood up and put my jacket on. "Wait," Diana said. "There's something else I've got to tell you."

I groaned. "No, Diana. I can't. No more. Please."

"But you've got to know this. It's about Roger's money. Walk out now and you'll wind up penniless." What more could Diana possibly know? I would soon find out, but I've got no energy left to write.

'Til next time,

𝒱

December 11

"I know you want to go. But we've got to talk about money." Diana held me by the sleeve. "Listen. Roger's a rich boy, baby. He's got money. And you're entitled to it."

"And I'm sure I'll get it," I said, pulling my arm away. "But that's something for me and my lawyer to deal with, okay?"

Diana wouldn't give up. "No, not okay. You have to hear me out. Please."

I just wanted to get the hell out of there.

"I know this is the last thing you want to deal with now," Eddie told me, "but if you don't shake yourself out of this stupor, honest to God, kiddo, you're going to wind up flat broke."

Diana stepped in. "Before I worked at the Center I was at Epstein Browne. Family law. You can't imagine the stories I heard around that office. It made me happy to be a bean counter, I'll tell you. Disgruntled wives going around the house with chain saws, cutting everything in half, the dining room table, the mattress. Husbands who poisoned the family dogs to get back at cheating wives. People who'd sooner kill their own kids than go through a custody battle. It's sick. I'm not saying Roger's about to hurt Petey, but I wouldn't put it past him to do something really big, really bad. Especially when it comes to money. Whatever he does, he's set for life."

"What do you mean 'set'?"

"I mean, he never has to work a day in his life. He's got assets, baby. Everywhere. Stocks. Bonds. Mutual funds. He's got money in the Cayman Islands. He's even got gold bullion."

I laughed out loud. It all sounded so ridiculous, almost surreal. "You're kidding, right?"

Diana just stared at me, sober as a gravestone. "They're hidden somewhere in your humble abode."

I reeled back in my seat. Gold? Hidden somewhere in my house? I mentally diagrammed every room, every nook. I thought I knew every square inch of that place, especially since I started cleaning it like a woman possessed, from baseboard to ceiling. I didn't even know what gold bullion look like. Bricks? Sticks of margarine? I had no idea. But I planned to find out, even if I had to rip every floorboard and ceiling tile out with my bare hands. That bastard.

"There are other things you can do now, you know," Diana continued. "I mean, I'm sure your lawyer will tell you all this, but you might as well start now, before Roger gets the chance to destroy any evidence."

I watched Diana and was suddenly filled with a surprising affection for her. She really knew her stuff. I was impressed.

"Your lawyer can help you dig up the hidden assets. And you need to figure out what kind of income Roger pulls in. Trust fund, income from teaching, royalties, whatever. But while you're rooting around in his files—and this is critical, baby—you've got to find anything that suggests he spent money on his lovers. Jewelry, clothes, gifts . . . all that gets deducted from his portion of the settlement, you understand? You've got to really look, okay?"

"Yes, yes, okay already." I was experiencing information overload. It was all too much. I looked at the clock. 5:30. I'd arranged to pick up Pete at my in-laws at 7:00 P.M. Roger supposedly had a meeting with his director. He said he wouldn't be home until 10:00 at the earliest. Perfect.

I grabbed the yellow pages and found a locksmith with emergency hours. I punched in the number. Asked the guy to meet me back at my house at 7:30

P.M. He asked if I'd locked myself out of my car. "No, I want you to change my locks. All of them." There were five altogether. Front, deck, basement, the door leading into the garage, and the one leading from the garage into the family room. This would cost me a thousand bucks at least. But hey, I have gold in my house.

"I'm not so sure that was a good idea," Diana said.

"Why not?" I asked.

"Because you don't want Roger to know you're cutting him loose. You need to buy yourself some time now. So you can dig up information, get to the records before he does."

I felt queasy. I didn't want Roger back in the house. "Look," Diana suggested, "if you're hell-bent on changing the locks, go ahead. I don't blame you. Just tell him you caught him in a lie."

"Yes," I interrupted. "Just the other day, in fact. He said he was late because of some accident on the road. I called the sheriff's office. There was no accident."

"That's it," said Diana, clapping her hands together. "When he starts pounding on the door, you tell him that. And say you're really mad and you don't want to talk about it. Don't even mention divorce. Let him think he has a chance with you. Let him try to weasel his way back into your life. In the meantime, you've got to plot your strategy. Nail him to the wall." Diana's eyes flashed. She was really getting into this. She asked me, "Do you have a good lawyer?"

"I've got a few in mind. Why? Do you know anyone?"

"Yes. The best." Diana grabbed the pen and scribbled on my paper. Omar Sweet. "He's a partner at Epstein Browne. A killer shark. Exactly the kind of guy you want on your side of the table." Diana's fighting spirit was contagious. I was actually excited about calling

Omar Sweet. I felt hopeful, even powerful. Diana turned toward the mirror and fixed her beret at a jaunty angle.

Then she pulled me into a suffocating embrace. "Now I've made my amends. And if there's anything else I can do, you know where to call. I've got a chain saw. And the Kama Sutra powder."

I groaned and she giggled. "Sorry. Couldn't resist." She gestured toward Eddie. "Hey. The room's on my dime. You kids have some fun, okay?" And with that, Diana was gone.

I had to meet the locksmith in an hour and a half. I still had to pick up Petey. And I had to ransack my house! Sex was the last thing on my mind. But Eddie apparently had other plans. He looked at me with beseeching eyes.

"Come on, love." He ran a finger slowly up my face, across my lips, and let it linger there. "Let's not waste this bed. You have absolutely nothing to lose now." I felt myself soften under his touch. He was right. I had nothing to lose.

I protested (halfheartedly) while Eddie kissed my neck. "Mmmm. I missed your smell," he whispered into my hair. "Estee Lauder Pleasures, right?"

"Eddie, I really don't think this is a good idea."

"It's not a good idea," he said, now slipping my jacket off my shoulders. "It's a great idea."

He pulled something from his back pocket. It was that little book of sex positions Diana had sent us both. I had to laugh when I saw that Eddie had bookmarked several pages with Post-it notes.

"You can't imagine how it turned me on to picture you buying this for me. Just picturing you flipping through the pages, holding it in your hands." He shook his head like a frisky pony.

I reminded him that Diana bought that book, not me. "True enough," he said, now working on my blouse, "but I'd rather think it came from you." He slipped off the rest of my clothes (with a little help from me, I must admit), then ordered me to sit on the bed and slipped off my tights. "You've been through hell today, honey. Why don't you just relax and let me take care of you, okay?"

I watched that sweet face staring up at me and thought, in another life, this man might have been my husband. We were two damaged souls. We needed each other, in all the healthy and unhealthy ways. I lay back on the bed and let him take care of me.

Over the next forty minutes or so, he managed to get us into four or five of the positions from that little book. He was tender, playful, and extravagant in his attentions. Through it all, he declared his love for me.

But I was distracted and, ultimately, never came. Lola Jacobson. Jackie Leland. Dara Rosario. My skull throbbed with images of every woman my husband screwed, fondled, or kissed. I pictured the computer repairwoman's head bobbing between his legs. Knowing Roger, he was probably typing while she serviced him. I thought of the actresses, the counselors. I thought of Alyssa, and felt the blood drain through me. I suddenly felt cold and achy. I wanted to go home and begin the business of dissolving my marriage.

Eddie came and eased out of me. He knew I hadn't climaxed and seemed disappointed. "I just want to make you happy, sweetheart," he said, brushing a hair from the corner of my mouth. I loved how he said that word, sweetheart. It's not a word I particularly like. Just looking at it on the page now, it looks so corny, so dated. But coming from his lips, there was always something sexy and loaded about the word. I could feel his longing in that word.

It was time to go. I dressed quickly while Eddie suggested he help me ransack my house. I was tempted. I wanted him to swoop down and take care of everything. But I knew this was something I had to do myself. I needed to purge and purify on my own. And I didn't want Eddie in the house when Roger started throwing himself against the door, as I knew he would when he discovered the key didn't fit. Eddie would undoubtedly beat the crap out of my husband. Frankly, I'd love to see that happen, but I know it would only hurt me later, when our lawyers start haggling.

I grabbed Eddie for one last, long kiss and ran to the Jeep. On the way home, I punched in Omar Sweet's number and left a message on his voice mail. I could tell from his voice he was a hell of a lawyer. He sounded smart and tough—and expensive.

I cringed when I thought of the legal expenses, but if this guy does his job right, money shouldn't be an issue. I fleetingly entertained the idea that I might actually wind up a rich woman—not merely comfortable, but actually loaded. I had no idea what Roger was worth, but I do remember his sister confiding (after a few too many gin and tonics) that the siblings once considered buying an island off the coast of Spain. My father once estimated that my in-laws probably had close to a hundred million in assets, maybe more. It seemed impossible. His parents lived so humbly. They wore old clothes, drove an old car, and never hired anyone to do anything they could do themselves, even if they didn't do it particularly well (which explains the windows patched with cardboard).

I picked up Pete from my in-laws, swung by the Burger King drive-through for dinner, and sped home. My heart thrummed as I prayed that I'd arrive before Roger did. I needed time alone in the house to search, not just for the gold, but for papers that could help me calculate my husband's worth. And I'd be on the look-out for anything to suggest Roger had spent money on any of his lovers.

As I approached the house, I saw that Roger wasn't there, and I blurted out, "Thank you, God." Petey asked me, "What are you thanking God for, Mommy?" and I almost started to cry. Is this what it's come to? That I thank God for my husband's absence so I can tear apart my house? I glanced at Pete in the rearview mirror. His world was about to explode. Only he didn't know it yet. Happy New Year, Petey.

The locksmith was a surprisingly bookish young man in an Old Navy sweatshirt. While he worked on the locks, I fed Pete, got him down for the night, and crept into Roger's study. The room, which I'd always felt comfortable entering, seemed alien now, almost dangerous. Twenty-four hours ago, the prospect of opening one of Roger's drawers wouldn't have caused heart palpitations, but now I felt faint as I tugged them open. I was terrified he'd walk in, then reminded myself that he was locked out. I was still nervous.

I pulled open a drawer of files and rifled through the folders. I didn't even know what I was looking for. I yanked on another drawer.

Locked. Damn. Futilely, I pulled at the drawer, then kicked it. I knew that it—whatever the hell "it" was—resided somewhere in that drawer. Rather than waste any more effort on the locked drawer, I grabbed a box of Hefty bags and headed for Roger's closet. I flicked on the light and sighed. Here, Roger's obsessive-compulsive inclinations came to life. Cedar hangers were arranged in neat rows, with hooks all facing toward the wall. Clothes, color-coordinated, ranging from neutrals to black. He'd designated a separate section for his racquetball clothes: there were soft white cotton polo shirts and gym shorts hung together in sets and a big mesh bag filled with balled-up white crew socks. Spring and summer garments were stowed away in cedar boxes on the highest shelves.

Oh, how Roger loved his closet! His was twice the size of mine, a walk-in with a vaulted ceiling and window overlooking the hemlock trees on the side of the house. Mine was tiny by comparison, with no lighting. It barely held more than a season's worth of clothes; I had to put some of my stuff in Pete's closet, and the rest in the basement. The first time we saw the house, Roger jumped into the bigger closet and said, "I've got dibs on this one." When I made a face, he held up a hand to silence whatever objections I might have considered expressing. "Don't even *think* of trying to talk me out of this." Truth was, I didn't have much of a case. What did I own, after all? Three pairs of black pants, six black skirts, a few tops, and a horrible blue plaid dress I bought at Talbot's that made me look like a rectangle with legs. And everything I owned wound up in a crumpled ball at the bottom of the closet anyway.

The real estate agent who showed us the house flashed me a confused look. She was a brave old gal: she risked losing the sale by reminding Roger that "usually the ladies of the house get the bigger closet." Roger just chuckled and shook his head.

My throat tightened when I saw the violet Jhane Barnes jacket Roger wore during his Alyssa period. I'd never thought to ask why he felt compelled to dress up for a bunch of loser students at the Learning Attic. Now I knew. He wasn't dressing up for a bunch of loser students, just for one whore.

The memory filled me with a manic rage. I pawed wildly at my prissy husband's clothes, yanking them off hangers, stuffing them into the trash bags. I heaved the bags down the steps and dragged them into the kitchen, then dumped everything I could find onto those beautiful garments. First the coffee grinds, then the tuna. I found moldy ricotta cheese, expired yogurt, and a full bottle of ketchup, and splattered everything over his clothes. I broke eggs onto the Jhane Barnes jacket and marveled at how lovely the bright yellow yolks looked against the violet knit fabric. I remembered Petey's paints in the cabinet under the kitchen sink, and gleefully dumped those in, too. Then came the bleach.

Never in my life had I experienced such gleeful nihilism. I felt no shame, no guilt, no reservations, and no recriminations. Something shifted inside me. I had my first taste of blood. I wanted more. I opened the door cautiously and checked for Roger's van. Except for the howling of the Saint Bernard on the corner, the street was completely still. I scurried out, threw the bags on the curb, and rushed back in.

Then the phone rang. It was the lawyer, Omar Sweet, returning my call.

As I gave him a frantic synopsis—Roger's pathological philandering, the money he's rumored to have amassed and stashed away, my decision to file for divorce—I listened for Roger downstairs. When he realized his key wouldn't open the door leading from the garage to the family room, he'd undoubtedly ring the bell. And when I didn't answer the door, he would pound and yell. I prayed he wouldn't smash the windows or wake up Petey.

I told Omar that I'd changed the locks.

"Big mistake," he said, and I felt like crying. "You've got to play it cool now. Can't let this bastard know you're onto him." *Bastard.* I was thrilled to hear the word. Already, Omar was my advocate. But then I panicked. I'd just destroyed most of my husband's wardrobe and changed all the locks. How could he possibly assume I planned to stay married to him?

"As your lawyer, it wouldn't be ethical for me to urge you to lie," he started, and my heart sank. "I mean, I wouldn't tell you, for instance, to say you came home and found the bags on the curb and figured someone was out to get him. And you got scared because there was a stranger in the house, which is why you changed the locks." He paused to let me absorb his meaning. "I'd *never* tell you to do that." My mind raced. What about fingerprints? What if he calls the cops and they find my prints all over the bag?

"My guess is, your soon-to-be ex will be scared shitless. He'll be wracking his brains trying to figure out which of his paramours went ballistic on him. He'll be so worried about you busting him, the last thing he'll want to do is pursue it with the cops. Take it easy."

I felt better already. I arranged to meet Omar at his office the following morning to plot our strategy. "It'll be like Normandy. We don't make a move until every last detail is down. Then BOOM!"

The phone clicked. Call waiting. It was Eddie. "Is the jackass home yet?"

"No," I told him. "Not yet. But any minute."

"So? How's the prospecting going?" he asked. I tried not to wonder whether Eddie seemed a little too interested. I told him I hadn't started looking for the gold.

"Hey. You know what?" he asked in a low voice.

"What?" Where the hell was his wife right now?

"I haven't showered yet. I can smell you on me. I don't want to lose it."

I felt a full-body flush. "Please," I whispered. "Eddie. Don't start."

"Okay. Okay. I'll be good. For now."

Then I heard the familiar hiss of the van's cranky engine. If this ruse was going to work, I couldn't wait for Roger to start fiddling with his key. I met him on the driveway and tried to look stricken. "Oh, thank God you're home!"

Roger looked at me warily. "Why?"

I pointed toward the Hefty bags. "Just look. It's awful." I watched Roger slowly walk toward the bags. I mentally reviewed my script. I've always been terrible liar; Roger says he can tell I'm fibbing by the way my lower lip twitches. Roger may be the playwright in the family, but tonight I had to be the actress. I couldn't let him know the truth. Not yet.

'Til next time,

$\mathcal{V}$

December 12

Roger pulled himself out of the van and the liquor on his breath wafted upwards like a hot air balloon. This feckless bastard wasn't merely a cheater, he was a drunk driver, too. I quickly eyed the inside of the van, expecting to find a pair of panties or a stray earring. I felt the disgust rise inside me. How I loathed him! But for now I had to play my part. If Roger suspected I was anything other than caring and kind, my plan was doomed.

I watched as he moved unsteadily toward the trash bags. The moon was full and resplendent, a shimmering disk in a deep indigo sky. What a waste, I thought. This gorgeous moon should have been illuminating a loving couple, not a drunk lech stumbling toward a pile of Hefty bags and a wife who pretended it was someone else who dumped spoiled ricotta cheese on his $100 silk shirts.

He turned toward me and asked, "Just tell me. Is it dead? It's not a dead baby, is it?"

"No. It's nothing like that."

"Well, then, is it a head, a decapitated head?"

"No, Roger, it's not a decapitated head."

My soon-to-be ex-husband picked up a fallen branch and began poking at the bag. What a sissy. I was beginning to grow exasperated, but reminded myself I was supposed to appear shaken and scared. After all, a stranger had just broken into the house and ransacked our closet. He squinted at the bag and poked again.

"Do I have to play goddamn twenty questions, or what? Can't you just tell me what it is?"

I shoved a knuckle into my mouth, as much to feign horror as suppress a smile.

"It's your clothes, Roger."

He stared at me. "My what?" He fell to his knees and pulled the cinched bag open. He reeled back on his palms. "Oh no. Oh no. Oh noooooooooooooo! Shit! Shit! Shit!" He poked his head into the bag, then pulled back again, gagging. "What the hell? What the hell? Shit! Shit! Shit!"

I'd be lying if I didn't feel the purest bliss watching Roger holding his nose with one hand, poking through his ruined garments with the other, alternating between moaning and gagging.

"Who would have done this?" he asked, his face darkening with rage.

"God, I don't know. Some sick, awful person," I answered. "I found it like this. The closet, ransacked. The bags at the curb. It was awful. I called the locksmith right away. I had to change the locks. All of them."

Suddenly, he began picking through the clothes with renewed zeal, as if he were looking for something specific. "Wait a second . . . just wait a second," he mumbled to himself. "I don't see . . ." I froze. I knew what would come next.

"Hey. How come none of *your* clothes are here?" He glared at me suspiciously. Now came the delicate part. I had to tell Roger enough to satisfy his curiosity, but make him back off.

"The cops had a theory," I began.

"What kind of theory?" he asked.

"Well, they say that whoever did it was after you, not me. You know, a vendetta." I took a deep breath. "They actually suggested it might have been a scorned lover." Roger held his face in his hands and began rubbing his temples. I forged ahead.

"You know, Roger, I'd hoped we could put this whole Alyssa thing behind us. But it just won't go away, will it? And now I come home, I find the closet ransacked. . . . "Someone broke into our house, Roger. Our house! What's next, Roger? Is she going to go after me next? Or Petey?"

Roger stopped rubbing his head and looked at me.

"Oh, God. What have I done? I am so, so sorry!" (Yes! And she scores!)

I remembered Omar's instructions. I couldn't let Roger know I was planning to leave him. I stepped forward and knelt beside him. I draped my arms around his neck. "It's going to be okay," I told him.

He looked bewildered. It had been a long time since I'd displayed any affection toward him. But he was relieved. Now I'd play the devoted wife. I told him I'd warm up some chicken soup and run a hot bath. "Oh, I feel so terrible for you. Those gorgeous clothes, ruined!"

"Ruined," he repeated, dazed.

"Why don't you go in and get undressed? I'll get your bath ready." I helped Roger to his feet and guided him toward the door. Roger stopped and put his arms on my shoulders.

"You are so good to me. I don't deserve you."

I hugged him. "Of course you do, darling. Of course you do."

While Roger soaked in the tub, I decided to make one quick pass through a filing cabinet in the basement. And there, tightly wedged between one dog-eared manila folder marked Medical and another marked Utilities, I found a folder with no label. I tugged until it popped out. My pulse quickened as I opened the folder. It was a document, stapled, slightly faded. I was certain Roger would come tripping down the stairs at any moment. I sensed that I'd found precisely the kind of information I needed. As I quickly scanned the page I felt something beyond shock, beyond horror. And I knew that what I'd found would forever change my view of marriage and men.

About the Author

Debra Kent writes the Diary of V for *Redbook* and Women.Com and has contributed to such magazines as *Cosmopolitan, Family Circle, Mademoiselle* and *McCall's*. She lives with her husband and children in the Midwest.